A BODY AT THE GRAND HOTEL

BENEDICT BROWN

Ebook ISBN: 978-1-80508-818-9
Paperback ISBN: 978-1-80508-820-2

Cover design: Rose Cooper
Cover images: Shutterstock, The Grand Hotel Torquay

Published by Storm Publishing.
For further information, visit:
www.stormpublishing.co

ALSO BY BENEDICT BROWN

The Marius Quin Mysteries

Murder at Everham Hall

The Hurtwood Village Murders

The Castleton Affair

Lord Edgington Investigates...

Murder at the Spring Ball

A Body at a Boarding School

Death on a Summer's Day

The Mystery of Mistletoe Hall

The Tangled Treasure Trail

The Curious Case of the Templeton-Swifts

The Crimes of Clearwell Castle

The Snows of Weston Moor

What the Vicar Saw

Blood on the Banisters

A Killer in the Wings

The Christmas Bell Mystery

The Puzzle of Parham House

Death at Silent Pool

The Izzy Palmer Mysteries

A Corpse Called Bob

A Corpse in the Country

A Corpse on the Beach

A Corpse in London

A Corpse for Christmas

A Corpse in a Locked Room

A Corpse in a Quaint English Village

A Corpse at a Wedding

A Corpse at A School Reunion

A Corpse from the Past

ONE

Sometimes, the only solution to one's problems is to forget about them altogether. I could have camped out at home worrying about my missing father until I was grey and old. I could have become obsessed with the idea that a shadowy organisation had taken him for some unimaginable reason. I might even have devoted my life to tracking down a disreputable character by the name of Lucien Pike who was the last known person to see him alive. But there comes a time when it makes far more sense to enjoy one's existence rather than worrying about things that are beyond our control.

To that end, I spent a mere three or four months involved in such gloomy and disheartening pursuits before a neat white envelope landed on my doormat, and I realised that I had become embroiled in an impossible task. The time had come for a change.

My basset hound Percy ran to the door to see what had arrived. He sniffed at the envelope and, rather than dutifully delivering it to his master, fell asleep on the carpet just next to it.

Happily, it wasn't a poison pen letter. I'd seen enough of

those to last a lifetime. In fact, it was the kind of communication that brightens one's week immeasurably. It said,

Dear Marius Quin,

I am writing to reveal that we at the Torquay Mystery and Detection Society have chosen you to become an honorary member. We are great admirers of your first two novels and will be holding a gala in your honour on the 12th October. It will be our immense pleasure to receive you at our town's luxurious Grand Hotel on the seafront. It is customary for authors to make a speech to our members on the topic of their choosing. In addition, you will be invited to stay at the hotel for two nights, make use of its fine facilities and attend our famous October Ball.

Please reply by post or call my assistant Miss Capshaw on Torquay 2465 if you have any questions. We must know your travel arrangements in advance.

I am sure that your visit will be a revelation.

Sincerely,
Mrs Angelica Thistlethwaite
Founder and Head of the TMDS

There was something about the tone of the letter that immediately made me want to meet the woman who had penned it. The presumptuousness of hosting a gala in my honour without first checking to make sure I could attend was not lost on me. However, I had a feeling that she was just the sort of person whom I, as a writer, was obliged to study. I hadn't written a single word of my third novel and yet, just from this short missive, I could start to imagine a plot revolving around the indomitable Mrs Thistlethwaite. I was eager to discover whether reality would live up to my impression of her.

I rang the number provided the very moment I finished reading. The operator connected me to Devon and then another, far chattier lady put me through to Miss Capshaw.

"Good morning, the Torquay Mystery and Detection Society. This is Mrs Thistlethwaite's assistant. How may I be of service?" It sounded as if she were talking to me from China or perhaps the moon. It wasn't just that the line was poor – that was a given – her voice was so soft that I had to strain to hear it.

"Ah, good morning." I tried to be clear and confident for the two of us. "My name is Marius Quin, and I—"

"Will be calling to confirm your attendance at next month's gala."

"That's right. I was wondering whether—"

"You could reserve a room in the hotel for the second weekend of October?"

"Correct again." She was so efficient that I almost didn't dare speak. She could take the words from my mouth before I knew what I was going to say. "I'll require—"

"A single room for the nights of the twelfth and thirteenth."

I couldn't muster a reply, as I was trying to imagine how she knew so much.

"My apologies, Mr Quin." She suddenly sounded more nervous. "I didn't mean to put words in your mouth. I'm only repeating what Mrs Thistlethwaite told me. I have a note here with those exact details. Are they correct, or would you prefer a double room?"

"No, a single will suit me just fine," I said with a touch of caution in my voice, which I tried to cover over with a joke. "Unless they have rooms for dogs. I'm sure that my basset—"

"That shouldn't be a problem, Mr Quin. I will tell the Grand that you will be travelling with your dog, and I'm sure they will do everything they can to accommodate you."

today." I knew she wouldn't listen, so I wasn't afraid of offending her.

"It's lovely to see you too." She breezed straight past me and into the lounge where my mother was reading a book.

It was not just any book, in fact. She was reading my last novel, *A Glimpse of a Blood Moon*. I genuinely appreciated the effort she had put into reading it. The only problem was that she'd started a month before and was still only halfway through.

"Oh, Bella." She was apparently most happy to be interrupted. "It is so lovely to see you."

"And you, Mary. It's been too long." They embraced warmly before my childhood girlfriend had the opportunity to interfere in my life again. "Now perhaps you can convince your son to tell us why he's smiling."

They looked at me as I stood in the doorway and Percy waddled past to sit on Mother's feet.

"I'm not smiling," I insisted.

"Look in the mirror, Marius, and stop being so contrary." Either one of them could have said this but, as it happens, it was Bella.

"My goodness," I said, staring across at my reflection above the mantelpiece. "You're right. I look quite the woodenhead. What's wrong with me?"

"Only you can answer that, old chum," Bella's tiresome boyfriend exclaimed as he stepped around me. I had to peer along the hallway to understand how he'd got inside.

"How did you...?" I asked, but no one was listening. I could only assume that Percy had got in the way of the door when I'd tried to close it. It would not be the first time this had happened, though he usually yelped in dismay.

"Gilbert, Marius has a secret that he won't tell us," Bella announced, and the newcomer looked almost as excited as the ladies did.

"You dark horse, Marius. Is it a woman?"

I wouldn't be pulled into their speculation. "There's no secret, and no woman, for that matter."

"A case then," Bella guessed. "It's been months since anything suitable came along. We really can't call ourselves detectives if you refuse every paying job."

They had arranged themselves on the sofa like a panel of judges and I stood in the dock in front of them. "I don't generally call myself a detective. I call myself an author."

I noticed that Mother winced a little at that, and I was tempted to force a confession out of her, but I'm not that cruel.

"And besides," I swiftly continued, "every person who has come calling to contract the services of the illustrious Marius and Co. has been a time waster. I've had men looking for lost girlfriends – who I very much doubt wished to be found – women seeking to confirm the good reputation of their future husbands, and an old fellow who had lost his pipe. They were hardly cases worthy of our time."

"Well, I'm not ashamed to admit that I enjoy poking my nose into other people's business and chasing down wrongdoers." Bella tipped her head back proudly. "If we don't accept a client soon, I will break out on my own."

I was going to tell her to do just that, but her boyfriend found our detective work most vexing, and I rather enjoyed putting his nose out of joint. "My apologies, dear Bella. I have been terribly busy, but I promise that we can go on another adventure before long."

Gilbert Baines, the born banker, leaned back in the comfy leather seat and passed judgement on me. "Your problem, Marius, is organisational. You will never make a name for yourself as a detective if you don't first define the objectives of your business. Second, advertise your services, and third, dress a little more smartly."

"I so greatly appreciate your generous advice." I had never in my life sounded quite so sarcastic. I almost made myself laugh. "However, I do not wish to make a name for myself as a detective. I wish to make a name for myself as an author."

"And a very good one you are, too," my mother presumably lied. "I'm enjoying your new book ever so much." She could only maintain her earnest expression for so long and changed the topic. "Now, about this secret. Is it anything to do with your father?"

I walked over to the back window and considered whether I should tell them. The problem with having nosy friends and family is that they tend to do the opposite of what a discreet person like me would wish them to do. Of course, not telling them at this stage would have led to even more questions, and I knew I would have to give in.

"It's not a secret, and it has nothing to do with Father in the slightest. In fact, it is the perfect antidote to everything the two and a half of you have been complaining about for months. It will require me to leave the flat, wear smart clothes and talk to new people."

"Then it must be a woman!" Gilbert replied. "What else could force you to take such drastic measures? I've met more sociable hermits than you."

"It is not," I contested very slowly, "a woman."

"Then please put us out of our misery." Bella's face had lit up with the game we were playing, and her happiness soon floated about the room to infect the rest of us.

I shook my head but submitted to her request. "Very well, I'll tell you." I licked my lips in anticipation. "I have been chosen as an honorary member of the Torquay Mystery and Detection Society!"

Not a sound came back to me. Not a sound!

"They're going to throw a gala in my honour," I tried again.

"Is that all?" Gilbert asked, and I wanted to throttle him even more than usual.

"Hello, everyone." These words carried down the hall, and I

wished that I'd shut the front door when I'd had the chance. My uncle Stan was pushing Auntie Elle into the room in her wheelchair. "What have we missed?"

"Nothing whatsoever," Gilbert replied, folding his arms sullenly across his chest.

Bella at least tried to sound positive. "A little society of some sort is throwing a party for Marius."

"It's not a party," I was quick to correct her. "It's a gala. There's a world of difference." No one looked convinced by my claim, and so I tried to change their minds. "I'll be staying at the Grand Hotel on the English Riviera. They say there is no finer town on the British coast than Torquay."

"In October?" Stan asked, somewhat dubiously.

"Well, I'm very proud of you, Marius." I can tell I'm losing an argument when my mother is the only person willing to support me. "Your new book is..." She still wouldn't say what she thought of it. "...deserving of high praise."

"Thank you, Mother. You are most kind." I glared at the others to imply that they were not.

The voice of reason, or Auntie Elle as she's commonly known, spoke up at this point. "It could be a marvellous opportunity for you. And it's so nice to have your work recognised by what sounds to me like a very worthy organisation." This would have been more persuasive if she had been in the house when I'd mentioned the name of the society that was throwing the gala, but I wasn't about to look a gift horse in its mouth, eye, or any part of the body if I could help it.

"Those are my feelings exactly. A 'worthy organisation' is looking to recognise my work in a beautiful place, and I am so excited about it that I'd like you all to come." As soon as I said it, I regretted the decision. Why did I think a petty squabble was so important that I'd invite my favourite loons and meddlers along for the weekend?

"Oh, that's a lovely idea." Bella sounded a little more enthused. "We'll make flags with your name on and sit at the back of the hall waving them."

"I'll knit some scarves like they have at football matches," Mother added, and suddenly the whole lot of them had warmed to the plan.

"I've always wanted to visit Torquay," Stan said with a far-off look. "It's a romantic sorta place, what with all them smugglers and mermaids." I could tell that his only knowledge of the area came from children's adventure books.

Realising what their presence at such an august event might mean, I subtly tried to rescind the invitation. "But what about your bakery at Hurtwood, Stan? Surely you couldn't leave it so soon after opening."

"Nonsense. Your old friends the Lyles have turned out to be fine apprentices. They're manning the fort for me today."

"Wonderful." I doubt anyone in the history of time had managed to express this word with quite so little enthusiasm. "Then it's a plan." I looked at Bella, who was already discussing the arrangements with my mother. "What about you, old friend? Surely you can't leave your father for so long."

"It's fine, Marius. Though I do appreciate your asking. My brothers spend their weekends with him, and they do a perfectly adequate job. Besides, he would want me to go away with you. He's always saying I should let my hair down more often."

"Yes, but not on the coast at this time of year. Your hair will get all wet." I have no idea why I would say this.

"Now that you mention it..." Gilbert spoke up, and just when I thought things couldn't get any worse... well, they didn't. "...I will be busy that weekend."

"Of course you will." I almost jumped in the air with glee. "The world of finance waits for no one."

He regarded me archly. "I beg your pardon, Marius, but I am not just a banker. I have a life outside my profession."

I admit, I was sceptical. "What is it? A lawn bowls tournament? Tiddlywinks? Or are you planning to get a head start on next year's income tax return?"

He stood up from his chair and looked incredibly patronising as he put both hands in his waistcoat pockets. "As it happens, I volunteer at an orphanage when I can."

"What do you do there?" I had never imagined him having such a charitable bent, and I struggled to make sense of the information. "Laugh at the poor creatures? Laud just how rich you are over them?"

"No, Marius. I do what I can to help. For example, I play with the younger children and listen to the older ones read," Gilbert clarified. "I've done so for years, and it was where Bella and I met."

It was at this point that his beautiful, charming and ever so compassionate girlfriend looked across at him with love in her eyes. I finally understood what she saw in the man whom I'd previously found quite charmless.

"Gilbert is being modest, as always," Bella told me. "He does not merely volunteer there. He helped raise the funds to build the place and brought several significant benefactors to the organisation."

Gilbert had done something which I didn't think possible; he had surprised me! I was starting to wonder just how much my opinion of him was shaped by my own preconceptions. I mean, I'd known the man for the best part of a year and learnt virtually nothing about him.

After a brief moment in which I rearranged my world views, I offered him my hand. "In which case, I must commend you on a good deed and ask how I can help in future."

He shook it profusely and even managed a smile. "That's jolly good of you, Marius. I suppose we all do what we can."

"Honestly, Baines, it is admirable behaviour, I'm just sorry that you won't be coming with us to enjoy the luxury hotel and its range of fine facilities."

TWO

My jolly to the coast had turned into a family holiday. I thought I might at least convince Percy that he could stay with a friend of mine for the weekend, but he'd got wind of the plan and was having none of it. Or rather, he'd twisted my mother around his little paw, and she fought his corner whenever the suggestion arose of leaving him behind.

By the time the month was out, my companions were more excited than I was about the trip. By the middle of October, they were champing at the bit to leave. Stan telephoned each morning to consult his sister-in-law on our plans for the trip and the best items of luggage to take. I had never realised that a weekend away could involve quite so much organisation. I felt fairly confident that my corps' attempt to take the Chipilly Spur at Amiens in 1918 had required less planning.

In time, the big day arrived, and I was eager to enjoy another foray outside the capital. I hadn't actually left London since the spring and, though I'd spent plenty of time rushing about the city, trying to locate a man who knew something of my father's disappearance, it had been too long since I'd enjoyed anything of the countryside. I was tempted to drive the two hundred miles to Torquay in my gleaming red Invicta, but the decision was taken out of my hands, and we piled onto the GWR Express at Paddington instead. As requested, the Mystery and Detection Society was dutifully informed of our plans.

"Now, this is what I call an adventure!" my dear old uncle cried as we sat down in our comfortable carriage. He immediately pulled the window down to stick his head out and survey the platform where we'd just spent the last twenty minutes waiting.

The compartment I'd reserved had two benches that faced one another and, from the curtains to the carpets and seat covers, everything was upholstered in vivid royal blue. I wouldn't normally have travelled first class, but it was worth the few extra d. to see the look on my relatives' faces.

"It is nice," my more restrained aunt agreed as I helped her into her seat, and the porter stowed her wheelchair in the luggage compartment. "I've always said there's something very romantic about trains."

Bella said nothing but smiled at my family, whom she had recently adopted as an extension of her own. Mother had brought a picnic, though I'd told her in advance that we could enjoy the Pullman dining carriage.

"It will save us all a lot of money, Marius," she reminded me as she raided the hamper and passed around neat packages wrapped in checked cotton napkins.

"I'm quite literally famished," Bella announced, and her eyes widened at the size of the sandwiches on offer.

"No, you are metaphorically famished," I corrected her, as I'm an author and I'm allowed to be pernickety.

My friend was unimpressed. "You sound like our old teacher."

"That's because Mrs Abbot was the person who taught me to use language accurately," I replied, before dropping my voice to a whisper, "unlike some people."

In reply, she delivered a well-deserved kick to my knee, but it did not stop me from laughing at her.

"Children, children," Auntie Elle said to get us under control. "This will be a very long journey if you insist on fighting the whole way there." She gave me a wink to show the spirit in which her comment should be taken, and we relaxed back in our seats to enjoy our early lunch.

"Long?" Stan said as he sipped at a bottle of dandelion and burdock. "Three hours and forty minutes from London to the south-west coast isn't long, my darling. It's positively miraculous." He could say no more, as his wife had seized a cheese and pickle sandwich to stop his mouth.

He was right about the speed at which we cut across the country. Once we'd built up a head of steam (literally), we raced past every station without stopping. I caught the blurred signs of Twyford, and Hungerford, Acton and Edington & Bratton, among others that didn't rhyme. I enjoyed the thought that England was one great map, and we were there to mark off the towns we passed like inspectors checking tickets.

The weather was bright and fresh, and patches of blue occasionally appeared in the cloudy sky. It was as if God favoured certain areas over others and blessed his favourite parts of Wiltshire and Somerset with sunshine. It was easy to imagine him singling out such places, and I marvelled at the views over multicoloured plains and hills that we were awarded from our fire-swift machine. It was not smooth or silent as it rattled through the countryside, but it was the kind of journey that might inspire a man to take up writing in order to capture the experience. Seeing as I was already an author, I simply took out a notebook from my bag and got to work.

By the time we crossed the border into Devon, I believe that I had the makings of a more than respectable first chapter. I don't wish to suggest that I hadn't written anything that year, but my grand idea for a mystery novel involving seventeen types of espionage and a circuitous plot was abandoned halfway through when real life turned out to be far stranger than fiction. What I would write in its place was still in doubt, but the seed of an idea that had come to me on the train was certainly intriguing.

"Don't you ever get tired of just writing about things rather than living them?" Bella said to tease, as she knew such a criticism no longer applied to me.

"I do indeed," I told her, "which is why I'm off to the luncheon car. Would you care to join me?"

"I think I'll have a rest." She looked at our napping companions. "Your mother's substantial picnic has tired us all out."

If we had still been in love, I would have kissed her then. I would have leaned forward to plant a kiss on the top of her head and, as Percy was the only one around with his ears open, told her how much I adored her. Sadly, or perhaps otherwise, I was making a concerted effort to remember that would not be my lot in life. I put my hat on so that I could tip it to her and then quietly left the compartment.

The train really was moving at pace, and I kept falling against the walls along the corridor. I almost tumbled into the open doorway of another compartment at one point, but I managed to steady myself just in time. I passed through the exquisite dining carriage, with its smart green seats and walnut panelling that showed scenes of far-eastern sunsets laid out in contrasting marquetry. It was a most attractive space, though I must say that the expensive lunch they were serving paled in comparison to my mother's contribution. From what I saw, the chicken soup looked a little anaemic. The pork chops had been carved from a scraggly pig, and I've never been one for *baba au rhum*.

"That will be thruppence please, sir," the curly-haired, red-cheeked girl in the pink apron told me when I ordered my cup of tea. She smiled but was unable to meet my gaze and gave a hesitant curtsey when I handed over the coin.

Just as I was doing so, I noticed that a man dressed all in black was looking at me from beyond his newspaper. He was sitting at one of the few small tables in the carriage, and I had the definite sensation that he'd been watching me since I arrived. I'd been planning to take my drink to the back of the train to watch the world pass by, but I decided to stay at the counter in the hope I might get a better look at him.

I sipped my tea and pretended to be looking at the menu on the wall opposite. He couldn't very well keep staring at me and, when he returned to his paper, I seized the moment to perform my own scrutiny. He was around my age but had mutton-chop sideburns and a pork-pie hat. His clothes were remarkable for their deep blackness. In normal circumstances, I felt that it would have been the outfit of a man who wanted to blend in, but the suit was a size or two too big for him and something about the way he wore it made me think the opposite was true. It was as if he wanted everyone to know that he was not a man to cross.

"Would you like anything else, sir?" the serving girl asked.

The man in black looked up again, but I was too slow to look away and our eyes met for a second, which made it rather obvious that I'd been watching him. I felt in that moment that this was his intention all along, and he'd managed to turn the tables on me.

"Sir?" the girl asked again, but I was concentrating on the stranger and don't remember how I responded.

I must have mumbled something as she set about fulfilling an order, and I handed her some money. With one last look over my shoulder at the strange figure in black, I left the carriage with my tea in one hand and my purchase in the other. It was only as I reached the dining area that I realised what I was holding. It was a clean white cardboard box which, judging by the weight, contained a rather large cake. Why do these things happen to me?

Next, I had to contend with the bone-shaking cakewalk back to my seat. Cakewalks themselves must be the least appropriately named attraction at the fairground, as they are certainly no cakewalk. Nor, it turns out, is the act of walking with a cake. Every time the train lurched one way or another, I nearly lost my footing. I spilt half of my tea and came inches away from burying my face in the box, but I was spared that embarrassment, at least.

Back in our compartment, everyone was fast asleep, and I didn't want to have to carry a cream-filled Victoria sponge around Torquay when we arrived, so I gave a morsel to Percy and helped myself to some.

When we were a short time away from our destination, we skirted the River Exe where it met the English Channel. I felt as though I could see for ever when the train turned to follow the coast, and we approached the small town of Dawlish. We shuttled along the seafront with a high street on one side and the splashing waves just beneath us on the other. I always felt a sense of great satisfaction when I spied the sea, and I couldn't be anything but sorry when the tracks pulled us back inland towards Newton Abbot.

"My goodness, Marius." Bella woke up at the worst possible moment and her sudden exclamation caused a chain reaction around the carriage so that my aunt, then uncle, then mother all looked at me in horror. "Why did you buy such a gigantic cake?"

I admit it must have been a trifle (if you'll excuse the pun) odd for them to wake up to the sight of me greedily tucking in to a whole cream cake.

"I could have brought you something from the bakery if you were desperate, my boy," Stan added, before dropping his voice as though someone might be listening. "Would have been a lot cheaper than the prices they charge you on here, I can tell you."

My mother could only parrot what Bella had already asked. "Why did you buy such a gigantic cake?"

I'd only had a few bites, but as the train was still far from smooth, I had crumbs all over my clothes and a small pile of them had reached the floor where Percy was making swift work of eating them.

"It's not all for me," I said when I'd swallowed the rather large mouthful I'd been working on. "I don't even like sponge cake that much."

Sitting on the bench opposite mine, Bella, my aunt and my mother all gave the exact same disapproving look at the exact same moment. I have no doubt they would have selected some words to go with it, but there was a commotion in the corridor outside, and we turned to see what was happening. At first it was just muffled shouting, but then someone sped past our door and, a moment later, a blur of black chased after him.

I was on my feet immediately and, when I got to the slide-down window and poked my head out to see what was happening, I saw two men fighting just a little way along the passage.

"Calm down now, both of you," I said in the hope that a simple dose of public outrage would be enough to resolve the situation. Before I could open the door, the train guard appeared and went to separate them. The two troublemakers had their backs to me, but they spun around as soon as the guard got there, and I saw the man in black once more.

"Now, now," the well-dressed employee of the Great Western Railway told them. "We'll have no trouble on my train. Who's got a problem with whom and why?"

The pair had gone from lamping one another to guiltily standing side by side, uncertain what to say to the man in charge.

"There's no problem, guv'nor," the second fellow replied. He was dressed in a reddish suit and matching hat, in much the same style as his pursuer. "Just a little misunderstanding between friends."

The guard stopped right next to them and poked them in the chest, one after the other. "I should hope so, too. Now, you're going to get along like good boys, or you'll be off at the next stop. And if you really feel like testing me, I'll sling you from the train between stations."

Bella had taken her place alongside me to watch the confrontation, whereas my family all stayed back in the safety of our cushy compartment.

"Have I made myself clear?" the guard asked, and the two men smiled at him as if they were having a perfectly lovely time.

"Crystal clear, guv'nor," the red-suited chap affirmed with a tap of the head and a sarcastic salute.

The man in black had not spoken a word, but he saw that we were watching and hesitated as his companion put his arm around his shoulder and the two of them walked off with a rather jaunty step. I believe the fellow in the red suit was even whistling.

"How very strange." Bella's voice was quiet and contemplative, but then the guard drew level with us, and she spoke more loudly. "I think you should check your pockets."

"I beg your pardon, miss?" He had a clean-shaven face but large bags under his eyes, as if he hadn't slept in days.

"I can't be sure, but I thought I saw one of them put his hand in your pocket when you were standing next to them. You should check that he hasn't stolen anything."

"Did he indeed." He looked at me then as though to confirm I agreed. Despite this short pause, he did as she'd suggested and appeared unable to find whatever had previously been there.

"That cheeky..." He thought better of speaking so rudely in front of a lady and cut the comment short. "I think I'll have a word, if you'll excuse me."

He didn't sound too upset by what had occurred and strolled off after the apparent pickpockets, humming to himself as he went.

THREE

I didn't give this scene a great deal of thought, and yet it unnerved me somehow. I believe it was the way the man from the buffet car had looked when our eyes met. It felt as if he knew I would be there. As for the run-in with the guard, that was only made stranger when we arrived at Torquay station to see the three men on the platform beside the waiting room. They had apparently made friends again, as they were all having a good laugh together.

Bella noticed it too, and I believe she was about to say something when we were interrupted.

"Mr Quin?" A man I took to be a chauffeur – based on the fact he was wearing a chauffeur's cap and brown and gold livery – gave a respectful nod and pointed us towards the street. I couldn't help wondering how he had known what I looked like. My publishers had a photograph taken of me for the odd public appearance I'd made, but, to my knowledge, it was yet to appear in print. "This way, sir."

He led us to a bay at the front of the station, and I called to Mother to check that she, my aunt and my uncle would be all right without me. They were busy dealing with their luggage, and we couldn't have all fitted in one car anyway – especially with Percy waddling along at my side in search of the luxury treatment to which he was accustomed.

The chauffeur's car was an unremarkable blue Baby Austin with a discreet white letter G on one door to signify his employer. No one had told me that I would be ferried to our destination, but I was more than happy that this would be the case. The gala would not be starting for some hours, and I was eager to make the most of our time in the hotel. I can only imagine that my dog felt the same way. He'd already slept at home that morning, on the train as we winged our way south-west, and he would now get a chance to rest on the no doubt thick carpets and springy sofas of the Grand.

"Palm trees!" Bella cooed as we pulled out of the station towards the crescent moon bay and its promenade. "I'd heard about them being here, of course, but it's quite another thing to see them in person. It feels as though we've come to some distant country."

"Your first time in Torquay?" our driver asked over his shoulder. The cautious, drone-like worker who had barely raised his eyes to us in the station was gone. In his place was a cheery human being. It was almost as if, now that we were ensconced within his realm of authority, he could be himself.

"That's right," I replied. "Our first time in Devon, in fact."

"Well, Mr Quin, may I say that you've made a wonderful choice? Torquay is the perfect destination for honeymooners like you." He was not just cheery, in fact, but cheeky with it. We stopped at a junction facing the sea to let a tram pass, and he took the chance to wink at me. "Forgive me for jumping to conclusions, but you certainly have the look of newlyweds. Am I right?"

Bella turned to me with a mischievous grin of her own just then, and I thought she would set him straight. "You are indeed.

My husband and I are very much in love and looking forward to our lives together."

I would probably have corrected him in an awkward manner that left a horrible atmosphere in the car, so this was just about preferable. For all Bella's apparent enjoyment of the misunderstanding, I pulled my head into my shell for the rest of the journey.

Torquay was evidently another of God's favoured places, and I could just have imagined him picking a spot on the beach to enjoy the autumn sunshine under a patch of blue sky. I could see it glittering off the perfectly smooth sea, where not a ripple or wave appeared through the glass of the Austin.

It turned out that our journey would be a short one. We manoeuvred around a small island in the middle of the road and back on ourselves towards an immense white building with fairy-tale towers on either side. It had approximately six thousand windows and plenty of grand balconies to go with them.

"You'll forgive my capriciousness," the driver stated confidently as we approached the back of the building, just yards away from where we had got into the car. "But I like to give new arrivals the scenic tour." He let out a chirpy laugh and brought the car to a halt in front of the steps up to the main entrance of the Grand Hotel.

"Hello there, Marius," I heard a man say as I stepped from the vehicle, and there was my Uncle Stan, his wife and my mother. "Fancy meeting you here."

"How was the traffic?" Mother asked.

Bella was still in a wonderful mood and joined in with their joke. "Terrible, but it was worth it for the views."

The driver passed our bags to the overly formal commissionaire at the entrance, who placed each one on a tall brass trolley with all the care of a nurse with a newborn baby. I believe this may have been what impressed my relatives most all weekend, as they nodded to one another appreciatively and proceeded into the building to make themselves known at reception.

Such menial tasks were below a noted celebrity of my standing – ho ho! When I mounted the steps, there was someone waiting to greet me.

"Good afternoon," the gentle voice I'd heard on the phone when I'd arranged my stay began. "I assume you are Mr Quin?"

"That's right," I replied. "And you must be Miss Capshaw."

I held my hand out, and she curtseyed with one ankle neatly crossed behind the other as though I were royalty. She was not how I had imagined her on the telephone. She had enchantingly blue eyes that were magnified by her thick glasses. Her dark hair was tied in a pleasantly messy pile on top of her head, and she wore the clothes of a woman much older than her twenty-five or so years. For all her obvious beauty, she did her best to hide it, and gave the impression of a meek and unimposing person.

"Please, call me Jennifer." She released my hand but kept her liquid eyes on mine.

"Then you must call me Marius," I replied, though I was uncertain whether she was allowed to be so informal in her job.

It appeared that neither of us knew what to say after that, so I cast my gaze about the elegant foyer. Its design was very much of our century, while also influenced by more ornate styles of eras gone by. There were white plaster columns here and there and a small fountain in the middle of the hall which released two fine jets of water in an arch from its centre. All that was missing were a few white doves and some orange trees and we could have been in a Spanish courtyard.

Further into the building, I could see the entrance to a dining room and the base of a grand staircase. The floor was tiled with an ornate mosaic pattern and the same scrolling letter G that I'd seen on our car was worked into it. All in all, it was a thoroughly welcoming sight from which Jennifer apparently wished to whisk me away.

"This way, please. Someone will see to your bags." She led me past Bella and my family all the way to a lift that looked as if it had been installed fairly recently. I would not have expected such modernity in an old Victorian building like the Grand, and it immediately caught my attention.

"If you think this is impressive," Jennifer told me, "wait until you feel the central heating in your room. It does an exceptional job at fighting off the cold."

"I was hoping that you would tell me that it is sunny here three hundred and sixty-five days a year."

She smiled and, in a whisper, said, "We actually only manage three hundred, but the local council has been trying to keep it a secret."

There was a pleasant ding, the brass concertina doors were opened by the attendant inside, and we entered the lift.

"Good afternoon, sir. Good afternoon, Jennifer." The young man within wore the same brown and gold uniform as the commissionaire had. It had a high collar and long hem, and I had to imagine that he was boiling, but he certainly looked the part. The only difference, when compared to the clothes his colleague wore, was the colour of his gloves and he now extended one white finger to press the button for the second floor.

"Good afternoon, Newbury," Jennifer closed and reopened her eyes by way of acknowledgment. The attendant blushed and pretended that he wasn't sneaking a glance at her, then the lift juddered into life.

I had the eerie sensation for half a second that someone had tied a string to the top of my head, and I was being pulled up through space before gravity weighed down on me again. We rumbled past the first floor and another ding greeted us as we reached our destination.

"Here we are, sir," Newbury chimed, much like the apparatus in which he worked. "Second floor." He tipped his hat to us, and we set off towards my home for the weekend.

The corridor snaked about, and I wasn't confident I would find my way back there when the time came, but I enjoyed the rich red carpets and perfectly clean white wallpaper with its oak dado. I'd visited plenty of grand buildings before, but there was something curiously showy and artificial about the hotel that I found quite pleasing. There wasn't a morsel of dust on the floor, and it was easy to see that every surface had been given a thorough clean in the last day. Though I don't personally have such high standards, I could appreciate the appeal for regular guests. It was the knowledge that everything was shipshape and as it should be. I had no doubt that this level of service would extend to every aspect of the hotel, from our toast at breakfast to an after-dinner snifter before bed.

"I chose room two-one-six for you, Marius." Jennifer produced the key and pushed open the door at the far end of a long corridor.

My only comment when I'd stepped inside the spacious parlour with doors leading off on all sides was, "Didn't I tell you that I only required a single room?"

"You did, but... Well, this is the nicest one in the hotel." She blushed and led me towards the front of the suite, where a spacious lounge offered the most wonderful view across the bay and all the way to the harbour in the centre of town.

"I am not complaining," I told her as I took in that magnificent sight. "It's hard to believe that Christmas is only two months away. It feels as if I've travelled to the south of France."

Her expression immediately turned to one of concern. "You do know that I was only joking about the sunshine here. We get bad weather just like everywhere else in Britain. You must make the most of it while you can."

Her warning served to draw my attention to a thick bank of

cloud on the horizon. It was an unusual contrast to the rows of elderly sun-worshippers on deckchairs on the terrace below my room. They were arranged in a semicircle around the edge of a large swimming pool that had been drained for the off-season. Yet more people were spilling out of the restaurant with cups of tea and pastries, ready for a sunny afternoon snack.

"Thank you. I will do what I can."

"To be perfectly honest," she added, "I've never known such a warm October, but the forecast says that it won't last a great deal longer."

I turned away from the window to look at her. "Then I've arrived at just the right moment." I can't imagine she knew how to take this comment, as it didn't actually make a lot of sense.

She politely changed the topic. "The head of our society, Mrs Thistlethwaite, will be here to greet you before the gala begins." There was the definite implication that I should take this as a great honour. "Until then, I hope you enjoy your time at the hotel."

I would have liked to ask some questions about the curiously named Torquay Mystery and Detection Society, but she was already moving to leave.

"Thank you, Jennifer," I said almost experimentally, and I was pleased that she responded just as warmly.

"You're very welcome, Marius." Those gorgeous blue eyes ignited for a moment, and she hurried from the room, no doubt to attend to one of the myriad duties for which she was responsible.

When I heard the sound of the door to my suite firmly shutting, I looked back at the view and the grey clouds that appeared to have already moved closer. Even the nattering ladies and gents from the sun terrace had noticed the approaching storm, but there was one person who paid it no heed. Beside the far fence of the property stood the man in black. He was deep in conversation with a rotund man in a dull grey suit. I was too far away to see their expressions, but from the way he moved his hands about and pointed aggressively, I got the sense that he was extremely angry about something.

FOUR

Oh, the joys of a little relaxation. I can't tell you what good it did me to lie down in a bed with plump pillows and a feather mattress. A thirty-minute snooze was enough to set me up for the evening ahead, and I still had the rest of the hotel to look forward to. I realised as soon as I'd changed into my bathing costume and dressing gown that I hadn't seen Percy since I arrived, so finding him would be the first task.

If the truth be told, I hadn't taken a holiday since I'd published my first novel. In my dream of what a novelist's life would be like, I had imagined a peaceful existence with perhaps a few hours of writing every week, followed by regular rounds of golf and a host of other leisurely pastimes. No one had told me that being an author was a full-time job and that the plots of my novels would leak into my waking existence. I had spent the last year and longer thinking about my books, investigating the odd crime for inspiration, or writing in brief spurts. So a weekend away from such stresses was very appealing indeed, and I was determined to enjoy it.

"Ah, Mr Quin," a rotund man in a dull grey suit intoned as I reached the reception. I recognised him immediately, and unlike the view I'd had of him out in the gardens, his demeanour now was most welcoming. "My name is Timothy Travers. I'm the manager here at the Grand Hotel, and I must say how honoured we are to receive you."

As you can probably tell, he had a terribly grandiose manner, and it was hard to know whether anything he said was sincere. Nonetheless, he played the part well and looked like the right sort of person to run such an establishment. Even as I stood there, a few sweet-hearted old dears with chintzy dresses and a lot of make-up waved at him as they passed. It was hard to estimate his age, but he hadn't a hair on his head and the bags under his eyes were so large that I imagine he required the commissionaire's assistance to carry them about.

"You are very kind, Mr Travers." I nodded my thanks. "Now the first thing I'd like to know is where my dog Percy has got to."

He patted his pockets much as the train guard had an hour before. "Ah yes, your dog. Now, where did we put him?" He smiled as he made his joke, then lifted the wooden counter to escape from his booth. "This way, please, sir."

He led me across the foyer and, rather than taking the lift this time, we walked over to the stairs opposite and were soon on the lower ground floor. It was noticeably warmer down there, and I could smell a particular chemical which suggested that I'd killed two birds with one stone and located the indoor pool. I could have followed the waves of heat to find it, but we turned off the corridor and there was my dear puppy, wrapped in a fluffy white towel, being terribly spoilt by a young lady dressed in incredibly clean nurse's whites.

The manager left us to it with a brief, "If there's anything you should need, sir, I will be at my post." He really was the definition of the faithful servant, which made the first glimpse I'd had of him all the stranger.

"Hello there, Mr Quin." Percy's smiley attendant had a

warm manner. "I'll be one of the staff who's looking after your little friend while you're staying with us. There are two other dogs arriving tonight, and I'm sure we'll all have a lovely time together."

I swear that a guilty look crossed the pampered puppy's features just then. His tail was whipping uncontrollably as she dried him after his bath.

"I can see that he is in good hands," I replied and winked at the spoilt doggy who sighed with pure contentment as I left.

"This place really is heavenly," I said aloud and practically skipped along the corridor to the misted glass door that I was one hundred per cent certain would lead to the swimming pool. There were other doors with porthole windows and, in each of them, I could see hotel guests enjoying personal treatments. Through one, I noticed a member of my family. Auntie Elle was enjoying a much-deserved massage of some description, and so I decided not to interrupt her.

"This place is heavenly," Bella told me when I found her laid out in a deckchair beside the kidney-shaped pool.

"I couldn't agree more," I replied, looking over at her. "I intend to spend every minute I can down here. It's a shame I have that gala tonight, but I will be back here first thing tomorrow morning."

There were potted palms in one corner and taffeta screens for changing. The floor was made up of red and white chequer-board tiles arranged on the diagonal, and the sides of the pool itself were an Athenian blue mosaic. I could not wait to jump in, so I didn't.

"Don't mind me," I told my elegant companion – whose exceedingly modern embroidered bathing attire I am too much of a gentleman to have noticed. I tore off my dressing gown and dived into the middle of the perfectly still water with my arms outstretched to part the way. I stayed under for as long as I could and made it right to the other side. For those twenty seconds, I considered what a lucky man I was even to peek into such a sumptuous world. And then I thought to myself, surely it won't last for much longer.

I emerged from the water with barely a breath left in my body and, when I'd wiped the water from my eyes, I realised that we were not alone. The man in black was sitting in a low chair on the opposite side of the room from Bella. He was still in the same clothes he'd worn on the train. His hat, pulled down as it was over his eyes, was particularly out of place in that almost literal steam bath, and I could only imagine that he would soon cook in his thick woollen suit.

At first, he just stared at me. He made no effort to hide it. He stared right at me, and I'd rarely been so uncomfortable. His penetrative gaze made me feel more naked than I already was and, had I not been stunned by the very rudeness of the gesture, I would have climbed from the pool, wrapped myself in a dressing gown and returned to my room to escape from that singularly unpleasant experience.

"My apologies, Marius," Bella called to break into it. "I should have introduced you. This is Augustus."

"Pleased to meet you, Mr Marius," the man in black laughed. His voice was not as I would have imagined. He looked like an American gangster but spoke with a London accent.

"Are you here for the gala this evening?" I held on to the side to avoid treading water.

"Gala?" he replied as though the word offended him. "I wouldn't know what that was if I was named after it." He allowed himself a silent laugh. "No, my friend. I di'n't come here for no gala. I've got a little business to attend to."

I was about to ask him what his business might entail when I had second thoughts.

Bella soon spoke to cover the silence. "Augustus was just telling me that he comes to Torquay every year at this time."

She made it sound as though they'd been having a perfectly friendly confab before I'd arrived.

"How nice." I hadn't taken my eyes off him. "It does seem a lovely spot."

"Lovely." Augustus held me in his gaze for another five seconds before he finally blinked. Even this slight movement appeared designed to intimidate, but then he pulled his hat even tighter on his head and rose from his chair. "It was a pleasure speaking to you, Lady Isabella."

He looked at me once more as he swept from the room, and we didn't see him again that night.

"How very odd indeed." I turned to my partner in crime-solving and expected her to have that lively expression that she wears whenever we come across something suspicious.

"In what way odd?" she asked, and the look on her face was far from how I'd imagined it. "I thought he was rather charming."

"Charming?" I waded through the water to get to her. "Do you really mean that?"

"Yes, I do." She adopted a tone to tell me that I was being ridiculous. I was very used to that tone. "We had a perfectly civil conversation about our homes and family, and he came across as a perfect gentleman."

"A perfect gentleman who we saw fighting some ruffian on the train today?"

She was about to answer back when the truth of my words must have hit her. She sat bolt upright in the chair and turned to look at the door through which our new acquaintance had just hurried. "No, surely not." She opened her mouth to say more, but nothing emerged. We had identified our first mystery of the weekend.

FIVE

I swam laps of the pool and tried to make sense of the strange figure. The best conclusion I could come to was that he was some sort of clown who was playing with me for the fun he could extract. He'd been perfectly civil around Bella, then put on his tough-as-nails act with me. The less appealing idea was that he thought he could charm the pretty young lady who was sitting by the pool in nothing but a three-piece crêpe de chine pyjama suit. If that were the case, it would explain his hostility towards me, though not his attitude in the luncheon car earlier in the day.

Well, mystery it may have been, but it was one that would have to wait for the time being. I had to change before the gala, and so I finished my exercise – feeling both stimulated and frustrated at the same time – and returned to my suite. I allowed extra time to find my way, and it was a good thing that I did. I must have wasted five minutes taking wrong turns around endless corridors which were lined with a hundred doors, before realising I had gone up one floor too many. After that, it was a doddle to find room number 216.

My possessions had made their way to my bedroom, and the

thoughtful, though perhaps a little intrusive, staff had removed my suit from its travelling bag to hang it in the wardrobe. I don't often get a chance to dress so formally, but I enjoyed the feel of my rich cotton shirt on my skin and the way that the cuff came to a stop on my wrist a perfect half inch beyond the sleeve of my dinner jacket. I added a pair of silver and opal cufflinks and regarded myself in the mirror. I looked a lot more like the photo my publisher had commissioned than I usually did. I felt quite smart, even if the curls in my hair had redoubled their springiness after the swim.

I hadn't a clue where any of the others were, but feeling as ready as I conceivably could, I took a deep breath and left my suite. I'm not hugely keen on talking in public, mainly because I can never imagine anyone wanting to hear about the topics of which I can talk with any authority. This time, though, I had more to concern me. It was not just the man in black, who, thanks to this mysterious epithet, had taken on fantastical qualities in my mind. Mrs Thistlethwaite's letter had left me with the definite sense that I was about to meet someone truly unusual. When the moment finally came, she did not disappoint.

"Quin," she barked across the foyer before I'd exited the lift, and I considered staying where I was.

Newbury, the overdressed attendant, pursed his lips as if to say, *Good luck out there, matey.* I noticed that, after I'd stepped into the foyer, he immediately closed the door behind me, and the lift shuttled away with no one inside except him.

"You are Marius Quin." This was not a question. Mrs Thistlethwaite knew exactly who I was and seemed to be reminding me in case it had slipped my mind.

"That's correct."

"I know it is." She shook her head in disapprobation and pointed towards a set of doors between the lift and the restaurant.

Before I could follow her instruction, I tried to take in the woman I had already built up in my mind as a colossus. She was around five foot tall, so not the world-destroying behemoth I'd imagined, and yet she strode deeper into the hotel with all the confidence of a young bull. She had the most remarkably complex pattern of lines on her face, as though she had lived a thousand lifetimes. I would have guessed her age as being around seventy, but she was not the type to let a number hold her back, and she positively raced ahead of me.

I was not the only person who was impressed by her commanding presence. The people we passed stopped to marvel at the human dynamo, in her buttoned-up silk blouse and long black skirt. I imagine that some of them were from the society she headed, but there was also a much younger woman whom I felt perhaps I'd seen before. She wore a sequined cocktail dress, satin opera gloves and beaded capelet and shone more brightly than the line of elaborate chandeliers above our heads. She had the kind of glamour that you don't expect to see in real life, and yet even she had to stand back to admire the tiny hurricane that swept through the room.

Mrs Thistlethwaite barged through the double doors, forcing the two people inside to freeze. Even her assistant, Jennifer, looked scared of her boss, and I soon discovered why.

"What is this?" Although I remember the terrifying septuagenarian screaming these three words, that isn't actually what happened. Everything that she said that night was delivered in the same low, intimidating growl, but it managed to travel across the room to the place where the manager of the hotel was standing with his back to a large artist's easel.

"Really, Mrs Thistlethwaite, it's nothing that can't be fixed," Travers informed her as I tried to understand why she was so angry.

The dragonish head of the society must have noticed something in the body language of her subordinates, but it was only as we drew closer, and the pair stood aside, that I knew why she was so upset.

Standing on the easel was a photograph that I have previously mentioned. My publisher had evidently provided it and, while I did not necessarily enjoy seeing my head printed at three times its normal size, this was not the only issue.

"In memoriam?" Mrs Thistlethwaite pointed to the two words at the bottom of the board. "What is the meaning of this, Jennifer?" Her eyes were so fiery that I'm surprised the poor girl didn't jump backwards to avoid being scalded.

"It's an honest mistake, Angelica. It must have been a mix-up at the printers."

"That's right, Mrs Thistlethwaite." Travers could only get this sentence out in a stutter. "No doubt there is a memorial service occurring as we speak with an image of the deceased and Mr Quin's name underneath it."

She didn't reply immediately. She looked between the two of them as if deciding who to blame. "It isn't good enough. You've made me look a fool in front of our guest."

"I really don't mind—" I tried to say, but she wouldn't be interrupted by the likes of me.

She held her hand up for silence and continued what she was saying. "You, Jennifer, should have made sure that the printers did their job properly. And you, Mr Travers, should have checked the board when it was delivered." She took a step closer to him and I couldn't help feeling sorry for the unfortunate man. "Don't forget the power I command in this town, Timmy." I'd never heard a diminutive wielded quite so brutally. "If you're not careful, I'll take our regular society meetings, and my various other enterprises, and find a new venue for them. I hear that the Imperial Hotel is exquisite."

"No, no," Travers was quick to respond, his hands flapping like the wings of a baby bird. "That won't be necessary. I will go personally to the printers this very moment to—"

Mrs Thistlethwaite's scowl only grew more venomous. "It's too late for that, you simpleton. Quin here will be starting his talk in fifteen minutes. What do you expect to achieve in that time?"

"Well... I suppose they could..."

"Get out this instant and stop bothering me. I'm tired of seeing your face."

"Yes, Mrs Thistlethwaite. Of course, Mrs Thistlethwaite." He was halfway across the large hall before he'd said a word, and I imagine he was only too happy to escape.

"As for you, Jennifer..." I'd never seen such a short person loom before, but that is just what she did in front of her young assistant. There was something vampiric about her; she seemed to rise up off the ground to strike fear in us. "I expected better of you. Now hurry along and corral our beloved members so that we can get started on time."

Jennifer didn't make a sound in reply. She simply nodded and scuttled away. Her legs beat a hurried retreat and her body was pulled along behind them. It was my turn to face the wicked creature before me, and I considered hiding behind a chair.

"Well, Mr Quin, I hope you are ready for what comes next." Had so ominous a phrase ever been uttered? The answer is yes, almost certainly, as everything the woman said bordered on the petrifying.

I attempted to remain calm and resolute before her, but instead I released an oddly melodious laugh and went to look at the picture that would be displayed at my funeral. I only hoped that day wouldn't come too soon. Of course, with the cold-hearted Angelica Thistlethwaite nearby, I could guarantee nothing.

The room was laid out with ten lines of white wooden chairs. There were approximately twelve in each row and, within minutes of Jennifer opening the doors, they were all filled. I felt there was a touch of theatricality at play here, as a woman like Mrs Thistlethwaite would have known how many people to expect. This only made the event she'd organised seem more popular, and extra chairs were soon located by the hotel staff to place at the back of the room.

The space itself was more similar to a town hall than any room I'd seen within a hotel. There was a small stage at one end, and the walls and ceiling were all painted white with large beams crossing above our heads. The floor was made of glossy pine, but there were so many people there that I couldn't see much of it. I imagined that it would be used for dancing at weddings and important functions, but I could tell my audience had more serious matters in mind. To a man, they were clutching copies of my two books. It was both encouraging and yet, thanks to the determined expressions they all wore, really quite intimidating – though this did explain a recent, unexpectedly large cheque I'd received from my publisher.

Bella and my family were there in the front row to cheer me on, but even with their loud and enthusiastic clapping, I would not receive the warmest reception of the night. When Mrs Thistlethwaite mounted the stage, it caused a sudden upswell of noise. This was not the polite applause of the awards evenings and literary dinners I'd previously attended. This was the sound of a group of people who adored their leader. For a moment, I was put in mind of the foreign rulers who have come to dominate their countries. As she raised her hand to silence them, she had the profile of a stern monarch or a zealous revolutionary, calling her subordinates to order.

"Good evening, ladies and gentlemen, and welcome to the forty-seventh meeting of the Torquay Mystery and Detection Society. With us this evening we have a young author who has won not insubstantial recognition for his first two novels, with which many of you will now be familiar. *A Killer in the Wings* I found to be a particularly enigmatic novel with plenty of surprises, whereas *A Glimpse of a Blood Moon* increased our knowledge of Mr Quin's detective Rupert L'Estrange and introduced a new group of suspects."

She was an accomplished public speaker. She did not hesitate or consult the notes in front of her, and I could only think that she'd memorised the short speech to avoid any such slip-ups. As it reached its conclusion, she gestured towards me with one hand. "Without further ado, I would like to introduce our special guest for this evening, Mr Marius Quin."

This time, the clapping was very much of the polite variety. It was as if the audience wanted me to know that I would have to prove myself if I wished to earn their plaudits.

I took the few steps up onto the stage at a clip, which gave me a fraction too much speed so that it looked as though I was in a hurry to be done with the whole thing. Mrs Thistlethwaite did not shake my hand or mouth words of encouragement, but she did stay on the stage beside me, as though she thought she might have to step in to correct me at any moment. She was a disconcerting presence at the best of times, and her loitering set me on edge.

I sought out Bella in the audience, as I knew that one look from her could make my nerves disappear. Sadly, she looked just as anxious about the goings-on there as I felt. There was something not quite right with this meeting. Perhaps it was the atmosphere, or the way that the audience seemed to lean forward as I took my place at the small lectern in the centre of the stage. It felt as if they were waiting for me to slip up. I cast a glimpse at my memorial before speaking and instantly felt worse.

"Good evening, ladies and gentlemen," I managed without a stutter or hiccup. "I thought that I'd talk to you this evening about the importance of character in a good mystery novel. Mrs

Thistlethwaite has already mentioned the detective in my books, and I believe that Inspector L'Estrange is a good starting point for us."

I paused then, but it was the wrong moment. I should have pressed on just a little bit longer to establish the thesis of my talk more clearly. The audience's response hit me in waves. I was yet to impress them, and I could feel it in the air.

"The thing about L'Estrange... what makes him unique is his uncompromising attitude, not just to the suspects on the cases he investigates, but to life itself. L'Estrange is a mirror that I hold up to society. He is not an everyman figure to whom we all can relate, but a cipher whom I can manipulate depending on the needs of the book."

They weren't enjoying it.

I'm not being insecure or overly self-critical; I could tell from their expressions that my audience had no interest in what I was saying. They clearly felt that they hadn't dressed in their finest and travelled to the hotel that evening to hear me rattle on about what makes a good character. They were waiting for whatever came next.

"To contrast with this implacable detective, the suspects in my books often go to the other extreme. They appear larger than life, however such impressions are undercut when L'Estrange probes deeper into who these people really are. This brings into question not just the personalities that the characters show to the world, but our own falsehoods too. The little lies we tell about ourselves are of great interest to me, and the chance to examine these unspoken contradictions was one of the reasons I became an author in the first place."

This at least brought a stirring of quiet discussion. The noise passed through the room like a breeze, though I couldn't make out what was said.

"If you take my first book as an example, which happens to be set in a seaside hotel, not so dissimilar to this one, we can see in the character of Edward Buxton that—" I stopped myself then as there was a man in the third row with his hand raised. "We can see— I'm sorry, but I'd prefer to leave any questions until I finish my talk." I cleared my throat, thinking that would be the end of it. "The character of Edward Buxton serves as a metaphor for human weakness in the novel. He is both a—"

I stopped again, and the room fell silent. The man was in his sixties with bright white hair and a hard face. I could tell just how determined he was from where I stood on the stage, and knew that I would have to give in.

"Very well. Ask your question."

He didn't hesitate as he stood up to do as I'd commanded. "My name is Robert Milton. My question is about your detective's methods of investigation. He relies a lot on instinct which, I think you'll accept, is not a scientifically recognised technique. There is no way that a criminal would be convicted based on hunches."

I could have responded directly, but his malignant tone made me disinclined to do so. "You haven't formed a question," I told him instead, and I was aware just how picky I sounded.

"Very well. How can you defend this? In my mind, L'Estrange is not a realistic detective. As such, in the real world, he would not be a successful investigator."

"Defend it?" I was knocked by his question. I hadn't realised until then that I'd been called to Torquay to defend myself. "I can defend my characters and my books because the stories are tightly plotted and make sense. My detective may use instinct when it comes to interviewing suspects and choosing which threads of a case to investigate, but he is able to secure a conviction thanks to the evidence he uncovers through the course of the novels."

He gave nothing but a curl of the lip in return. Before he could respond vocally, another member of the audience clambered to her feet.

"You say that, Mr Quin, but isn't it also true that three quarters of the way through *A Killer in the Wings* L'Estrange picks the wrong culprit?" She was a good decade older than Mrs Thistlethwaite and held onto the chair in front of her for support. "It is only because the real killer is so desperate to complete her plan that she is eventually caught."

"That may be true," I began, "but the fact is that my primary motive with that book was to set the reader off guard. L'Estrange himself goes through a crisis of conscience in the course of the investigation, and it is that failure which leads him to—"

"Now, now, Mr Quin," a third person interrupted and a woman in the front row prodded my book over and over again as she contradicted me. "That is a rather convenient explanation for what, ultimately, must be considered a flaw in the work. Like all of my acquaintances in this room, I have read a great many mystery novels, and I have never come across one which grounds its plot in the lead detective's own inability to identify the killer."

I wasn't even offered a chance to reply this time. Another spectator rose to confront me on my poor writing, and the scene continued like this for some time. I hoped that someone might come to my defence, but the subsequent forty minutes were given over to disparaging and deprecating my work. A brief respite came when my mother attempted to say something complimentary about the books, but as she was one of the very few people there who did not speak with a Devonshire accent, I very much doubt that anyone believed her to be impartial on the matter. Our family likeness can't have helped either.

"There we go, ladies and gentlemen." Mrs Thistlethwaite propelled me from the lectern as though we were magnets, and I was facing the wrong way. "I'm sure we all agree that was a fascinating discussion. We can now cross off another of Great Britain's detective writers from our list." This inspired a rather smug titter from some in the audience. "Thank you so much for coming, Mr Quin. I can't tell you how... enlightening it has been."

I noticed the woman's assistant as she stood at the side of the stage. Jennifer Capshaw looked truly sorry for me, but her pity only made me more determined to hide how bruising the experience I'd just endured had actually been.

"Thank you for a most enjoyable time. There is nothing like a little constructive criticism to help a writer improve," I told Mrs Thistlethwaite very loudly so that the audience calmed down to listen once more. "I'll recommend your little event to Carmine Fortescue."

I didn't mention this name because it belonged to one of the most famous authors in the country. Carmine Fortescue was my committed rival, and I loved the idea of that thin-skinned bore suffering up on that stage. We share a publisher and, with the help of a few well-chosen words, it would be only too easy to flatter the odious chap's ego and get him down to Torquay. I could imagine him finding common ground with Mrs Thistlethwaite, as they shared an apparent antipathy to everyone around them.

"There is one more thing I'd like to say," I told my host when she looked ready to usher me from the stage. "You see, there's something you evidently haven't discovered about me. Though I appreciate your effort reading my books to prepare for this evening, what you don't seem to know is that I am not just an author. With my associate, Lady Isabella Montague, who has kindly accompanied me here this evening, I have established a detective agency. We at Marius and Co. have already investigated a number of high-profile cases, and our success has even been described in several newspapers."

It was hard to say exactly why, but Mrs Thistlethwaite had grown increasingly angry as I spoke.

I paused to enjoy her reaction. "I have no doubt that you are all extremely knowledgeable when it comes to police investigations but, regardless of what you think of my fictional detective's investigative skills, I have certainly learnt a thing or two from the six murders we have already solved."

It was Mrs Thistlethwaite who began the clapping, presumably to precipitate my departure from the stage.

SIX

"You handled it all very well, Marius," Bella told me as the audience flowed out of the hall, "but I don't understand a thing that just happened."

Before I could answer, an old friend appeared. To my genuine surprise, Inspector Lovebrook was moving towards us, against the tide. "Marius, that was outstanding. You were fascinating from beginning to end." His supportive presence there was definitely Bella's doing, and I must say that I appreciated it. "I'm afraid I missed the first few minutes as my car was causing me trouble, but you really gave those doubting Thomases what for." The always enthusiastic policeman's passionate response drew a few tuts from some of Mrs Thistlethwaite's acolytes, but he didn't mind.

Uncle Stan was the only member of our party who looked a little deflated. "I made flags to cheer you on, Marius," he said, raising two paper pennants that had been glued on to a couple of sticks. "The moment never seemed right, though, and I didn't end up using them."

"I will happily respond to everything you have all said, just as soon as I have a drink in my hand." This was the only response I could give, as my energy reserves were flagging after the unexpected onslaught of criticism.

There was something of a bottleneck to leave the room, and so Uncle Stan loudly announced his presence and then pushed his wife through the crowd in her chair. Under normal circumstances, I would have told him to behave himself, but I didn't mind his being rude to members of the Torquay Mystery and Detection Society.

"It was a trap, and I fell for it," I explained once we'd cut a path through the masses to get to the bar. "I should have known from the name. They aren't interested in books; they meet to discuss crime. They evidently believe themselves far more capable sleuths than I am."

"Do you mean to say that they invite mystery novelists here just to show them up?" Lovebrook asked in a suitably disgusted tone.

"It would seem that way. I even sensed that there was something out of the ordinary from the tone of the letter they sent me. The whole experience has been thoroughly chastening."

My mother blushed a little as she made an observation. "Yes, but did you see the look on that harridan's face when you revealed that your detective work is not just theoretical? From what I could make of her, she deserves to be taken down a peg or two."

"It's her assistant I pity." I looked back across the crowded lounge to the doorway where Mrs Thistlethwaite was berating poor Jennifer. "It makes me terribly glad that I don't have a boss of my own."

"That's nice that you would think that, m'boy," Stan told me in a theatrical whisper so that all could hear. "But I'd say you have at least two bosses in your immediate vicinity as we speak."

Mother just laughed at him, whereas Bella had something to add. "There's no doubt about it. Your name may grace our little enterprise but, without me, you'd never leave your flat. In my book, that makes me the head of the operation."

"And I wouldn't have it any other way." I tried to look angelic, but I doubt she believed my act.

"Come along, all," Lovebrook declared once we'd enjoyed another slug or two of our drinks. I'd ordered a negroni and was pleasantly surprised by the barman's skilful preparation. "If the society of know-it-alls and cynics are paying Marius's bill this weekend, I think we should all enjoy a hearty dinner."

"That sounds like a grand idea," I replied, and we moved across the bar towards the main room of the restaurant.

One thing that I could not fault were the fixtures and furnishings of that delightful hotel. I had once dined at the Savoy with Lord Edgington himself, and though we were now two hundred miles from London, it did not feel like it. In the summer season, the English Riviera had become a home from home for many visitors. Hotels like the Grand could offer all the luxuries rich travellers enjoyed in the city, but with the blessing of the sea on their doorsteps. It really was the acme of style and comfort.

The restaurant itself was decorated in a classic style with white pilasters on every wall. Scrolling metalwork contrasted with ornate plaster flourishes above eye level and, most impressive of all, an immense crystal chandelier stood in seemingly implausible suspension over our heads. Every tablecloth was spotless, white and perfectly pressed. Equally neat waiters zipped about the place carrying silver trays, and in one corner, a four-piece band played at a discreet volume. If it weren't for the clientele that night, I might have said that it was very much my kind of place.

We were seated at a table that looked over the sun terrace and out towards the sea. It was too dark to make out a great deal, but a tram would occasionally pass on the distant street and its lights would bounce off the water. I could just make out the waves as they came crashing towards the bay. It was a charming spot.

"Here's to Marius!" Stan announced with a raised glass once we'd ordered our food. "The best detective I know." He was about to drink when he realised that this might not have been the most diplomatic thing to say, and so he continued speaking. "Along with you, Bella... And you, Inspector!"

"It's lucky you've never attended a police convention, or we'd be here all night," I quipped, but everyone was drinking, and so I did the same.

There was no set menu, so we could each enjoy the food we desired. My first course of giblet pie was delectable. The China chilo was to be savoured and for dessert there was a new recipe from the United States that I'd never even heard of before; the baked Alaska was exquisite. Sadly, I could not enjoy my cheese board nearly so much, as Bella tutted at my gluttony throughout. I thought this fairly rich considering the dimensions of her beau's waistline, though when two people have been friends for as long as we have, it's natural that old behaviours become ingrained.

"Isn't that Idris Levitt?" she asked as she looked across the restaurant to a smaller table at the far side of the room.

"It might well be," I replied. "Though, as I haven't a clue who Idris Levitt is, I can't possibly tell you."

"Oh, come along, Marius." Lovebrook looked disappointed in me. "You must know. She's one of those racing drivers you read so much about in the newspapers."

"Do I?" I was still bemused. "I have no recollection of any such thing."

Even my family disagreed, and Auntie Elle would be the next to tell me I knew a person of whom I had no recollection. "Of course you know her. She's a scorcher. You know, a real speed demon. She's forever trying to break records and drive from here to there faster than her competitors. I've always found her rather admirable."

I put my hand across the table and placed it on hers. "Yes, thank you, Elle. I'm aware of what a racing driver does for a living. I simply don't recall reading about her."

Bella was still sitting in quiet awe of the apparently famous young lady. I glanced across the room to see why she would cause such a fuss and immediately noticed what a striking figure Levitt cut. She was tall and sun-kissed, which made me speculate that she had recently returned from some expedition across the desert. She wore a silken batwing gown with a gigantic peacock-feather print upon it, and whenever people passed her table, she looked a little shy, then waved at them so that her sleeve would billow. At other moments, she seemed quite amused by something and would hide her smile behind her hand as if someone had said something entertaining.

"I'm going to say hello," Bella announced out of the blue, and before I could tell her to leave the poor woman in peace, she'd tipped me from my chair, and I was accompanying her across the room. It had got to the point in the evening at which early diners' tables had been cleared away and a dance floor was revealed. We had to wait a few times for a foxtrotting couple to pass but soon made it across the room.

"I'm terribly sorry to interrupt," Bella announced in her most polite voice before holding her hand out to the lone diner. "I'm Lady Isabella Montague."

Miss Levitt took her hand tentatively in her own. "It's very nice to meet you, Lady Isabella."

I'd never seen my dear friend look quite so in awe of someone before. Her cheeks took on a sudden redness, like a baby's bottom that has just been slapped. I doubt she would have enjoyed this comparison had I said it aloud.

"I was dining with my friends on the other side of the room, and I noticed you here." She was a little tongue-tied and struggled to get to the point.

"Oh, were you?"

I felt some sympathy for both of them for different reasons. Bella was apparently so overcome on meeting her heroine that she didn't sound like herself, whereas Idris Levitt was having a hard time understanding what the elegant though awkward woman before her actually wanted.

"That's right. I saw you over here, and I just had to say hello. I'm a great admirer. I was there when you won the speed trials at Southorpe-on-Sea. My father, the Duke of Hurtwood, accompanied me." I could tell she must be nervous if she was babbling about her mighty forebear.

"Oh, how nice of you to say such a thing." Levitt seemed to relax at this moment, as though she now understood the situation more clearly. "I always enjoy meeting my public, and even more so when they come from such a notable family. I believe I remember meeting your father..."

She kept talking, but I was distracted by something at the next table. Sitting just behind Miss Levitt was a man I felt that I recognised. I could only see half of his profile, but I was sure that I knew him. He seemed to have taken an interest in the conversation Bella was clumsily conducting, as he kept taking cautious looks over his shoulder.

"Dicky Prowse!" I went over to say. "You are the cricketer Dicky Prowse, aren't you?" I sounded just as debonair and eloquent as my friend hadn't.

"That's right, do I—" He looked a touch startled by my sudden appearance.

"No, no. I apologise. We've never met personally, but I've seen you play many times. I've always been amazed by your bowling. I was there at Lord's the day you took eight wickets off the Aussies."

It was a close copy of the conversation I had just overheard, and he clearly didn't know how to react to my effusive interruption.

"I'm terribly sorry," I said when he didn't respond, and then I pointed to the empty chair across from him. "Were you expecting company?"

"No, no, it's not that... In fact, I'm quite alone here," he reassured me. "I didn't catch your name, Mr...?"

"Quin, Marius Quin. I'm an author and... that sort of thing." Though I'd proudly proclaimed myself a detective in front of a room full of amateur sleuths earlier that evening, making such a statement in day-to-day life made me feel as though I were a boy playing a game.

"I will have to look out for your books... and that sort of thing." He clearly had a good sense of humour, and this, coupled with his incredible sporting prowess, made him the kind of person I would have happily counted among my friends.

A waiter placed a bowl of soup on his table, and it was clear that the time had come for me to leave, but I had remembered something else about him and couldn't go just yet.

"I won't keep you, but I must say that we have a friend in common."

"Oh, really?" It appeared his soup was piping hot, and he was in no hurry to get rid of me after all.

"Yes. I believe we've both met Lord Edgington and his grandson. I spent some time with Chrissy last autumn and he spoke very highly of you." When he didn't respond, I continued. "Weren't you caught up in one of their cases?"

He raised his eyebrows and sat back in his chair. "I know who you mean, of course, but I can't say that I've ever crossed paths with them."

"You must have. It was in a manor house somewhere with a ridiculous name. Mistle Thrush Manor... no, Mistletoe, that was it. An old police commissioner was murdered, and you were there at the same time as—" I caught the look of fear on his face and it finally dawned on me that he would rather I stop talking.

"I'm afraid that you're mistaken," Prowse said, and he looked away from me entirely.

"Yes, of course, you're quite right; that wasn't you at all. It was the chap who plays for Surrey. Jack Hobbs. That was the fellow. I'm really terribly sorry to disturb you, Mr Prowse."

He gave an artificial laugh and dipped his spoon into his bowl. "It's really no trouble. That sort of thing happens all the time."

"My apologies. Have a nice... soup." I didn't wait for his response but turned on my heel and hurried away.

Bella was having a better time of it at the neighbouring table, but I could tell from Idris Levitt's strained muscles whenever she spoke that she would like to cut the conversation short.

"Come along, my darling," I said, placing a hand on my friend's arm. Why I decided that the only way I could get her to come with me was by pretending that we were in love, I cannot say. "We must be getting back to our friends."

Bella said her goodbyes and Levitt nodded politely to the pair of us.

"What were you thinking, Marius?" My companion did not hide her anger as I led her back to our table. "You made me look a total fool in front of a woman I greatly admire."

"My apologies, Bella." The dance floor was busier now, and we kept getting stuck between sashaying couples on our jagged path. "I was trying to save you both from embarrassment."

She pulled her arm free and turned to look at me. "What on earth do you mean?"

"The man I was speaking to is the cricketer Dicky Prowse. And I know for a fact that he and Miss Levitt are acquainted."

"So then why were they sitting at separate—" She cottoned on far more quickly than I had. "Oh my goodness. You mean they're here together, and they don't want anyone to know?"

"That's exactly it, and we almost ruined it for them."

SEVEN

I watched Levitt and Prowse for a few minutes after we returned to the table, and I now understood why she kept laughing. With his chair pressed close to the back of hers, they must have been talking to one another the whole time.

What surprised me more, however, was the fact that, as soon as she had finished her first course, Levitt got up to leave. The cricketer gobbled down his soup and followed her out a few minutes later. I doubt that anyone else would have noticed, but then we might well have been the only people there who knew they were together.

Lovebrook really is a sweet-hearted chap and had been regaling my family with tales from his life on the Metropolitan Police Force. I was glad to hear that his time on the job had improved since he'd first moved to London, but I couldn't pay enough attention to his anecdotes. I was still distracted by the scene around me.

A few tables away from our own was the young woman I'd seen before the gala. She had changed into an even more glamorous rig-out, covered with shiny beads and sequins that seemed to catch fire in the low lights of the restaurant. It wasn't just her beauty that caught my notice, though her eyes were so large they seemed to take up half of her face, much like an idealised image of a person in a young child's picture book. No, what really made me look at her was that creeping sense I'd had when we'd passed in the foyer. I didn't understand at the time how I could have recognised her when I was equally certain we'd never met, but after I saw Prowse and Levitt, it became clear.

The explanation for this apparent paradox was that she was famous, just like the couple from the secret rendezvous. Once I realised that, I remembered who she was in a flash. Her name was Clemmie Symonds, and she was one of the most beloved singers in Britain. She'd performed all over the world and people talked of her as the Jenny Lind of our day, though her repertoire and style of voice were far more modern. I must have seen those incredible dark eyes of hers staring out of the illustrated papers at me a hundred times over the last few years, and I was surprised I hadn't recognised her instantly. She was such a miraculous and mythical figure that it was hard to imagine coming face to face with her in real life.

These three weren't even the only celebrities there. When we'd finished our drinks and were on our way to the lift, a man we couldn't help but notice stormed into the room and up to the bar as though he was dying of thirst. It was my mother who pointed him out, as she tends to look at the men with handsome faces in the paper, rather than the women.

"There's that young firebrand who everyone is talking about," she told us, and she wasn't the only one to notice him. All around the room, people stopped to look at Alexander Fraiser. I don't believe it was because of his brooding looks, so much as his rare magnetism. Well, that, and the fact he was engaged to the richest woman in Britain. I would certainly have to look out for any more famous figures who happened to be at breakfast.

As we left the restaurant, I noticed that Mrs Thistlethwaite was still there, and she was still putting a flea in poor Jennifer's ear. There was a line of her devoted followers waiting for a word with her, but she was busy insulting her subordinate.

I said goodnight to my charming companions (and my Uncle Stan – ho ho) and went to the reception to find out where Percy had got to.

"I'm afraid I don't understand the question, sir," the apparently not too bright child behind the desk told me.

"My dog. He was having some kind of hydrotherapy treatment in your medicinal waters earlier. I'm going up to bed, and so I thought I had better fetch him."

The boy with closely cropped hair stared back at me with eyes agape. "But he'll be in his room, sir. I wouldn't want to wake a sleeping guest unnecessarily."

"His own room?" I had to repeat back to him in case there was some interference on the line. "A dog with his own room?"

He smiled at this, and I felt guilty for being short with him. "Yes, sir. When a guest brings any pet to the Grand Hotel, we treat them with the same level of hospitality as if it was a famous actor or perhaps a royal. We once had a woman with a peacock."

I laughed and, perhaps not so dim after all, the boy joined in before looking about the foyer in case anyone was listening. "I must admit, I find it a little excessive myself, but I've only just started working here, and the manager insists that we show every courtesy to our clientele, whether they have two legs or four."

"I wonder how he feels about millipedes." This fairly average quip sent the waistcoated boy into hysterics and, as I appeared to have won his trust, I dared ask another question. "I don't suppose you can tell me whether the cricketer Dicky Prowse is staying here tonight?"

He made the same nervous gesture of looking about him before he replied. "I'm not allowed to provide any information about the people we have staying here, sir." There was one more glance into the office behind him, which he'd already checked twice before. "Though, as he left fifteen minutes ago, I don't mind telling you that he left fifteen minutes ago."

"Followed by a tall lady with a loud, confident voice, I imagine?"

He straightened up and looked more formal again. "No, sir. Miss Levitt had already signed out five minutes prior."

I fished into my pocket for a shilling and laid it on the desk. "Thank you..."

"Paul, sir. And you're very welcome."

"Thank you, Paul. I hope you have a pleasant night."

I must say, it was a relief to get back to my room and that huge comfortable bed. I was ever so excited at the thought that I might sleep through the dawn and not be woken by Percy scratching at the door to leave my bedroom or, even worse, getting into bed next to me. There's nothing quite so unappealing as waking up in the night to find your pillow is covered in dog slaver.

As I lay there in the darkness, trying to fall asleep, my head swam with the images of that strange, discomforting evening. It was almost like dreaming without having to drift off. A mix of the glamorous and the terrifying swirled and combined so that, at one point, Mrs Thistlethwaite was dressed in the beaded attire of a flapper, and my dog was up on stage giving a talk on how to solve a crime. It was around then that I realised I really had fallen asleep. Nothing from that point on made any more sense than the rapturous reception Percy's howls received from the Torquay Mystery and Detection Society.

My plan sadly failed, and I woke at five in the morning. I suppose that I'm so used to my lovably bothersome dog disturbing my sleep that my own habits have begun to copy his. I tried thinking about the night before to help me drift off, but this time it didn't work. Instead, my head was full of questions. I had to ask myself why Mrs Thistlethwaite would set up such a society in the first place. What were her intentions in bringing successful (or at least comparatively so) authors to Torquay if she only wished to embarrass us? The celebrity guests had made the evening feel even less real, and I wondered whether there was something drawing them to the English coast other than fresh air and autumn sunshine.

In the end, I gave up altogether and decided to have a dip before anyone else could get to the pool. There was a cleaner already rolling a Bissell carpet sweeper outside my room. I felt sorry for the poor woman having to start work so early, but perhaps hotels of high standing like to get such tasks out of the way when there aren't too many people around. As I navigated the corridor towards the centre of the building, the hotel was beautifully quiet. To avoid disturbing the lift attendant, I took the stairs down to the lower ground floor, and it felt as though I had the whole place to myself.

I put my towel on a deckchair, removed my dressing gown behind one of the screens and stepped into the warm water. As I ducked my head under, it felt rather like the summer sun was kissing my body, and I wondered whether the hotel's state-of-the-art central heating system heated the water too. It was only as I came back up for air that I realised I was not alone. There was something lying in the depths a few yards from me. I hadn't noticed at first because of the shape of the pool, which curved round at both ends like a baby in the womb. It took me another few seconds to realise that it was almost definitely a woman and at least one more to accept that, considering how long I'd already been there, she was almost definitely dead.

My first thought was to call out for help, but there was no one else there. And so, with a sudden thrill of fear and perhaps vulnerability, I dived under to retrieve her. The water seemed to push back against me, and I had the ridiculous sensation that it was protecting me from the terrible sight. I pushed on nonetheless and caught hold of the fully clothed woman's arm. When I managed to pull her to the side of the pool, I didn't have to turn her onto her back to work out who was floating there. Her clothes had turned darker in the water, but the gleam of her silk blouse told me all I needed to know. Mrs Angelica Thistlethwaite had breathed her last breath and bullied her last victim.

With that same unsettling emotion running through me, I manoeuvred her to the side of the pool. Thanks to the water trapped in her clothes, she weighed more than I would have thought possible. I had to try twice to get her onto the ledge, but I eventually managed it. I had just pulled myself out and was about to place one shivering hand on her eerily pale skin when I heard someone come through the door behind me.

"No, this isn't right," the man in black declared, pointing across the water. "That was supposed to be me in there. Why would—" I don't know what he noticed at this moment, but he stopped speaking and lifted one hand to his mouth.

"She's dead, man. You'll have to call the police."

I can't imagine that he heard the end of this sentence, as he'd already turned to go.

"Wait," I shouted, and my voice echoed back to me from around the room. "Where on earth are you going?" This did nothing to stop him, and so I sprinted after the stranger who surely knew something of the bizarre string of events that had unfolded over the last day. "Come back, you blighter!"

EIGHT

Accident or murder? It was jolly hard to tell. Murder is never pleasant, even when the victim was thoroughly unpleasant. And I could well imagine that Mrs Thistlethwaite's nasty attitude had upset people her whole life, so perhaps someone had finally had enough. Her assistant would be the likely suspect, which made me sad for Jennifer. Her now deceased employer had not been the kind of person to elicit much sympathy, but the downtrodden woman who had perhaps been forced to kill her certainly could. I was jumping ahead of myself, and I could only hope I was wrong. Either way, I had more pressing worries as I ran up the stairs, leaving wet footprints behind me.

"Paul?" I ran up to the reception in the hope that the boy from last night was still around.

The manager stepped from his office as I approached. "Is there a problem, Mr Quin?"

"The man in black!" I garbled the words, then realised that he was unlikely to know what I meant. "I've seen him several times since I got here. He wears a pork-pie hat. You were talking to him in the garden yesterday."

He narrowed his eyes in uncertainty. "I'm terribly sorry, sir. I can't imagine who that might be. Is he a friend of yours?"

This was getting us nowhere, and I was leaving a puddle in front of his desk, so I changed tack. "Mrs Thistlethwaite is dead. I found her face-down in the swimming pool. It looks as though she must have drowned, and then that man came in there and said something strange that I couldn't understand."

"Mrs Thistlethwaite?" His voice sounded more confused than shocked. "Surely there must be some sort of mistake. And to which man are you referring?"

I was out of breath, as much from having to explain the unexplainable as my short run from the pool. I was about to answer when I heard someone moving behind me and turned towards the restaurant. "That man!"

The still pork-pie-hatted fugitive saw me, and I felt a fool for shouting. He ran into the lounge where we'd had our drinks the night before, but I was quick to follow. Perhaps the scantiness of my outfit helped, as I was a tiny bit quicker than him, though he had a head start.

"There's no getting away," I shouted overconfidently. "Stop where you are. I only wish to talk."

He seemed to know the place well, as he ran straight for a door on the right-hand side of the bar, and it opened with no trouble. Once outside, his shoes made the going easier, but I was determined to catch him. It had rained in the night and a thick bank of cloud had snuffed out the possibility of more blue skies, which left me feeling really very cold as I chased him around the lawn to the stone wall on the edge of the hotel grounds. He climbed on top of it and looked as though he would jump down to the pavement twenty foot below.

"Don't be a fool. You could break your neck." I was full of good advice and, just before I arrived, he put his legs over the edge of the wall and slid down without incident.

There was no way I could follow in my tight-fitting shorts

and swimming vest. I would have cut my legs and then had to run after him with no shoes on my feet. I didn't stand a chance, and he couldn't resist lifting his hat to me as he disappeared in the direction of the station.

I suffered this minor defeat more than I should have and could barely summon the energy to return to the reception.

"Have you called the police?" I asked Travers, but he was staring into space and looked truly heartbroken. At least he had a telephone in his hand.

"No, I rang Miss Capshaw."

I nearly shrieked then. "Why would you do that?"

He looked at the receiver in something approaching bafflement. "I assumed this was all some sort of game. I thought she might know what I was supposed to do." To be fair, he sounded sorry for his mistake, but there was still something not quite normal about him, as if he couldn't comprehend the bad news.

"Seriously, Travers, telephone the police this instant. Mrs Thistlethwaite really is dead. Her body really is laid out beside the swimming pool, and that man I just chased was our best hope of finding out what happened."

"Which man?" he whispered, but the phone had connected to the operator, and he had to speak. "Oh, yes, hello, Irene. Yes, it is a shame about the weather." He put his hand over the mouthpiece of the candlestick receiver to talk to me. "Irene is rather chatty. Sometimes she can— Yes, that's right... No, not this morning. I'd like the police." He paused to hear her response and I could just about make out her surprise from five feet away. "Yes, we've had a bit of an accident. Poor Mrs Thistlethwaite has drowned in the pool. No... No... Yes... You're absolutely right. She once told me that she'd never learnt to swim and—"

"The police, Travers. Ask Irene to connect you to the police."

"I know, I know. A great tragedy... so perhaps you could put me in touch with Sergeant Stainsbury at his home." There was another short wait as Irene did her job. "Yes, good morning, Sergeant. Timothy Travers here at the Grand Hotel. Yes, it is a shame about the weather changing, but I hear that—" Travers evidently saw my look of consternation at this moment as he cut the sentence short and got to the point. "I'm afraid I'm calling with some bad news. Mrs Thistlethwaite is dead." Now it was the sergeant's turn to natter. "No, I haven't seen the body myself... I totally agree. I thought she was indestructible. Now, if you could come down here with your men, I would certainly appreciate it."

There were more pleasantries to observe, but he eventually hung the telephone back on its hook on the wall, and I was free to ask him an important question. "Can you tell me Inspector Lovebrook's room number?"

"I certainly can, though, if you prefer, I could send someone up to explain that he is needed."

I had managed to catch my breath by now. "That would be most helpful. Thank you." I turned to walk away, but another thought occurred to me. "If you could do the same for Lady Isabella, I would greatly appreciate it. I'll be with the body."

He smiled as though I'd just told him that I'd enjoyed my breakfast or was considering playing croquet after lunch. Not knowing what else to do, I shrugged and walked back towards the stairs. The lift was open, and the attendant was peering out expectantly, so I decided to have a word with him.

"Lower ground, please," I told him, and he pulled across the handle to close the door. "Your name's Newbury, isn't that right?"

"Yes, Mr Quin."

"I don't suppose you saw Mrs Thistlethwaite this morning or late last night?"

"No, Mr Quin. I finished my shift at nine and started again a few minutes ago. You are my first passenger of the day." The slim, red-haired youngster with a freckled face had been very formal until now but relaxed a little as he delivered this final comment.

"What about a man in a black suit and pork-pie hat?"

"Oh, yes, I saw him in the foyer when I arrived for work. I don't know his name, but he's a jolly fellow."

Another person's perception at odds with my own.

"Did he tell you anything in particular when you saw him?"

We'd arrived at the lower floor by now, and Newbury took his time to consider the answer before sliding open the folding brass door. "Not really. He said it was a shame that the weather had changed, and that he'd heard a storm was on its way."

"That is a shame," I found myself saying without wishing to. I was soon brought back to the information I needed to know when the attendant added another detail.

"And then he said something like, *No rest for the wicked*, and so I assumed he had to get to work. He waved and sauntered away."

I stepped out of the lift. "When was that exactly?"

He scratched his fuzzy red beard. "I'd say it was less than ten minutes ago. It couldn't have been fifteen."

"Thank you, Newbury." I nodded to him and would have given him a tip, but I was still wearing my bathing costume and there were no pockets to keep a wallet. "Be sure to tell the police if he appears again."

This panicked him somewhat, but I'd already stepped from the lift. "The police, sir? What have they got to do with anything?"

He would find out soon enough and didn't need me to tell him. "I'm sure that Mr Travers will tell his staff in good time."

I walked past the empty dog-pampering room and back to the pool. I almost felt guilty for having left Mrs Thistlethwaite on her own for so long, but she hadn't moved an inch. It didn't quite feel real. I couldn't put my finger on the reason, but there was something so jarring about all that had happened since I'd arrived in Torquay that I half expected her to be sitting in one of the deckchairs smoking a cigarette.

Ha, call yourself a detective, I imagined her telling me. *You didn't even realise I was only pretending to be dead.*

But she was dead. She really was. She lay with one arm folded over her body and her previously neat hair sodden where it lay across her forehead. I decided not to touch her again without the police there, not that it would have made a great deal of difference. She'd presumably died in the water, and I'd had to grasp her clothes when taking her out.

I could see no sign of any wound, and I had to wonder whether she was conscious when she fell into the pool or not. I remembered from some old cases I'd read that there were tests for such things. The coroner would check to see whether water had entered the lungs and that might make the difference when determining whether Mrs Thistlethwaite's death was an accident or she'd been murdered.

I sat with her for some time, as even a dragon like Angelica Thistlethwaite deserved that much respect.

"Did someone do her in?" a voice from behind me eventually enquired, and I didn't need to look over my shoulder to know that my associate detective had arrived.

"I can't say for certain," I told her, and Bella stepped closer to take a look for herself.

"But instinct tells you that—"

"Instinct tells me I'd like to have breakfast. It is not a good indicator of whether this unfortunate woman slipped into the pool or was pushed."

She knelt down beside me and was already struggling not to be excited by the prospect of a new case.

"You're terrible, Bella. Mrs Thistlethwaite may have been an absolute horror of a person, but she didn't deserve to die."

"She looks as though she had a good innings." Lovebrook

had appeared alongside us, and it was his turn to say something inappropriate. "How old was she? Ninety?"

"Don't you start." I looked up at him with the same stern expression. I don't like being the most mature person around, but needs must. "I would say closer to seventy and, as yet, we cannot be certain whether there is even a case to investigate."

They both watched me then. I could tell they were expecting something more, but I really didn't want them blowing things out of proportion.

"Oh, fine!" I eventually gave in. "There is one suspicious thing. The man we saw dressed all in black on the train yesterday was here shortly after I found her."

"Go on." Bella balled her hands together nervously.

"Well... when he saw the body, he said that he should have been the one in the pool."

Lovebrook tipped his head back to think. "You mean that he was hoping for a swim?"

I tried to make sense of it myself for a moment. "No, I don't think that was the idea. He didn't have anything with him, for one thing. He had no towel or dressing gown and he was fully dressed, but it was more than that." I couldn't quite put my finger on it, but I did my best. "He made it sound as though he should have died in her place."

"How curious." The tension in Bella seemed to break at this point and she stopped prodding me for information to cast her mind over what we knew. "Perhaps he felt guilty for what he saw. Perhaps he's her son or something like that, and he feels he should have prevented her death."

Lovebrook could add nothing more to this hypothesis but waited for me to respond.

"If that was the case, why did he turn tail and run through the hotel to escape?"

"He literally ran away?" the inspector asked.

"That's right. I tried to catch up, but he went over the garden wall."

This was all so bizarre that my friends had to keep checking that I meant what I said. Bella put one hand out to stop me. "Do you mean he literally went over the garden wall, or is that a metaphor I've never heard before?"

"I mean it literally. There was no way I could follow him in my bathing costume."

"And very fetching it is," the inspector replied with a mischievous nudge.

"What a bizarre way to die," Bella muttered, and then silence settled over the three of us as we considered Mrs Thistlethwaite's sad fate.

Lovebrook eventually moved around me to inspect the body. "From the look of her, she's been dead since late last night – though I've had very little experience of drownings in my career." He knelt down to examine her more closely. "As far as I can tell, there are no bruises or wounds on her head which could immediately suggest that someone had attacked her. The coroner will do a better job than I can, but for the moment, there's nothing to say for certain that her death was anything more than an accident."

Bella was clearly never going to accept this. "Which is what any killer would want us to believe. The fact is that she was still alive when we went up to bed around midnight, so what was she doing down here after that?"

"I'm afraid I can't say." Lovebrook truly is one of the most polite young gentlemen I know. "Perhaps she came down here for a night swim."

"She didn't know how," I stated quite confidently, though this information was extracted from overheard snatches of a phone conversation.

"There you go then!" Bella continued brightly. "That shows

that someone she knew well is responsible. They got her down here and pushed her in the water."

"Why do you say that?" Lovebrook asked across the body.

"Because only someone close to her would have known of her lack of natational prowess."

I had to make a small correction. "Only someone close to her, the manager of the hotel, the local telephone operator, and, judging by *her* chattiness on the phone, everyone in town by this point."

She let out a long breath. "That's disappointing."

I hated to see Bella sad and, as the only way to cheer her up was to confirm that an old lady had been murdered, I tried my best to do just that. "Perhaps we don't have enough physical evidence to say what happened, but Mrs Thistlethwaite was a difficult person. From what I saw of her, she was a real tyrant, and just the kind to drive someone to snap."

Lovebrook, who was still kneeling beside the corpse, must have been taught not to speak ill of the dead as he added a brief, "May God have mercy on her soul," under his breath.

"Oh, undoubtedly." Bella was more like me and mainly worried about the living. "The question is, what should we do next?"

I had just pulled back one of Mrs Thistlethwaite's sleeves and released a yelp of excitement, but before I could say anything more, we were interrupted.

A man in a blue uniform with shiny silver buttons had come through the glass doors at just the right moment to answer Bella's question. "What you should do next is tell me why you're here loitering over a dead woman."

NINE

"I don't care who you are, Inspector," Sergeant Stainsbury told the Scotland Yard man in a gruff, booming voice. "That doesn't give you the right to go poking about in other people's business. I happen to know Mrs Thistlethwaite very well. This is my town and my case to investigate."

My friends and I looked wordlessly at one another, trying to decide who should be the person to tell him how wrong he was.

I was happy to see Lovebrook stand up for himself – in the most genteel way possible, of course. "I'm afraid that's not true, Sergeant. I am an officer of the Metropolitan Police Force and rang my superiors when I heard the bad news. They have put me in charge of finding out what happened to the poor woman."

Stainsbury was almost a polar opposite of my friend. Brawny and slow, where Lovebrook was brainy and lithe, he shouted each word as if it were a command and appeared to view the world through a dark lens. I knew the inspector well enough to say that he would never be so negative... I didn't know him quite well enough, however, to have learnt his first name.

"Why would you do that?" Stainsbury demanded. "Her death was clearly an accident."

"It's possible," I said to interrupt the back and forth. "But then why would she have a bruise on her wrist? I say that someone pushed her in."

Lovebrook eyed the corpse for a moment but opted for a diplomatic response. "We can't know for certain until the coroner has done his job."

The big man in blue came closer to look down on the officer who, based on rank at least, he should have looked up to. "I've been a policeman for over twenty years. I can just tell."

"I greatly appreciate your help, Sergeant, but as I said, we'll have to wait for the coroner's expert opinion."

I'm surprised that no steam came from the immense man's nostrils just then. He was as angry as a dragon on a rainy day.

"If you think that's best, Inspector, then I will be upstairs doing the real work of a policeman; I'll be consoling poor Mrs Thistlethwaite's loved ones."

He turned and didn't look back as he thundered away across the room.

"What a nice man," Bella said before I could make any such joke.

"To be fair to him," I replied, "we don't exactly look the part of an investigative team *par excellence*." I glanced down at my bathing costume which gave the others cause to inspect the pyjamas they were wearing.

"I suppose that tells us what our next task should be." Lovebrook paused for effect. "It's time to change our clothes."

"Wait one second." I held a hand up to freeze them in place. "Did you really call your superiors, Lovebrook? Wouldn't you normally look at the body before contacting them?"

His cheeks went quite rosy, and I doubt it was down to the heat of the pool. "Ah, yes, about that... I may have told a tiny fib there. But as soon as I have the chance, I will be on the phone to

Chief Inspector Darrington, and I have no doubt he'll agree. Especially if he knows that you're here, Marius. I think he'd recruit you in a crack if you were interested in a job with us."

I laughed, and we drifted over to the exit. "You never know. If my next book doesn't sell well, I may need another occupation."

"Shouldn't someone stay here with Mrs Thistlethwaite?" Bella asked when we reached the door.

Lovebrook sighed. "This is when I realise that I should have tried to make friends with the local police to avoid having to wait around with a dead body in the heat of an oven." He trundled over to the nearest deckchair and collapsed in it to wait for the coroner.

"Have a lovely time, Lovebrook," I told him as I picked up my dressing gown and put it on. "We'll keep you abreast of anything important we discover."

It felt wrong to call him by his rank or surname, but Bella and I had been trying to discover his Christian name for some months without luck.

We zipped off to the lift before he could object but, as I was about to press the button to call Newbury, I noticed Percy through one of the porthole doors. He was running – a rare enough sight in itself – on what looked like the kind of treadmill they used to use as a punishment in Victorian prisons. I couldn't quite believe what I was seeing, and so I opened the door to talk to the woman charged with his care. It took me a moment to realise that it was a different person from the day before, as their white uniform and hat made it hard to distinguish between them.

"Excuse me," I said in a quiet voice. "What exactly are you doing to my dog?"

The machine on which the normally apathetic hound was running had a large wheel beside it to make the belt turn. For his part, Percy looked perfectly happy. His tongue wagging, he sprinted on the spot and released the odd yelp of satisfaction. At his side, there were two more machines with a similarly short, stout dog on each. Their overseer occasionally turned or held the wheels to speed up or slow the pace.

"I'm making sure the little darlings have enough exercise," the woman said without looking away from the controls.

"That's..." I went through a number of adjectives – *bizarre, insane, ludicrous* – before I settled on the right one. "...wonderful! I don't suppose you could come to London once a week to keep him trim? It's hard enough getting him to walk, let alone run."

She laughed and shook her head at the suggestion, much as Bella was doing in the doorway.

"That's excellent," the handler called, and I eventually realised that she was talking to the dogs. "Good work, all of you." She slowed them down and gave them each a crumb of biscuit. Goodness knows how much they charge for such a service, but I was glad not to be paying the bill.

After that, we did make it to the lift, and I was surprised to see how sad Newbury looked at the bad(ish) news.

"I'm sorry, sir, madam. I don't mean to show such emotion, but I can't believe that she's actually dead."

"Were you very close to Mrs Thistlethwaite?" Bella knew how to talk to grieving people, whereas I know how to write silly stories with lots of dead bodies, so I felt we were more or less even.

He looked at her as though she'd just claimed that Cornwall was prettier than Devon. "No, of course I wasn't. I couldn't stand the woman. She once hit my brother with her car and told him that it was his fault for getting in her way. And as for the way she treated poor Jennifer." He suddenly looked quite irate. "She viewed every single person in this town as if we were her inferiors, and yet some of them worshipped her like a... well, you know!"

He had a curious manner, and I felt that we were getting a glimpse of the person that most of his passengers never saw. I'd rarely wondered about the private lives of lift attendants, but this certainly got me thinking.

"Then congratulations are in order," I said, hoping this might cheer him up, but Bella looked at me as if I'd said that Kent was more beautiful than Surrey.

"That they are," Newbury told me despite my haughty friend's disapproval. "The Nag's Head in town will be doing a roaring trade tonight, and my brother will be there buying the drinks."

He lost his composure again, but we'd reached our floor. Bella patted him awkwardly on the shoulder and we left the lift.

"Mrs Thistlethwaite certainly seems as bad as my first impressions of her suggested." I opened each dividing door we reached in order to curl around the corridor towards my suite.

"So there must be plenty of people who would have wanted her dead."

I considered her point and attempted to formulate a list of the suspects we'd already met. Jennifer Capshaw would be at the top, seeing as she appeared to have suffered more than anyone at her boss's hands. But perhaps the hotel manager was tired of being pushed around, too; he had looked oddly out of sorts when I'd broken the news.

On the other hand, one of her followers could have turned against the leader, and we still hadn't heard an explanation for the collection of celebrities we'd spotted. There were any number of people at the hotel who might have wanted the battleaxe dead, without even considering the fact we were a short distance from a large town where many thousands lived.

"I wonder if she had any siblings," I said out of the blue, which drew a blank expression from my companion. "I just mean that siblings often fight... Never mind, I'm probably being silly."

Bella must have been travelling down a similar path of thought as her sudden exclamation was, "We have to talk to her assistant. There's a good chance that she could take no more of the wicked woman's complaints, arranged to meet her beside the pool and just pushed her into the water. From the way Mrs Thistlethwaite was berating her last night, I really wouldn't blame her."

We'd reached my door, and I took my key out to open it when I remembered that I was not alone. "Bella, my dear, is your room in this part of the hotel?"

She looked around her and realised that this was not the case. "Oh, blood and thunder. No, it's not." She started to back away from me down the hall. "I'll change my clothes and we'll meet downstairs. I shouldn't be too long."

I was barely listening to her, as just inside the entrance hall of my suite was a small card that someone had slipped beneath the door.

I must have breathed in sharply as Bella halted her retreat. "What is it, Marius? What's happened?"

I picked it up to show her, and she read it aloud.

"*He died because of you...*"

TEN

"This is becoming ridiculous," Bella exclaimed when we sat down in my lounge overlooking the bay to think things through for the seventh time that morning.

"No, this started off ridiculous. It has passed through absurd, and I imagine we are currently at the stage of mild insanity, which leaves us room for things to get even worse."

We had both read the single line of text on the small rectangle of card several times before I'd gone to my bedroom to get changed. Bathing clothes really aren't designed for comfort – or criminal investigations – and I can't tell you how much better I felt in a crisp, clean shirt and smart black trousers.

"He died because of you..." Bella repeated once more for good luck. "What can it possibly mean?"

"It means..." I couldn't answer her question. "It means that I don't know what it means."

She tapped the card on the ball of her hand and then clicked her fingers as though she'd worked out what had happened. Her optimism soon faded. "Actually, no. That doesn't make sense."

"We can't just expect the answer to come to us." I thought

this was a reasonable thing to conclude, but she didn't like my tone.

"Don't be so defeatist. I'm certain that most puzzles can be solved if you think about them hard enough."

I considered mentioning the Whitechapel Murders or any number of elusive criminals who the police had never caught, but instead I just waited for her to put together the apparently unconnected fragments of evidence we'd so far gathered.

"Really, Marius, you mustn't look at me like that or I won't be able to do it."

To give her the time and freedom she required, I walked over to the window and looked across the bay. The tide was out, and I could see a spit of sand that stretched along the coast, but this was not enough to attract bathers. Even a month earlier, the place would have been jam-full of holidaymakers, and now there wasn't a soul along the whole promenade.

"Well?" I finally prompted her.

"You're hurrying me, but..." A moment later, she raised her hand once more, and I knew that she had an answer. "I've got it! The man in black told you that he should have been in the pool in Mrs Thistlethwaite's place; that's it!" She stood up and walked towards me with all the confidence in the world. "What he meant was that she planned to kill him, but he fought her off. Whatever nasty business they're in together, the evil old woman who brought you here wanted him dead."

I considered the three or four hundred holes I had already spotted in this theory but focused on the most important one. "So you're saying that Mrs Thistlethwaite was murdered by the man in black—"

She interrupted before I could get to the point. "Yes, but I'd prefer it if we call him the man in the pork-pie hat. The man in black makes him sound like a villain from a film about pirates. I keep imagining Douglas Fairbanks playing him."

"Very well, the man in the pork-pie hat killed evil Mrs

Thistlethwaite." I spoke very calmly as I'd rarely seen her so excitable. "And then she returned from the dead to post a card under my door expressing her plan to murder him."

"Now you're just being bloody-minded. Of course she didn't come back from the dead." I waited for her to think of an explanation. She would need more time. "What happened was that she planned to kill him and paid one of her minions to take the card up here to shift the blame on to you." She breathed in quickly, as she was so happy with the idea upon which she now struck. "That explains everything. You were invited here because they needed someone to blame for their wicked deeds."

"Wicked deeds? I think perhaps you've been watching too many pirate films."

She stopped her nervous pacing and looked straight at me. "I'm trying my best, Marius..."

"I know you are, my dear, but I'm afraid that you're looking for an easy solution when there simply isn't one."

"Go ahead then. Tell me why I'm wrong." She returned to the spot where she'd previously been sitting.

The sofa was a large affair, rather cruise-ship-like in its dimensions, and she sat in the middle of it with her legs crossed. In her red silk pyjamas, with a painting of a Middle-Eastern scene on the wall on either side of her, she looked like an Arabic princess. She was frankly rather lovely at that moment, and I continued in a soft tone.

"Well, for one thing, the diminutive victim did not look as though she had the strength to murder a chicken, let alone a fully grown man, so I doubt she would have put herself in charge of despatching Mr Pork Pie."

She made a clucking sound of disapproval. "No, no, no. Mr Pork Pie makes him sound like he has a butcher's shop on the Finchley Road."

"Bella, my dear, this minor detail is unlikely to have a major impact on the case."

"Well, then we should at least call him Augustus. He did tell me that was his name, after all." She had a point.

"Very well. Mrs Thistlethwaite wouldn't have killed Augustus herself." I did prefer this name to Mr Pork Pie, not that I wished to tell her that. "And I also don't think that his reaction when he saw her dead body in any way suggested that he was justifying a murder. It sounded much more like... like he... Oh, I don't know."

I went to sit next to her, and we both sat musing until our heads were sore.

"What we must do," she eventually huffed out as though she were incredibly tired, "is stick to the original plan. I'll get changed and meet you downstairs. And when that's done, I think we should have breakfast."

"Breakfast?" I had to wonder whether the excitement of that morning had all been too much, and she already needed a break.

She was backing away from me again, but this time there would be no sinister note to delay her departure. "That's right. It will be the perfect opportunity to watch our fellow guests."

She fled from my suite and, by the time I'd put on my tie and jacket and gone down to the foyer, the coroner had arrived. I sat on a bench opposite the reception and tried to gauge the feeling in the hotel. It was still early, and the place was noticeably quieter than it would be in an hour or two when many overnighting guests would leave. From the look of the people I saw drifting to the dining room, I could only think that a good number of them had attended my gala. I noticed several of them peering in my direction and couldn't imagine what interest they'd have in someone like me. Surely they'd extracted all the fun that they could from a hack mystery novelist with an unconvincing main character.

Miss Capshaw arrived in a terrible state. I rose to speak, but Sergeant Stainsbury intercepted her before I could do so.

"I'm sorry, Mr Quin," she told me, already shifting her gaze towards her next port of call. "I can't talk now, I have to..." Her words faded out, and the sergeant took her by the arm and left me with a particularly filthy look.

"Don't go disturbing the poor woman." He even tutted, though I hadn't said a word. My only crime was to stand up in a young lady's presence, which my father had always told me was good manners.

With his guard duty complete, Lovebrook appeared and called me over to the reception. He didn't ask for the man on duty's permission but lifted the hinged wooden counter and moved towards the phone. Such authority was a privilege denied to private detectives like Bella and me, and, for a moment, I could see the appeal of being a real police officer.

Before the inspector could lift the receiver, we both noticed Travers in his back office. He was sitting in a green leather chair, looking thoroughly blue.

"My apologies for interrupting, Mr Travers," Lovebrook said. "I'm afraid I need to use your phone to call Scotland Yard."

Even when Travers saw that he was not alone, he couldn't lose the distant expression on his face. "Yes, yes. Of course, Inspector, go ahead."

I had imagined he might move away, but he stayed right where he was and went back to staring into space as Lovebrook picked up the receiver, and I moved closer to listen.

"Hello, yes, this is Detective Inspector Valentine Lovebrook. I need to speak to Scotland Yard at Whitehall 1212."

I almost jumped in the air with glee. I'd known the man for the best part of a year and only just discovered his Christian name. I can't tell you how happy it made me. I felt as though I'd solved the case in time to enjoy a nice, relaxing, murderer-free weekend away.

"Oh my golly gosh," the overly talkative operator replied, and I had to wonder whether she worked twenty-four hours a day. "I've never had to connect a call to Scotland Yard before. It's so exciting. Are you a real inspector? A really, truly real Scotland Yard inspector?"

"I am," Lovebrook replied in a comparatively stern tone for him. "But I'm afraid I'm in something of a hurry."

I could hear Irene's excited responses quite clearly, even though I was a few feet away from the phone. "Yes, sir. Of course, sir. I won't be a moment connecting you."

Lovebrook was finally put through to the right person, but I stopped paying any attention to what was said as something had caught my eye on the desk of the reception.

There was a paper folder with a picture attached to the outside. It was a photograph of a man I instantly recognised. He wore a black suit and a matching pork-pie hat.

ELEVEN

"I'm only asking how the file came to be here on the desk," I explained when Travers took exception to my enquiry.

"I don't like what you're insinuating, Mr Quin. If you wish to suggest that I have lied or withheld information, that simply isn't true." He'd gone from frightened to defensive in the space of a few seconds.

"That's not what I'm saying in the slightest. I have no wish to offend you, but you must admit it is curious that I should find the police file of the very man who appeared at the scene of Mrs Thistlethwaite's murder right here on your desk. The same man you denied seeing in the garden yesterday, even though I saw the two of you together. The same man..." Yes, I'm aware this was getting repetitive, but I'd started, so I had to finish. "...who rather than calmly explaining what he'd been doing here, ran away to escape over the wall of the property."

Travers took a step backwards and looked even more agitated than before. "You're doing the very thing that you just said you had no wish to do. You're accusing me of keeping secrets when that simply isn't the case. I do not know how that document came to be on the desk. The only explanation I can conceive is that Sergeant Stainsbury put it there."

Lovebrook had finished his telephone call and came forward to calm us both down. "That's all cleared up then. Mr Travers doesn't know anything about the file, and we will have to question the sergeant when the chance arises."

I seized it from the desk and held it up so that the manager could see the photograph. It was an unusual image, and not the kind I would have expected to find in a police file. It was too well taken, for one thing. The lighting was stark, and its subject was looking at the camera side on, as though he'd been interrupted in the middle of a deep thought.

"Do you at least now remember seeing him here yesterday?" I asked, and Travers would need a moment to think.

"I do, as it happens. I had escorted a party from the Mystery and Detection Society out to the sun terrace, and he asked to speak to me. I couldn't remember who you meant when you asked me earlier, but now that I see the photograph, it has come back to me."

"Very well," Lovebrook began, "what did he say when you spoke?"

Travers's eyes flicked back and forth between us. "When we spoke," he stretched these words out unnaturally, "he said that he wished to have some information on Torquay and its attractions. It was the usual conversation that you might have with anyone who is new to the area. He was perfectly civil."

I looked at the inspector then to see whether he had any feeling for the truth of what we'd just heard. He gave no sign one way or the other but came closer to look at the file. I put it down on the desk before us so that we could both flick through it. There were no more images, but we did get a glimpse at the criminal history of one Augustus Black from Hornsey. Yes, the man in black's real name was Mr Black.

"It doesn't sound as though he's been convicted of anything particularly violent," Lovebrook observed, taking a slightly more charitable perspective than I would have.

"Yes, but it's surely true that small crimes can lead to bigger ones. A young boy who has been in trouble with the police all his life is presumably more likely to go out and kill a man for his wallet than a boy who's never seen the inside of a prison cell."

He considered this for a moment. "You may be right, but in my experience, anyone can do anything, and they normally do."

It was tempting to take the file with us, but I felt that the grumpy sergeant might have objected and we'd butted heads enough already that morning.

"You know, Valentine, breakfast is included in the price of the room," I told my friend, making sure to drop his Christian name into the sentence as if I'd known it ever since we'd met. "We should probably discuss the latest findings over some toast and jam."

"What a superb plan." This was Bella speaking. She'd popped up behind us, looking resplendent in a blue and white striped dress. It had long sleeves and was presumably warm enough for the colder weather despite its summery appearance.

"You seem very pleased with yourself," she told me. "Let me guess... Someone else has been murdered?"

"No, of course not. Why would you think such a thing?"

A guilty look crossed her features. "I just meant... I really only wished to say that it might provide another clue. I didn't mean for a second that—"

I nudged her with my elbow to show I was only teasing, and we walked towards the breakfast room. She wasn't her usual confident self that weekend, and I couldn't say what had come over her.

The main restaurant was not used in the morning, but this new, far larger space would do us just as well. Its decoration was less ostentatious, but it still had the hallmarks of a Victorian hotel. The long ceiling was divided up by plaster-clad beams and, within each square, a ceiling rose held a glass lamp with tulip shades. The only thing that I didn't like about it was the bright magenta carpet, which made me want to close my eyes. Had I done so, I would not have witnessed the sight of my mother, aunt and uncle rolling themselves from the room after a more than hearty meal.

"Good morning, Marius," my mother said as she held her stomach to stop it from bursting.

"Overdone the buffet breakfast, have we, Mother?" I asked with an innocent smile.

"Not at all," she lied. "Though if you wouldn't mind pushing your auntie's chair, Stan and I will sit in her lap, and you can help us back to our rooms."

"I'm afraid I have to attend to other business this morning but do enjoy lying in bed, groaning because you ate too much bacon."

"And sausages, and liver, and porridge..." Stan added, and I have no doubt he would have gone on longer if my mother hadn't taken him by the arm and escorted him away. I would have told them about Mrs Thistlethwaite's murder, but it seemed they had enough on their plates – if you'll excuse the pun.

"You didn't answer my question," Bella said when we'd collected a far more reasonable amount of food from a line of tables that were covered with wonders.

You know, a hotel breakfast is really not so dissimilar from the excessively indulgent dinners with approximately seventeen courses that rich Victorian families used to host. There is far too much selection, everyone ends up eating more than they should, and you wonder at the end whether it was actually worth the effort.

"I'll tell you why I'm smiling, my dear Bella," I eventually replied after I'd drunk my first thimble of apple juice and gone back for more – the glasses were so small they made me look like a giant, "I am smiling because, together with our friend Valentine here, I found a police file on one Augustus Black."

She immediately seemed brighter than she had all day. "Oh, Valentine! Well done. That really is exceptional work, Detective Inspector Valentine Lovebrook!"

I don't think she'd taken much from what I'd said beyond the fact we finally knew his first name. For his part, the inspector looked confused.

"It was really Marius who found the file, and I must say it's odd that it was just left there in reception. I already had a negative impression of the sergeant, but this really is a poor show."

"Oh yes, Valentine, you're quite right." Bella was over-egging the pudding. "So, Valentine, what should we do about it?"

He realised at this point that something was off. "What's happening here?"

It would have been wiser of Bella to keep her mouth shut, but she couldn't resist. "*Happening*, Valentine? Whatever do you mean?"

There was a fair bit more staring from his side of the table to ours. "You keep repeating my name." He paused then to calculate what this might suggest. When the truth hit him, he had to gulp for air. "Really! We've known one another for nine months, and you didn't even know what I was called."

Bella was the first to buckle. "You never told us, and we didn't want to be rude." She sounded quite upset, but he was worse.

"I considered you my friends! I don't actually know many people in London, and so whenever I telephone my mother, I tell her all about the pair of you." He looked truly sullen, and I felt a touch sorry for him.

"We didn't mean to upset you, old boy," I said, dropping my voice and the ends of my mouth in sympathy. "We'd discussed the possibility of asking you outright, but we didn't want you to feel the way you do now."

His always floppy fringe seemed to droop lower, and his baby blue eyes turned down to his plate, which was mainly filled with crumpets. "You two really are a gullible pair if you fell for that." His gloomy expression disappeared, and he laughed at us. "I was well aware that you didn't know my name. I hardly ever tell anyone. Though I must say, I've enjoyed seeing you squirm."

"Valentine, you brute," Bella said almost admiringly. "I didn't think you had it in you."

"There's clearly a lot you don't know about me." He relaxed back in his chair and looked very pleased with himself.

"Like the reason why you don't use your first name, for example," I was quick to point out.

His laughter fell to a hush, and he took pity on us. "I doubt it needs a great deal of explaining. My parents failed to consider the ramifications of calling me Valentine Lovebrook. It makes me sound like a hero in a particularly trashy romance. I was the baby of the family, and all my cousins took to calling me Valerie, which was even worse. I couldn't stand it so, since joining the police, I try to go by Detective Inspector Lovebrook to avoid revealing my full name."

"None of your colleagues know it?" I asked in amazement, and he left us in suspense for a few moments.

"Only the ones that matter... and the operators who connect me to my superiors."

Bella and I were evidently both transfixed by this unexpected oddness, and it was Lovebrook who would have to get us back on track. Well, first he took a bite of buttered crumpet, but then he prodded us onwards.

"Now, what can we say about Mr Black?"

"Wait," Bella interrupted, "I was sure that we'd decided to call him Augustus."

"Try to keep up, Bella. His surname really is Black." I grinned as she expressed her surprise.

"What were the chances that the man in black is called Mr Black? He's back to sounding as though he's a pirate from a bad film."

"Thank you for that helpful observation, Lady Isabella." Lovebrook was becoming increasingly sarcastic. "And now that we've established everyone's names, perhaps you can tell me what you believe happened to the wretched woman."

I decided to give a nice clear answer, as we'd definitely got distracted from our task. "Black is evidently involved in the crime somehow, but I don't get the impression he's the killer."

"Based on what evidence?" The inspector cocked his head and rather reminded me of Percy.

"Based on his demeanour when he saw me with Mrs Thistlethwaite. Perhaps he knew that someone could connect him to the murder, but he didn't strike me as guilty."

"Have you already discussed the card we found in your room?" Bella asked and when I shook my head, she revealed what had happened and our various theories on the matter. "Personally, I think that Black is the obvious suspect, and he's done all this to confuse the facts."

I found a problem with her theory. "Since when have any of the murders we've investigated been committed by the obvious suspect?"

In response, Lovebrook pointed at me as if to say, *That is a very good point.*

Bella was less impressed. "Let's say he killed Mrs Thistlethwaite and then ran to your room to see when you would emerge. As soon as you were gone, he slipped the card under the door and made his appearance downstairs to suggest that he had nothing to do with the murder. The flannel he regurgitated about the wrong person being in the pool was designed to distance himself from the crime. It all ties together nicely."

I took a slightly larger bite of sausage than intended and nearly died. Well, that's an exaggeration, but it was a good long while before I could answer her point. "Oh, I suppose that he was waiting outside my door disguised as the cleaning woman, was he?"

She would not be dissuaded from the idea. "It's possible. Did you get a good look at her?"

I realised that I'd barely noticed the cleaner's face and, as unlikely as it was that Black had donned a pinafore to hide his identity, I couldn't disprove Bella's theory. "Very well. What about the swimming pool?"

"What about the swimming pool?"

"If he was waiting for me to leave so that he could post the card through my door, how did he know where I went?"

"That's easy." She needed a second to think this time. Lovebrook was happy to listen and enjoyed the conversation as it pinged back and forth across the table. "What were you wearing?"

I'm not normally the sort of person who hates to be wrong, but I admit that I groaned in frustration at this moment. "Touché. I was in my bathing costume and dressing gown."

"Exactly, and you said in his presence yesterday afternoon that you intended to spend as much of your time here as possible swimming in the downstairs pool." She was very much enjoying herself. "Game, set and—"

Lovebrook helped save match point in the nick of time – though the fact that the extension of this sporting analogy would suggest we were playing two against one should be ignored.

"What neither of you seem willing to consider is why a minor criminal from London would have come to the seaside to murder a cantankerous old lady who ran an amateur crime detection club."

Bella looked at me and I looked at her, and neither of us said anything. I was struggling to summon a response when I noticed something out of the corner of my eye.

"You have a point, Valentine. And we will answer that question by talking to the heartbroken young lady who just entered the room."

TWELVE

I didn't want to ambush Jennifer Capshaw, so I went over to the buffet table to speak to her on my own. Even then, she practically jumped in the air when I spoke to her in as soft a voice as I could muster. "Excuse me, Jennifer?"

"My goodness, Marius!" She held her hand to her chest and began to breathe more heavily. "Why did you just whisper like that?"

"I'm so sorry. I was trying not to scare you."

"You sounded like a ghost." She took another moment to catch her breath, and her attitude relaxed. "No, it's my fault. I'm terribly skittish after what happened. I really can't understand why anyone would have killed poor—" She stopped herself then, but it wasn't just because she had begun to cry. What she had intended to say clearly wasn't true. "Who am I trying to fool? I know exactly why someone would want to kill her. Angelica was a monster."

Her sorrow took hold of her body as the sobs grew louder, and I had to step forward to support her.

"There's no need to cry." This seemed like a supportive

thing to say. Sadly, it wasn't true, and the look she gave me suggested I was something of a fool.

"What else can I do? The whole situation is a nightmare."

"Then come and have breakfast with my friends and me. We're just over there." I pointed to our table and Bella offered a sympathetic frown and approximately half a wave. I was beginning to think I should have let her speak from the beginning.

Jennifer collected a plate and then piled it high with the various essential elements of a cooked breakfast. She evidently knew the staff there as she flagged down the nearest waitress by name and ordered some fried eggs to go with her mountain of food. I was frankly impressed by her appetite, or at least her ambition.

Lovebrook rose from his seat to greet her as I introduced my two companions. "Miss Capshaw, this is Detective Inspector *Valentine* Lovebrook."

Bella copied the inspector and stepped forward to introduce herself. "And I'm Marius's friend Bella Montague."

"You're very kind to let me share your table. I've been with the sergeant ever since I got here. He made me confirm the identity of the body, as if he didn't know her just as well as I did. I was down beside the pool for what felt like hours and... and I..." The emotion got too much again, and she had to swallow it back down.

Lovebrook did his best to comfort her as we all took our places around the table. "I can only think that Sergeant Stainsbury is a good officer, but he may be a little old-fashioned in his work. Rest assured that, if you feel uncomfortable talking to us at any time, you only have to say, and we can stop."

She looked a little disappointed at this. "I see, so this is an official conversation." She let out a sigh and soon rallied. "To be perfectly honest, it might do me good. I'm not normally the most talkative person, but I've been turned back to front and upside down by the news. Discussing what happened with you might help to make things clearer in my mind." She looked back to the door through which she'd just entered and seemed to shiver. "So long as I don't have to see her cold, dead eyes again, I think I'll just about manage it."

It was at this moment that the professional detective – the one who would no doubt be reimbursed for his time spent working on his weekend away – looked at Bella and me to show that we should ask the first question. In turn, I let Bella speak because, just occasionally, I remember to act like a gentleman.

"Perhaps you can tell us about the organisation which you help to run?" When Jennifer remained quiet, she continued. "The truth is that Marius came here thinking he would be speaking to a literary society of some description. Yet, it is rather more distinctive, wouldn't you say?"

Jennifer looked from one to the other of us. She took her time, and I assumed that she was considering whether to trust us with her secrets.

"I wasn't involved in Angelica's society at first. She set it up when I was still finishing my studies." Perhaps she was aware that this sounded rather formal, as she added an extra detail. "I completed a course at a secretarial school in Exeter."

The three of us were good enough interviewers by now to know not to rush a witness and, in time, she continued.

"From the outside, I thought that Angelica's society merely offered the opportunity for the retired citizens of the town to chinwag and meet up from time to time, but their leader... or rather, the head of the society, saw it very differently. She really believed that they could do a better job at solving crimes than the police. They would select a novel or sometimes real cases and pick them apart like detectives. Sometimes they would spend weeks on one investigation, and I must admit, they were successful on a number of occasions and identified culprits where the police couldn't."

"They solved open cases?" Lovebrook asked.

The nervousness I'd noticed in Jennifer the night before controlled her every word and movement so that even the slight nod she gave in response was affected by it. "That's right. There was a murder that occurred in Dartmouth a couple of years ago and another case of a woman who turned up dead on a beach near Plymouth. They sent in their findings to Scotland Yard and several arrests were made. It really burnished the reputation of the society."

Something about the way she said this suggested that this outcome was not a positive one.

"Did their success go to their heads in some way?" I put to her, and that quick, anxious nod came back once more.

"That's right. The most outspoken members of the organisation had always been prone to arrogance, but it only grew after that. They moved on from discussing crimes to comparing their success to that of others who failed to live up to their standards. There was an intensity to everything they did and eventually, they began to harass the authors they invited here under the pretence that they were coming to speak to admirers of their novels." She turned to me then and – still slow, still hesitant – offered an apology. "I must say that I'm sorry I did nothing to warn you, Marius. I tried to hint that there would be plenty of questions for you, but if I'd said any more, Angelica would have... Well, she was an angry person, and I don't like to think what she would have done."

Bella knew when to ask a question and when to leave something unsaid. She leaned across the table to squeeze Jennifer's hand, as it was clear that such comfort would be welcome. "We saw her barracking you as we left the restaurant last night. Was she a terribly cruel employer?"

I believe that the compassion in my friend's voice surprised our witness. Jennifer took a deep breath before answering. "I never like to complain of my lot. My parents, God rest their souls, brought me up to look for the positive in each person, but I can't deny that it was difficult at times with Aunt Angelica."

I'm glad to say that I wasn't the first to react. "She was your aunt?" Lovebrook had been sipping a cup of coffee and nearly spilt it all over himself. I was far more restrained and merely choked on a piece of mushroom.

"I assumed you knew." Her wide eyes blinked as she composed herself. "Yes, Angelica Thistlethwaite was my aunt. I moved in with her when my parents died. I was eighteen at the time."

The three of us looked at one another in the hope that someone else would ask the awkward question. Luckily, Jennifer could read the discomfort on our faces and solved the problem.

"If you're wondering how they died, I don't mind telling you that it was a car accident. The brakes on my father's Austin must have worn through. The car went straight off a cliff and into the sea. They hadn't wanted me to go out with my friends that day, and the last conversation I had with them was an argument."

If this was the root of the young lady's nervousness, I found it quite understandable. Her emotion came to the fore once more, and it was my turn to strike a sensitive note.

"That really is tragic," I said and was pleased that I sounded as though I meant it. I did mean it, of course, but I find it difficult to communicate my sincerity at times, and I'm glad I'd managed it for once. "What was it like living with your aunt?"

"I'm sure she meant well." This response was fired over the table at me, and I wondered if it was an instinctive reaction. Dancing bears are really only reacting to the sound of the music that was played when they'd previously been tormented into moving, and I could imagine that Mrs Thistlethwaite had conditioned her subordinate in a similar fashion. "Living with

Angelica came with a lot of conditions. One of them was that I had to work for her."

"You mean that she didn't pay you?" Lovebrook stopped eating and awaited her answer. I can't say that I'd generally recommend interviewing a suspect when there's so much food around. It makes it more difficult to concentrate... and speak.

"She said that the essentials she provided were payment enough." I was about to ask how she could afford to have a life of her own when she anticipated the question once more. "I also work at a solicitor's office in the town. My duties for the society don't take up all of my time."

It felt as though we'd slipped away from what we really needed to know, and so Bella reined in the conversation in that soft but insistent manner of hers. "You described how Mrs Thistlethwaite treated visiting speakers. Did any of them react badly to their experience here?"

"They weren't all as strong as Marius." Jennifer smiled at me then, but there was no cheer in it. I think she probably still felt guilt over what had happened. "The reason that my aunt was so angry with me last night wasn't because of the 'In Memoriam' board that stood beside him when he was speaking. In fact, I believe she did it on purpose to unnerve him. She once boasted how she liked to knock down our guests' defences before her hounds could rip them to shreds."

She shuddered then at the thought of the despicable woman's habits. "No, what really upset Angelica was the fact that you weren't cowed by what happened. She told me that I should have found out about your detective work and chosen someone weaker to invite. I've rarely seen her quite so furious."

Her tone became a touch lighter, and I could see what this minor victory would mean to a person who had been belittled and browbeaten for years.

"So then you were the one who chose Marius," Lovebrook replied, the pieces falling into place even as he spoke. "You knew what he'd achieved in previous cases and brought him here to give the old harridan—" He stopped himself and chose a kinder description. "I'm sorry, you brought him here in the hope that your aunt would meet her match."

I think she must have taken this as a criticism, as her normally quiet voice suddenly rose. "No, it wasn't like that. Or rather... I didn't hate my aunt – though I don't blame you for thinking otherwise. I just wanted her to stop acting the way that she did." She paused to search for her words. "You have no idea what she was capable of doing. She had so many schemes on the go at any one time. I struggled to keep up with them."

"For example?" There was a certain toughness to Lovebrook that I hadn't noticed before, and I could only think that his time in the police had changed him.

Jennifer turned to me, perhaps hoping for a milder response than the inspector could offer. "She played little games with the visiting authors."

"Like the slogan under Marius's photograph you mean?" Bella put to her.

"Yes, and worse. She always made sure that they stayed here at the hotel, and then she would do things like turning off all the radiators and opening the windows before they came so that they were half frozen." This was hardly the most diabolical crime I'd ever encountered, but there was worse to come. "One of the authors had written a book about his mother who had been murdered when he was a child, so she noted down what the woman had worn when she was killed and made one of her followers dress up in the exact outfit and linger at the back of the hall. The man broke down in tears. It was a terrible spectacle."

"Why didn't you stop her?" Lovebrook could have phrased this more sensitively. It was the kind of thing that I would normally say, but he seemed more upset by the tales of a crotchety woman's petty schemes than some of the murders we'd investigated.

"I didn't know about them until it was too late. Perhaps she thought I would stand in her way. What I can tell you is that she was like a child trying to upset her chosen foes, but I never discovered why she held so much against them."

"Do you even know why she set up the society?" I asked, as this surely lay at the centre of all the strangeness we'd witnessed. "What attracted her to mystery and detection in the first place?"

Jennifer had ignored her food until now, but the waiter had brought the eggs she'd requested. She cut them into neat triangles, much as if she were dividing up a cake, then ate the first piece. I got the impression that she was famished, as she savoured the mouthful and sipped her tea before answering.

"It depends on who you're willing to believe. If you ask me, she just wanted to climb inside people's heads and feel superior, but she had another story." She held the cup of tea to her mouth without drinking. I imagined that she was enjoying the warmth it gave off. "She said that it was because of what happened to my parents. You see..." Her speech was punctuated with long pauses, and this was the most noticeable one yet. "...the police suspected her of being involved in their deaths. She'd been in debt before it happened and benefited greatly from her sister – my mother's – demise, but there was nothing to prove she'd had a hand in the accident."

"So she inherited your mother's estate?" Bella surmised.

"Not exactly. Half of it would have gone to me when I turned twenty-one, but there was very little left once my aunt's debts were paid."

Bella and Lovebrook exchanged glances then. I knew what they were thinking and so did Jennifer, who was quick to give her thoughts on the matter. "I never blamed her for it. She did what she had to in order to stay afloat."

Bella tipped her chin back a fraction to look at the suspect before us. "What about your parents' deaths? Did you suspect your aunt of being involved?"

"I..." Jennifer looked about the breakfast room and her eyes came to rest on a rather tragic figure sitting alone in the corner. I had to wonder if she saw a parallel between her own sorry state and whatever had happened to the singer Clemmie Symonds to make her look so sad. "I was too naïve to have an opinion at the time, and I had no one else to look after me, so I didn't have the luxury of suspicion."

Bella glanced at the inspector and then back to me. She was about to ask a question when the emotion overwhelmed our first suspect and she started to cry.

"That's why I'm so frightened." Jennifer tipped her head down and stared at her hands in her lap, where they were tightly gripping her white cotton napkin. "I know everyone must think that I'm to blame, but I promise that isn't the case. I promise I didn't kill her. When I left here late last night, I swear that Auntie Angelica was still alive."

THIRTEEN

When Bella and I had reassured the young lady that we would try our best to find the real killer – and she'd finished her sizable breakfast and gone on her way – the three of us sat in silence around the table.

I don't think it was the facts of the case that silenced us, but the idea that the shy, delicate girl we had interviewed could be a killer. Though I'd originally placed Jennifer at the top of my list of suspects, and I now knew of even more reasons why she would have wanted her aunt dead, I no longer believed that it was a possibility. It wasn't her alibi that convinced me – I knew from experience that they were easy enough to construct or confuse. What made it very difficult for me to believe that she was the killer was the level of distress that still ran through her.

Bella kept looking at me as we sat there, and I felt that her expression was saying, *Be careful, Marius. I don't think you can trust this girl*, but I couldn't have disagreed more. I don't know whether Jennifer was mourning the death of her relative or just afraid for what might happen next, but the tears she cried were real. There was no doubt about it. Her wicked aunt had been murdered. Well, that was how it looked anyway, but until we heard from the coroner, we couldn't—

"Excuse the interruption, Detective Inspector," the sergeant came to say in a particularly cautious voice. "I've just heard from the coroner. He can confirm that all signs suggest that Mrs Thistlethwaite was alive when she fell into the water. There is also some bruising visible to her wrists and upper arms, as Mr Quin noticed. This might imply that she was manhandled into the pool. The coroner will have to do more work at the mortuary to be certain, but for the moment his hypothesis is that she was murdered at around one in the morning. She had no reason to be down beside the swimming pool, especially as she couldn't swim. No one had seen her in the vicinity before, and so it's my thinking that she had gone there to meet somebody."

"Thank you, Sergeant Stainsbury." Lovebrook bowed his head in appreciation and, his message delivered, the local man stomped from the breakfast room.

This revelation didn't exactly spark us into life, it merely underlined the challenge we faced. It was still too early to know much for sure, and so I continued my musing. I peered around the restaurant just as Jennifer had a few minutes earlier. Also just like her, my gaze became locked on the famous singer, who still looked as though she wanted to run to the nearest cliff and jump from it. I could tell from the way she stared at the empty seat in front of her that her eyes saw nothing, and I wondered if she'd heard the news about Mrs Thistlethwaite.

Before I could ask the others what knowledge they had of Clemmie Symonds, I was distracted by the appearance of the hotel's other well-known guest. Alexander Fraiser entered the room far more gingerly than he had the night before. It was hard to tell if it was the lingering impact of the alcohol he'd drunk that slowed him down, but he did not look happy to be there. This reticence only increased when he approached the maître d'hôtel to give his room number. He glanced across the tables as if choosing where to sit, then changed his mind and walked out again.

"I still can't tell what sort of place this is," I muttered to myself before Lovebrook interrupted my thoughts.

"The manager must be in on it!" He looked at us both, then realised how this sounded and corrected himself. "I don't mean the murder, though that is also possible. I'm talking about the games that Mrs Thistlethwaite played with people. Jennifer told us that her aunt made one of the invited authors terribly cold by turning off the heating."

The only thing I could extract from this was just how kind Jennifer had been to give me a nice, warm room, but the inspector had more to say.

"Angelica Thistlethwaite wouldn't have been able to achieve any such thing without help from the staff here, and I'm willing to bet that Travers went along with her plans."

"He certainly knew about the ominous sign with Marius's photograph on it." Bella sat up straighter and the same heightened sense of excitement that I'd noticed ten times over the last day returned to her. "He must know more than he's let on so far."

"He may even have had reason to want her dead." I hadn't truly considered this statement before uttering it, but having spent some short time in Travers's presence, I rather liked the idea. "Think about it. If he was involved in her plans and wanted them to stop, he might have taken drastic measures. Mrs Thistlethwaite wasn't the kind of woman who would like it if people backed out of her schemes."

Lovebrook had finished his mound of food and got up from the table. He was not convinced by my theory. "I'm afraid it's much too early to come to such a conclusion. There are too many possibilities before us. We don't know anything about the victim's wider circle, and we must still investigate her family. This could all be linked to money, or perhaps one of her followers that we keep hearing so much about did her in because he or she wished to take over the society."

He was right, of course, but this rather threw cold water on our usual technique of thinking the worst of everyone we met until we'd narrowed down the suspects to just one person. "Very well, so what should we do next?"

He didn't answer my question directly but seemed distracted. "That's up to you. I'm going to call Scotland Yard again. There's a fellow I know there by the name of Simpkin. He's a real demon when it comes to finding information on people. I'm going to see what he can turn up on Mrs Thistlethwaite, and I'll ask him about Augustus Black while I'm at it. I'll be sure to let you know if I discover anything."

There were no goodbyes. He just nodded and walked in the direction of the reception. My long-suffering companion looked at the last mouthfuls on her plate as though she never wished to see another rasher of bacon, and I knew that it was time for us to leave.

"I imagine that you've noticed the positive glut of celebrities that are at the hotel this weekend?" I asked as we left the restaurant and strolled outside onto the sun terrace.

"That's just the word for it. It's as if there's been an outbreak of them. Do you think it's connected to the killing?"

We came to a stop beside the fence that surrounded the outdoor pool, and I rested my arms on it to look across the gardens. "I think everything is connected to the killing until we can prove that it is not."

"Very well, then. Perhaps what I should have asked is whether you've any idea what brought them here."

"Not yet, I don't, but I'm determined to find out. In actual fact, I'm feeling quite motivated to catch Mrs Thistlethwaite's killer. We won't be paid for our time, of course, and it seems unlikely that I could place any such improbable character as her within the pages of a novel, but I'd rather like to show this upstart society of meddlers that they're not the genius detectives that they think themselves."

She didn't smile as I had hoped, which made me realise for possibly the fortieth time this year just how much I seek her approval. To be fair to little old Marius, it was a real challenge to make her happy just then. As I'd sensed since we'd arrived in Torquay, she was not quite herself. Even as we lingered there, she seemed to be breathing more awkwardly than normal, as though she couldn't find a comfortable position in which to stand.

"Bella, my dear, are you perfectly all right?"

She looked down at me as if I'd said something horrid. "Why wouldn't I be?" I was terribly glad when she retracted this question, as I hadn't a clue how to respond. "I'm sorry, Marius. I don't know what's come over me. You were only trying to be kind, and I practically bit your head off."

It was nice of her to apologise, but she still hadn't answered my question. I am a glutton for punishment, so I asked her again. "But are you? All right, I mean."

That same fierce expression came back to me and, once more, she soon softened it. "No, I don't think I am. I think I've become a person who gets very excited when we have a juicy murder to investigate, and I'm not sure that's a normal way to behave."

I didn't rush her. My eyes wandered the empty pool before us, and I waited for her to say more.

She turned her body ninety degrees to look at me and, when she next spoke, her voice was full of passion. "I love the thrill of our investigations, but I don't want to be the kind of person who ignores the suffering that a crime can cause. I don't want to become insensitive to such things."

"And I suppose this was reinforced by our conversation with Jennifer Capshaw."

Another fifteen seconds went by with only the cold wind

talking before she could say anything more. "It reminded me of the impact that a death can have. Even when a cruel person like Angelica Thistlethwaite dies, it sends shockwaves through the people who remain."

I was doing my best to follow what she was saying and show some real sympathy, even though I'd failed to understand how this could have brought about her bad mood. "I can see why you would say that, but you were already a little unsettled yesterday. This can't just be about a dead woman who most people didn't seem to like."

She let out a melancholic groan and held on tighter to the fence. "Of course it's not. It's about the world in general. I really believed I would have more in my life by twenty-eight years old. I didn't think I would need weekends away and the odd slaying to make me feel as though I were alive."

I didn't speak this time, not because I was afraid of stepping on her toes, but because I didn't want to show just how eager I was to hear what she had to say.

"The great hope that we possessed when we were younger seems to have faded. My family is... Well, I'd rather not talk about them to tell you the truth. But even if my father wasn't ill and my brothers weren't all living in worlds of their own design, what would I have to look forward to in the future? Perhaps I'll marry Gilbert and become a banker's wife. Maybe we'll get a flat in Belgravia and I'll spend a year redecorating it just to have something to do until children come along, if they come along, which is never guaranteed. And then they'll grow up and leave me and—"

"Bella," I finally interrupted, "I can't imagine you having anything but a brilliant life. Even if everything you've just said turns out to be true, you will make the most of every opportunity that comes your way, because that is who you are. You'll raise the greatest children in the whole of Britain, who'll love you so much they'll never want to leave home, and when they finally do, you'll throw yourself into the next challenge with just as much verve as everything else you've ever done."

I'm sure she was looking for an argument to prove me wrong, but she stayed quiet, and so I kept talking.

"You do love him, don't you? You do love Gilbert. Because if that is your problem, then maybe you're asking the wrong questions." My plan to seem cool and aloof had just failed, but she didn't seem to notice.

Her voice dropped, and her eyes met mine. "Yes, I do. I love him very much. He doesn't know how to talk to anyone but me, and he's outright terrified of you, but the truth is that Gilbert has a terribly kind heart. How many bankers spend their weekends volunteering to help the needy?"

I scoffed then. "As a matter of fact, I know literally..." I pretended to count. "...one, and his name is Gilbert Baines." I think I might have drawn a brief laugh from her, which was better than nothing. "I'll tell you what, Lady Isabella, as you are the most kind-hearted person that I have ever met, I'll make a promise: when we go back to London, I will be especially nice to your boyfriend."

Her good humour faded. She reached her hand out to me, and I think I already knew what she was going to say. "Actually, Marius, he's my fiancé. He asked me last week, and I agreed."

I smiled at her; there was nothing else I could do. My insides felt as though they'd been pricked approximately nineteen thousand times with an irritatingly sharp fork, but I smiled all the same. "Then I'll be especially nice to your fiancé. If it makes you any happier, my dear Bella, Gilbert and I will become the very best of friends."

"It would." Her shoulders rose and fell, and I believe that she laughed again without making a sound. "It really would. Thank you, Marius." She wiped an invisible tear from each eye. "I can't tell you how happy I am to have you in my life again."

For a moment, I rather wished that I was the kind of man

who would do whatever it took to steal a woman away from her beau, but even though I'd loved Bella since childhood, that would never be my style. Whatever I felt for her now was irrelevant. She wanted to marry Gilbert, not me, and all I could do now was feel happy for her.

I straightened up and tried to make light of the whole conversation. "You are a treasured friend, Isabella, and I must offer my congratulations."

She really must have been emotional as, rather than shake my hand or kiss my cheek, she wrapped two arms around me and held me where I stood.

I tried my level best not to enjoy the feel of her hair against the skin of my neck and, when the embrace had gone on for too long – and I was at risk of turning into a rotter after all – I forced myself to interrupt. "Now, it's time to get back to what we do, if not best, then at least comparatively well. Let's solve a murder, shall we?"

She pulled back and looked a little embarrassed. "What a sensible idea. Where shall we start?"

I already had an answer, as crime is a lot easier to fathom than love. "With the manager of the hotel, of course. And I've a plan just for you. To make a change and provide you with the adventure you so crave, why don't you be the rude, oafish interrogator for once, and I'll be the kind, softly spoken one. It certainly works when we do things the other way around."

She flexed her eyebrows... if such a thing is possible. "That does sound like a lot of fun. I hope I don't scare him."

"Bella, my dear, I'd like to see you try."

FOURTEEN

Mr Timothy Travers had been forced to vacate his office so that Lovebrook could make his calls without being overheard. As a result, the manager of the Grand Hotel was hovering near the front entrance, greeting the newly arriving guests who presumably hadn't heard anything about the dead woman in the indoor swimming pool.

This idea was confirmed as, at the very moment he was charming an elderly couple who had entered the hotel with great big smiles on their faces, two coroner's assistants carried Mrs Thistlethwaite's body past them. To say the joy they had felt instantly dissipated was an understatement, though I can't say I didn't enjoy seeing Travers's embarrassment.

Bella and I stood aside respectfully as the corpse was removed. Sergeant Stainsbury followed the convoy rather like an undertaker at a funeral precession. He was certainly tall and gloomy enough for the job, though instead of a look of quiet concentration that typified such gentlemen, he wore a scowl as he passed. Luckily, we were close enough to overhear his deep grumble to the manager.

"Travers, tell the usual busybodies and society members

that I'll be hosting a meeting in the centre of town at noon to inform the local community of the terrible news. People have begun to talk about the motive and the like, so I thought I'd nip any nasty rumours in the bud."

Travers had an apprehensive manner and could only muster a "How very thoughtful of you," in reply. The sergeant tipped his helmet and continued out of the hotel as the old couple quietly debated whether a weekend by the seaside was really such a good idea after all.

"Mr Travers," I said when he turned into a waxwork from Madame Tussaud's. He hadn't shown any sign of life for some moments, but he jerked and blinked when he heard his name and finally realised that I was the one who had spoken. "If you could spare us a few moments of your time, I would be most grateful."

He bowed his head to the good Lady Isabella, and nodded very quickly to me, but the two actions were far from complementary. I was afraid that he had come over a little queer and needed to sit down.

"Mr Quin, there you are." He put both hands out as though introducing me on a stage. "I always have time for my guests, and may I say what an honour it is to have two such reputable persons staying with us? Lady Isabella, your father's name is very familiar to me. I have often heard good things spoken of the Duke of Hurtwood, and it is a pleasure to make your acquaintance."

There was something practised and phony about his speech. As Bella was eager to show that she could be even ruder than I was, she responded with a curt, "The pleasure is all yours."

Travers's gaze remained on her for a moment, as though he were unsure whether he had heard what he thought he had heard.

"Perhaps we can go somewhere more private?" I suggested, but he would need a few seconds longer to acquiesce.

"Of course, of course. Please, come this way."

He took us along the wide corridor that led through the foyer to the bar. On the way, we passed one of the white-overalled pet attendants with Percy and two other dogs on leads. They were pulling her towards the gardens, and that fickle hound barely looked at me as he passed.

Before we reached the bar, Travers signalled us towards a door I hadn't noticed before. "The library should suit our needs perfectly. We don't tend to have too many people in here at this time of day."

We filed in ahead of him to enter a small but charming space. Below a white marble mantelpiece, there was a roaring fire in the grate, which was guarded by two brass griffins. The one thing that the library did not have, however, was a selection of books. The only reading material was a pile of newspapers on a low table, though I had a feeling they were kept there to make spills for lighting the fire. The room was not short of bookshelves, but aside from a few china ornaments depicting ladies and shepherds, they were entirely empty.

"Now, how may I be of service on this sad, sad morning?" Everything Travers said sounded as though it had been decided in advance. He had the manner of someone who knew it was his job to show certain emotions, but he lacked the conviction to make anyone believe he actually felt them. "If there is anything I can do to make your stay more enjoyable, I am at your disposal."

"We'd like to know what part you played in Mrs Thistlethwaite's death," Bella responded, and I could tell that our plan would not work as I'd hoped.

Taking a seat beside the fire, I laughed in the hope he might not notice her forceful tone. "What my friend here means to say is that we're helping Inspector Lovebrook to look into the killing, and we'd like to know..." I couldn't think of an end to this sentence that would explain Bella's clumsy phrasing, so I finally went with, "...where you spent the hours between twelve and six in the morning."

Travers's mask appeared to have slipped and the emotion he felt was now visible. He looked angry and sad at the same time. "There is a room behind my office where I tend to sleep at the weekend. I chose not to go home last night, so I would have been asleep in there until I started work just after six."

"Then perhaps you can tell us who might have wanted Mrs Thistlethwaite dead."

His wide, round face wobbled, and he reminded me of Humpty Dumpty, perched on that wall. "Ah... yes, that is a point which merits discussing. I can see why you would ask such a question."

Bella said nothing at this moment, though she did drill holes in the man's head with her eyes alone. I believe he got the message but, just in case, I helped him along.

"Thank you. Now could you perhaps share your thoughts on the matter?"

"My thoughts, yes."

We were sitting in rather uncomfortable chairs around a small table that, come the afternoon, would be occupied by bridge players and tea drinkers. No one spoke for a few moments, but our silence finally prompted him to answer the question... more or less.

"Mrs Thistlethwaite was a beloved member of Torquay society. Her husband, the late Major Thistlethwaite, was awarded for his valour in... well..." He ummed and hesitated for a moment. "...one of the colonial wars. Unfortunately, he died comparatively young, but his wife has been just as much a presence in this town as he ever was. In fact, through her society, she rose to become a treasured figure."

"You haven't answered the question," Bella finally stated

with a hint of menace in her voice. If she scared me a little, she terrified Travers. His jaw opened and closed again, and Bella grew even more impatient. Or at least, that's what she wanted him to think. "You know that we'll get to the truth in the end, so please stop wasting our time."

"I'm merely trying to express that many people loved dear Angelica."

"Many but not all," I pointed out. "So who did she truly infuriate most strongly? Who found it intolerable to be around her?"

He tried to hide his fear by keeping as still as he possibly could. He placed both hands on the bare arms of the chair, but a slight shaking was still visible. I felt that he knew something of what had happened to Mrs Thistlethwaite, but whether that made him the killer or not was another matter.

"I can honestly say that no one I consider a friend would have wished her any harm. Many members of the society adored Angelica. They just adored her. In fact, they followed her about as though she were one of those eastern wise men."

"Stop trying to be clever." Bella only whispered these words, but each one appeared to cut through him. "We know you're ignoring the question, so tell us the truth or you will not like the consequences."

I'm sure she would have liked to wink to show what fun she was having. As this was impossible without giving the game away, she remained in character and Travers was forced to respond.

"Fine, I admit it!" His voice was suddenly loud and high-keyed. For a moment, I thought that he was confessing to his part in the crime, but we really aren't that lucky. "She wasn't everyone's cup of tea."

"That is an understatement," I said before Bella could utter anything worse. "Even her niece told us that she couldn't stand her." I was paraphrasing, as Jennifer had never been quite so blunt, but he didn't need to know that.

"Very well. The truth is that she divided opinion. People either loved or hated her, but there's a big jump between disliking a person and murdering her."

The problem with Bella playing the attack dog was that it didn't allow room for the tense silences that were so important in a good interview. Now that the initial skirmish had concluded, I would have preferred to sit there moodily regarding our suspect so that the pressure could build, and he would let slip every last detail that he was so desperately trying to hide. Sadly, that wasn't possible, and so I pushed on with my questions.

"We know that the two of you were involved in..." I sought a good word for Mrs Thistlethwaite's sadistic form of troublemaking, but before I could find it, something happened that I really hadn't been expecting.

The rather staid and affected manager of the Grand Hotel burst out crying. "It's true. I loved her!" As he buried his head in his hands, I looked at Bella, but even she didn't know what to say. "I loved Angelica Thistlethwaite. There, I've said it. I kept it a secret for far too long, and I can't tell you what a relief it is to say it out loud. The only person I ever told was her, but I'm glad you discovered our secret."

He calmed down a little as he travelled back in time. "Perhaps it surprises you to hear that a person like me could adore so fervently a woman like her, but she was so capable and driven. I have never met another person like her. When I confessed my love, I told her that, whether she could bring herself to return the feeling or not, I would be her devoted servant."

There were many questions in my head just then. The age difference between the approximately fifty-year-old manager and his *petite amie* was definitely high on that list. But the one on which I finally settled was, "What did she say in reply?"

He looked away to stare into the flames of the sputtering fire. "I suppose I should lie and tell you that she let me down graciously, but it wouldn't be true." His sobs grew louder, but he kept talking. "The truth is that she laughed. She said that she was in love with a far more masculine and assertive man, but as I'd sworn to be her servant, she would very much enjoy giving me my orders."

"And you still loved her?" Bella had dropped her act by this point. She was clearly taken aback by the revelation.

Travers turned his bright red face to look at my companion. "Tell me, Lady Isabella, have you ever loved someone so much that you couldn't sleep at night for thinking about him? Have you ever wished the world would explode because you missed him to the extent that you would rather not live than go on for another second?"

I had to smile as I looked at her; I really couldn't imagine Gilbert making any woman feel that way. For her part, Bella kept her eyes fixed on the suspect and replied without a hint of emotion.

"As it happens, yes. I have."

This led to some raised eyebrows – not just from Travers. I was really surprised that Baines the banker had it in him. It was yet another way in which I had evidently underestimated the fellow.

Travers nodded seriously before responding. "In which case, you know." There was something wistful about his manner then. I really must learn not to judge people by first appearances; I would never have imagined hearing such things from him in a thousand years. "You know how I felt when Angelica crushed my heart with her bare hands. I was truly distraught and wished that I could take back every last word I'd uttered. But when faced with the choice between fulfilling her every whim and never speaking to her again, I chose the former."

"That's terribly sweet," Bella said, and her eyes turned

glassy in the light of the fire. It wasn't like her, so I nudged her with my elbow for being such a softy.

"Wait a moment," he said, and a frown reshaped his features. "How did you know that I was in love with her?" He dug his nails into the arm of his chair. "Was that another cruelty she inflicted upon me? Did she tell everyone how pathetic I am?"

Now he even had me feeling sorry for him. "No, Mr Travers, it wasn't that at all. You were the one who told us."

"But that can't be. You said that you knew about my involvement with Angelica." He switched emotions every few seconds and had now become audibly nervous. "I know that's what you said. I wouldn't have said anything otherwise."

I looked at Bella in the hope that she would explain, but I was supposed to be the nice one, so I did what I could. "Yes, Mr Travers, but you misunderstood me. I wasn't talking about a romantic entanglement. I was referring to the schemes that Mrs Thistlethwaite enacted. We know that you were involved."

I thought he would rush to deny it or at least issue an explanation, but he stayed perfectly still and said nothing.

Bella must have enjoyed her previous role, as she adopted her sullen tone once more. "She only invited speakers to her society so that she could torment them. But now we know why you went along with her perverse ideas."

"Ah, yes. Her schemes." He sounded unexpectedly relieved to discuss the matter. "Angelica really could be cruel to the guests that she brought here. Do you know that she once made me turn off the radiators in the room where one of the authors was staying? She even broke off the controls to make sure that they couldn't be turned back on. The poor lady in room 323 got so cold that she had to ask for extra blankets. I wasn't so mean that I would refuse her that." He paused again, clearly thinking back over the happy memories of the insane woman he had loved. "And as for the way Angelica treated you, Mr Quin..."

He didn't finish that sentence, but I personally thought I'd got off lightly. At least no one had dressed up as my missing father to make me think he was still alive.

"But why did she go to those lengths for such a petty result?" I was apparently sensitive to the idea of mystery writers suffering mistreatment.

He moved his teeth from side to side over his top lip as he considered the question. "Do you know that I never actually asked her? I am aware that she had some trouble with the police after her sister and brother-in-law died. I know that she blamed them for her niece's low opinion of her, but I don't know exactly why. I suppose you would have to find the man she loved in order to discover such information, as opposed to the fool who chased around after her."

"Then you don't know who he is?" I guessed, and he dropped his hands into his lap and shook his head.

I felt that Bella would have liked to shout or perhaps upturn the table to produce a reaction, but Timothy Travers was not the sort of person who would respond to such pressure, and so she said nothing more.

"Let me just tell you this... Angelica Thistlethwaite was not an easy woman to like. There are people in this town who believed her the devil incarnate, and I can't say I totally disagree with their perspective. She was cunning and manipulative, but the truth is that she had more impact on our little world here than anyone else I know. She gave the aging population of Torquay a shot in the arm and helped bring this sleepy town back to life. For every person she chose to hurt, there must be ten more she helped."

"Then what about the others?" I replied. "What about the ones who didn't feel that way? Could the thug I saw here – Augustus Black – have been paid to kill Mrs Thistlethwaite by one of her enemies?"

He actually rolled his eyes at me then, which I thought

rather rude. "This is Torquay, not New York City. Devon is hardly a hotbed of gangsters and assassins." In the middle of dismissing my suggestion, something occurred to him. "And yet, there is one particular person who took umbrage at the way that Angelica ran the society."

"Oh, really?" Bella seemed quite taken by the idea that one of the respectable ladies and gentlemen from Mrs Thistlethwaite's club could have bumped her off.

"Yes, his name is Robert Milton, and he's a monster." Travers made no attempt to hide his distaste for the man whose name was familiar to me from the gala. "He once threatened to 'seize control' of the society that my dear Angelica had done so much to establish. Those were the very words he used."

"What caused them to argue?" I didn't really believe that such a neat solution would present itself, but I would keep my mind open for the time being.

Travers became reticent once again. "You would have to ask Mr Milton."

"Then how can we find him?" Bella leaned forward and placed one hand on the table as if we had reached a key point in the investigation.

"Go to the town hall for the sergeant's meeting at noon. Milton will be there bossing people around and expressing his opinions nineteen to the dozen. If that man knows how to close his mouth, I've yet to see the evidence." His already round face had become so puffed up that he had to pause to prevent himself from popping. "Robert Milton is an out-and-out reptile. If Angelica really was murdered, the only thing I can think is that he is to blame."

FIFTEEN

"It's hard to fit together anything we've learnt this morning," I told Bella as we walked along the immense, curving promenade towards the centre of the town some twenty minutes away.

She didn't reply for a good ten steps or more, and when her response came it was quiet and contemplative. "I agree. There were times when Travers made me think he knew everything we needed in order to identify Mrs Thistlethwaite's killer and just as many points at which I felt we should give up and talk to someone else."

For the moment, the black clouds had retreated to the horizon and, except for a few drops overnight, the weather had remained dry. However, there was a cold wind that hurried us along the road like a mother pushing her children out of the house when they were late for school.

I allowed myself a few moments to think. "His identification of the potential killer didn't sound right to me, either. He spent half of the conversation telling us that no one would want to hurt the woman he loved, and then suddenly, at the end, he knew exactly who would have killed her."

"I quite agree. The idea that Mrs Thistlethwaite had been

murdered over a feud with one of her fellow amateur sleuths appealed to me at first. But something about the way he spoke made me doubt the whole thing. It was just too..."

"Convenient?"

"Exactly. It made me wonder whether Travers has his own reasons for shifting the blame onto Milton."

"Great minds think alike." I increased my pace a fraction to get a better look at her as she motored along beside me. "Obviously, the biggest revelation of the morning is that Angelica Thistlethwaite was actually Helen of Torquay. All men adored her, and her various suitors would risk their lives for her love."

"That isn't exactly how Travers described her, but it did surprise me. Who do you think her secret lover was? I was rather wondering whether Sergeant Stainsbury could be our man... or rather, her man."

I couldn't help smiling at this curious idea, and she didn't like it one bit.

"What's so funny? Stainsbury is certainly very masculine. He's older than Travers, too – sixty if he's a day. So there wouldn't have been so much of a difference in age between them."

"But that doesn't prove anything. We have met approximately eight people in this town, and Mrs Thistlethwaite must have had a life outside of the hotel. We can't identify her sweetheart based on that small sample."

"Very well. Then I'll be looking out for prospective culprits at the meeting." She nodded as if to show that she had made a resolution and would stick to it.

As we approached the town and a large hill rose up to our left, it occurred to me that several of the old couples out for a stroll had observed us closely as we passed. It was dreadfully unnerving and added to a feeling that had been simmering inside me all day.

"You know, I have the most uncanny sensation that the

people of this town are watching me to see what will happen next. I felt it at breakfast this morning, and it hasn't stopped since."

"Perhaps they were secretly impressed by your speech and wish to see whether you've got it in you to catch a real killer." This was far from the worst idea she'd had that day.

"I very much doubt it. I think it's far more likely that they're looking forward to seeing me fail, but I refuse to satisfy them on that score. Now that I think about it, I felt a lot of eyes upon me at dinner last night, too. Whenever a couple danced past our table, it seemed that their eyes lingered upon me just a little too long."

Bella was unswayed by this theory. "You know, Marius, there is the very real possibility that you are simply too modest."

"Yes," I replied quite seriously, "I have often been told that an excess of modesty is my one failing. If only I were a touch more vain, I'd be perfect."

She realised that I was joking and poked me playfully in the ribs. "That's not what I mean, and you know it. I'm saying that you always ignore the possibility that people might like you. There were over a hundred society members in that room last night and, though fifteen or twenty of them chose to tear your books apart, it's more than likely that plenty more enjoyed the brilliant mysteries you have created."

Rather than respond to her point, I asked her a question. "By chance, my dear Bella, have you found the time to read my second masterpiece?"

"No, not yet." She showed no guilt at her response. "But I have every intention of doing so."

She had failed to notice the irony of the situation; however, I decided not to draw her attention to it and changed the subject. "Everything would be simpler if it weren't for Augustus Black. For a start, it makes no sense whatsoever that we were the only ones in the hotel who noticed him, especially as one of the police officers must have brought his file there this morning. Now that I think of it, if the sergeant knows about Black's criminal record, why isn't he out looking for him instead of organising this chinwag in the village hall?"

"Are you sure that Black is important in the grand scheme of things?"

"Well, he popped up at the scene of the crime and claimed that he should have been the one face down in the pool, so I don't think it's too great a stretch of the imagination."

"Perhaps he just meant that he was hoping for a quick dip but couldn't because there was a dead woman in there." She paused as a noisy tram passed with its bell jangling. "I can imagine it being quite the inconvenience if one was desperate for a swim."

I knew she was only half serious but, with each retelling of the story, it was more difficult for me to know exactly what Black had said and the tone he'd used to say it. Was it possible I'd placed too much significance on an innocent comment?

"He did run away from me," I reminded her.

"Yes, but he's been convicted of other crimes before. Perhaps he was scared that he would get the blame for this one."

I kicked a stone along the paved promenade as I thought about the perplexing case before us. "When you spoke to him in the swimming pool yesterday, you said he was different. 'Civil' – wasn't that the word you used?"

As soon as we question our memories, they begin to lose their strength. Just by asking this, I'd made her doubt herself. "It was something like that, yes. He was perfectly cheery and talked about his life in London and how he'd been here once before. It was only when you arrived that he became a little sullen."

"Well, that helps us a great deal."

I'd heard a voice calling in the distance but hadn't imagined that it was of any relevance to us. When I caught my name on the breeze, I turned around to discover that our good friend Inspector Lovebrook was running along the prom in our direction.

"Marius, Bella, I..." He stopped when he reached us and doubled over to pant. "I..."

"Take your time, Valentine, old boy," I told him. "Whatever you have to say can wait. It will only take longer if you pass out first."

He took my advice and did his best to recover his breath. "I ran all the way from the hotel."

"Oh, really?" Bella replied with a hint of her new boldness already apparent. "We would never have guessed."

"Augustus Black..." He put one hand on my shoulder to steady himself and delivered a more urgent message in one short breath. "Augustus Black doesn't exist."

SIXTEEN

"I don't see how that's possible," Bella replied for the both of us.

"My colleague at Scotland Yard spoke to the officer on duty at Hornsey police station. They've never heard of an Augustus Black in that parish. There are no records of him being arrested there in the last decade, and the old chap on duty knows every last criminal in the area. He says that he could not have missed someone like Black."

"So the file was a fake," I concluded, but Bella had more questions.

"Did you mention it to Sergeant Stainsbury? Does he have any knowledge of how it found its way to the hotel?"

"He was busy with the body for most of the morning," Lovebrook explained. "I had planned to discuss the matter with him, but the chance never arose."

"It's Travers who lied about it." Bella had the same note of anger in her voice that she'd adopted in our interview. "He told you that Stainsbury had left the file there on his desk."

"That's not exactly what he said," I corrected her. "He told me that he could think of no other explanation for how it had got there."

"So where does any of this leave us?" the inspector asked, and I don't believe it was just the run that had knocked the wind out of him.

"Shouldn't we be asking that?" I replied. "You're the one who's spent the last hour following the threads of the case."

Bella launched into a precis of the facts. "The way I see it, whether he's a criminal or not, we don't know of any link between the man who would be called Black and the victim. He told me in a seemingly unguarded moment last night that he'd only been here once before. Perhaps he was just a holidaymaker who had a bit too much to drink. Perhaps he woke up this morning with a knock-out headache and decided to have a swim. The fact he blurted a bizarre statement and ran away doesn't make him the killer."

"I agree," I muttered, with my eyes on the harbour of the town we had almost reached. "For the moment, we must concentrate our efforts on getting to know the victim. And I believe we've set off on the right foot."

We soon made it to the centre of Torquay. There was an elegant pavilion by the harbour, a concrete pier stretching off into the water on the right of us, and a pretty garden just beside it. In the summer, the place would be full of children sailing their little boats in the pond and eating ice creams, but as it was October, we were the youngest people in sight.

I must admit that I had never imagined that the place would be quite so grand. There were several immense white houses on the hills on either side of the town and, when we wound our way up through the streets, which were lined with inviting shopfronts, our destination turned out to be equally attractive. Torquay town hall was an immense stone building that couldn't have been more than twenty years old, but it had been built in an overblown, perhaps even baroque style, and I wondered whether the mayor who had ordered its construction felt he needed such a handsome building to commemorate his impact on the town.

As we arrived, there were already plenty of people milling about outside, and I caught a glimpse of Sergeant Stainsbury's huge, hulking form. He cut a swathe through the crowd to enter the building with two younger officers in tow. He was not the type to stand on ceremony and had already mounted the stage and begun his speech by the time we entered the large assembly room.

Bella and Lovebrook took their seats in the back row, but I stayed on my feet to make sure that I didn't miss anything.

"You all know why I'm up here," Stainsbury told the townsfolk.

To be perfectly honest, there was not a great deal of difference in the make-up of the audience compared to the night before. The average age was around sixty-five and, except for a few young couples with babes in arms, none of them would have looked out of place at the society.

"I'm not one for speeches if I can help it, so I'll make this short." He paused then to show just how serious he was, which rather undermined what he'd just said. "You will all know by now that our dear Mrs Thistlethwaite was found dead in the Grand Hotel this morning. I've already heard the rumours going around, and I don't like a single one of them. So, for the record, she was not having a secret affair with a member of the royal family who decided to stop the news from spreading. She was not, to our knowledge, murdered by one of the criminals that the society helped put behind bars seeing as they are all, as I've just mentioned, behind bars."

"So then what did happen to her?" a man with pale white hair that matched his pale white skin asked from the front row. I recognised him as Robert Milton, one of my questioners from the gala the night before.

A woman sitting just behind him spoke up next. "Do you know that she was definitely murdered?"

Stainsbury grumbled to himself, as though he would have preferred not to answer. "Thank you for your interest, Mr Milton, Miss Elsbury. In turn, the answers are that we still don't know, and yes."

This sent a tremor through the room, which was immediately followed by a burst of discussion. I heard whispers of "Well, I never," and, "To think of such a thing happening here in Torquay."

Mr Milton, whose first name I already knew was Robert, rose slowly and rather majestically from his seat to speak again. "How is this possible? How could a woman have been killed in such a public place?"

A rage-filled voice from somewhere in the crowd shouted a response before Stainsbury could. "You must know what happened, Milton! I bet you were the one who killed her."

Half the audience seemed to agree with this assumption, while the rest remained quiet.

"Now, now, everyone." The sergeant raised both hands in an attempt to control the rabble. "We'll get nowhere by turning against one another."

The same angry woman stood up to rage some more. "We'll get nowhere until you find out where Robert Milton was at the time our poor, beloved Angelica was drowned."

Milton turned to look at his accuser. "I was at home in bed. Thank you, Mabel Grimage." Mrs Thistlethwaite's apparent nemesis did not look quite so devilish as Travers had made him sound. He was a short-statured but broad man with the look of someone's unwelcome uncle. His white hair was perfectly trimmed, and the brown, three-piece suit he wore was just so, as though he had carefully measured the dimensions between tie and waistcoat, belt and brogues before leaving the house.

It was at this point that a significant piece of evidence

exploded into Mabel Grimage's brain. "And how do you know what time she was killed if you weren't the one who did it?"

She'd silenced the room, and all eyes turned to Milton.

"I was..." He struggled for a moment to recall the details, but then his confidence returned. "I left the hotel soon after that hack author's speech, and I know for a fact that Mrs Thistlethwaite was alive at the time, which means that I could not have been the one to kill her." He crossed his arms in a very precise manner which reminded me of the much-detested captain under whom I'd served during the war.

"Unless you sneaked back there and did the deed." The delightful woman with the spittle flying from her mouth would not give up.

"Really!" I heard Bella whisper to Inspector Lovebrook. "Every Tom, Dick and Harriet is trying their hand at detective work these days." Which I thought a bit rich coming from her.

It would fall to Sergeant Stainsbury to intervene. "All right, Mrs Grimage. That's enough for now. My officers and I will be investigating every avenue that remains open to us. We will not leave a door knocker unknocked or a stone unturned. From now until the moment I lay my hands on the killer, we will be a constant presence on the streets of Torquay."

This led to a rash of appreciative chatter, but Milton was having none of it. "Then all you have for us are platitudes. Is that right, Sergeant?" He fixed his steely eyes on his opponent on the stage. "I'm beginning to think that we members of the Torquay Mystery and Detection Society could do a better job than the officers of the Devon County Constabulary."

There was a clear split in the audience between those who appreciated Milton's interventions and those who were dead set against them. I had to assume that the opposing faction had previously been commanded by Mrs Thistlethwaite herself.

"I will respectfully have to disagree with you, Mr Milton." The sergeant had found a more conciliatory tone at this difficult moment. I was frankly surprised that he was capable of such diplomacy. All I'd seen of the man suggested he was an implacable fellow. "The best you can do is to leave the investigation to the professionals."

"Then you should at least include Marius Quin," the first woman to have spoken suggested. "His books might not be very good, but my cousin in Surrey told me about one of the cases he solved, and it sounded impressive."

Some of the citizens of Torquay had evidently noticed me, lingering at the back of the room, as there were now calls for me to take to the stage. I had no desire to do any such thing.

"Go ahead, Marius," Lovebrook of all people told me, and I wondered whether this was revenge because I kept calling him Valentine.

"Ladies and gentlemen," I replied to the calls. "It would be arrogant of me to suggest I had the skills to solve this case when we are in the presence of one of Scotland Yard's youngest and most capable detective inspectors."

Before he could object, I pulled Lovebrook to his feet and escorted him to the stage. Bella led the cheering, and the people around us soon joined in with some well-mannered applause. When we arrived, I was surprised that Sergeant Stainsbury looked pleased to have us up there. He clearly didn't want to deal with the troublesome townsfolk any more than I did.

Poor Valentine stood looking stunned in the middle of the stage. The hall was not so very different from the hall where I'd spoken at the hotel. The ceiling was higher, and the walls were painted pastel green with contrasting white beams. I very much doubt it was the design scheme which concerned Lovebrook at this moment. The eyes of at least a hundred angry locals were on him, and it turned out that he was not greatly accustomed to public speaking.

"I am here as a representative of the Metropolitan Police Force." It was a faltering start, and this was as much as he could muster before coming to a sudden halt. To no doubt everyone's surprise, however, the words then began to flow more smoothly. "We mean to persist to the end, and we rely upon you, whom, I believe, we represent in this matter, to give us the sympathy, support, and loyalty which has never yet failed us. If we have..." He hesitated once more, and I had the definite sense that he was reciting this speech rather than composing it. "...concentration of purpose, unity of spirit, and unshaken firmness of resolve, then, long and stormy though the voyage may have been before it comes to an end, the ship will find her way with a full cargo into the desired haven."

Though this did nothing to explain how we find the killer, it was stirring enough to enliven his audience, and he soon had a standing ovation on his hands.

"You were quoting someone, weren't you?" I whispered as he accepted the resounding applause. "Was it Churchill? Lloyd George?"

He kept his eyes on the audience as he replied with ventriloquist-level stillness of the face. "No, it was Asquith's speech against tariff reforms from 1912. I don't know how I remembered it, but I've always thought him a wonderful orator."

In time, the hall fell quiet, and the next challenge began as the people of Torquay put their questions to us.

"Detective Inspector Lovebrook, what will your first task be?" Robert Milton put to him.

"My first task," he replied most confidently, "will be to inspect the victim's house for clues to the motive of this terrible crime." He'd very much grown into the role and spoke like a grandstanding politician.

"And after that?" grumpy Mrs Grimage demanded.

I'd got Lovebrook into this situation and decided to lend a hand. "We cannot possibly say where the case will lead us. Depending on the evidence that we uncover, we may veer off in any one of a hundred different directions. To make such predictions at this stage would be presumptuous."

I noticed that Bella was standing to enjoy our performance. She had a smile on her face that was surely visible from the peaks of the hills around the town.

"You can rely upon the fact that, together with Sergeant Stainsbury and my good friends Marius Quin and Lady Isabella Montague, I will find the killer." I believe that Lovebrook was hoping for another cheer in response to this bold claim, but instead he got more questions.

"Will you interrogate Robert Milton?" a young boy at the side of the hall demanded, though I had a feeling he'd been handed a halfpenny for the trouble by another member of the audience. "If anyone hated Mrs Thistlethwaite, it was him."

"Has anyone questioned the famous guests at the Grand Hotel?" another voice enquired. "I saw that Alexander Fraiser drinking himself into a stupor last night. Perhaps the booze made him lose his mind and Mrs Thistlethwaite suffered." This point sparked another barrage of comments from around the room.

"What about the staff there?"

"How can you say for certain that Mrs Thistlethwaite didn't commit suicide?"

"How do we know that this maniac won't kill again? He could be here right at this very moment."

Faced with this onslaught, Lovebrook had turned a shade that was not so very different from the walls of the hall in which we stood.

SEVENTEEN

A queue of people formed to make demands of the beleaguered inspector, whereas I only received searching glances and snide looks. I was tempted to tell them that I intended to solve the blasted case if it was the last thing I did, but I had other things on my mind. Mr Pork Pie, the man in black, Augustus, or however else you might wish to call him, was lodged in my brain and I was trying to understand what he'd been doing at the hotel.

As Lovebrook dealt with the locals, Bella and I had to talk to an apparently important person we'd never met before.

"Mr Milton?" she said to cut short the bad-tempered conversation he'd been conducting with another society member. "I'm sorry to interrupt, but it would be very helpful if we could have a word with you."

"Oh, yes?" he replied somewhat suspiciously as the man with whom he'd just been arguing threw one hand in the air like a vexed Frenchman and stormed off. "If you're here to accuse me of murder, I will repeat what I said in the meeting."

"No, sir," I said in a conciliatory tone. "It's because you seem to be one of the most knowledgeable people we have encountered. We believe you are well placed to explain the hierarchy within your society and the town in general."

He regarded us both a little smugly and I believe that it was the presence of my aristocratic friend that finally swayed him. "Very well, but not here and not now. I am a busy man and will have to meet you later. Shall we say afternoon tea at four o'clock in the hotel?"

"That would be a real treat," Bella replied, and he looked at her a little more keenly.

"No, it will be your treat. If you expect me to serve up gossip and hearsay on my neighbours, then the very least you can do is provide the refreshments." With his rude manner and apparent self-interest, he really was just like the captain who had led my unit in the war.

"We will see you at four o'clock, then," I replied before Bella could take exception to his curtness and put him in his place.

"I would have liked to tell him what for," she confirmed as I steered her away.

"I know you would, which is why I intervened. He may be a tedious grub, but we need him to tell us what he knows. And there's always the chance he really is the killer, as Travers insisted. The friendlier we can be to him, the better."

She did not reply but seemed to accept the sense of what I'd told her. We walked to the front of the building where Sergeant Stainsbury was shaking hands with a line of people, much like the father of the bride at a wedding. Not everyone was happy, and one or two of them told him just that, but, for the most part, the discussion remained polite.

"Thank you for coming," he told us once our turn had come. It was said in a far more pleasant tone than anything he'd uttered that morning. "I believe the meeting achieved its goal."

"How did you organise it so swiftly?" Bella sounded

genuinely impressed, and Stainsbury was happy to wallow in her implied praise.

"It was really no effort. We have a well-established whisper network here in the town. I told a few key people and sent my men out to inform others. They were all up in arms about the murder as it was. I suspect they would have congregated in Princess Gardens on the seafront and made a scene if I hadn't done something. Though I must say, Mr Quin, I appreciated your assistance. With a certain contingent in this town, things can quickly turn ugly if you don't say the exact thing that they want to hear."

"I don't suppose that contingent would be members of Mrs Thistlethwaite's detection club?"

He shifted from one foot to the other so that his large frame rocked like a ship in a storm. "I don't think it would be wise of me to answer that question, Lady Isabella. Of course, if there is anything else I can—" Before he could finish his sentence, an altercation broke out between two representatives of the rival groups.

"How dare you make such claims without any evidence!" one of the elderly ladies who had spoken in the meeting demanded, and Mrs Grimage was not afraid to offer a reply.

"I dare because I know what kind of person Robert Milton is. I know what Mrs Thistlethwaite thought of him, and I know that he's the likely killer."

The sergeant and two constables stepped in to prevent things getting out of control. It was a shame that this had happened at that very moment, as there were any number of questions I would have liked to put to Stainsbury. We would also have to wait to visit Mrs Thistlethwaite's house, as Lovebrook was still busy in the town hall.

"Does any of it make more sense?" Bella asked, and I acted for a moment as though I was supremely confident on the matter.

"Of course it does." I ran one hand through my hair to suggest that I was very fond of myself – which, I'll have you know, was also part of the act. "It's clear to me now that this pretty enclave on the southern coast of Britain is an epicentre of crime, violence, and afternoon teas. If we don't solve this case quickly enough, there's bound to be another murder."

"That's certainly positive thinking, Marius. Thank you."

Lovebrook eventually appeared, and we asked the one remaining constable how to get to Mrs Thistlethwaite's house. I must say that I had a brief pang of guilt for not bringing my loyal basset hound with me on the walk. This was quickly forgotten when I remembered that he was having a much better time in dog heaven back at the hotel.

"The mystery around Mr Black has only deepened, I'm afraid," good old Valentine informed us as the road we were walking along grew steeper. "I asked the sergeant what he knew about the man, and he'd never heard the name in his life."

"Then what about the file in the hotel?" I had to ask, though I could have worked out the answer from the information he'd already provided.

"Well, he wasn't too happy that I'd asked him such a question, but he insisted that he and his men are not in the habit of leaving sensitive papers about the place."

"How perplexing..." Bella mumbled, her eyes on the pavement as we pushed on up the hill.

Mrs Thistlethwaite had lived in a surprisingly lavish property some ten minutes' walk from the town hall. There were some real mansions up there. Some of the buildings belonged to schools and nursing homes, but the rest looked as though they were still occupied by wealthy families. To be quite honest, I'd seen smaller palaces in my time on the continent.

"Her husband was a major, isn't that right?" Bella asked. "Perhaps he brought back loot from wherever the army sent him. How else could an army widow afford such a home?"

There would be no answer to this question until we entered the house, and to do that, we would have to convince the officer standing guard outside it that we deserved any such privilege. It turned out that somebody had already tried and failed to achieve this. The dead woman's niece was sitting on the step of the property, looking forlorn. For a moment, the sight of her there kindled something inside me, but it was Bella who sought to comfort her.

"Jennifer, you poor thing," she said as we approached. "What are you doing out here?"

This kindness was enough to make the broken-hearted young lady whimper. "The constable says that I can't go inside until his colleagues have turned the place over. I'm not allowed in my own—" She stopped herself then as she realised that what she was about to say wasn't true. "I'm not allowed into the place I've been living for years, which will now go to my already rich uncle."

"Don't you get anything?" I asked far too bluntly, which, understandably, made her cry a little more loudly.

"Oh, yes. In one final slice of cruelty, my aunt told me that she has provided an allowance of the exact same amount that I would have been paid for my job, had she been so generous. I believe it's somewhere in the region of fifteen pounds a month."

On hearing this, Lovebrook marched along the garden path to argue with the guard. It wasn't much of an argument. In fact, the constable capitulated just as soon as the inspector mentioned Scotland Yard. He didn't even have to show his police badge, and I decided that I might have to try a similar trick should I ever need to access a building that a mere civilian was forbidden from entering. Of course, impersonating a policeman is an arrestable offence, so I hope that I will never find myself in such a pickle.

"This way, everyone," he called back to us, and I helped

Jennifer up to standing so that Bella could put one arm around her.

The house was surprisingly light and airy. If I'd tried to imagine where a person like Mrs Thistlethwaite lived, I would have pictured a dank cave or perhaps a castle teetering on the top of a Transylvanian mountain. The reality couldn't have been more different. The long hallway we entered was tiled with a white-and-terracotta diamond pattern. The walls were cream, the curtains light blue and there was a sweet smell in the air of perfume or freshly cut flowers. Nothing about the place gave the sense that its owner had just been slain, which made perfect sense, as how would a house know such a thing?

There was a moment of trepidation as my friends and I looked at one another to decide who would stay with the weeping witness and who would get to search the house for clues. Luckily for Bella and me, Jennifer caught sight of a photograph of her aunt on the wall and fell into Lovebrook's arms. He looked a little disappointed but was too much of a gentleman to dump her in a comfortable chair or pass her off to the constable outside.

"I wonder who she really was," Bella said once we were alone. She'd walked closer to the wall of photographs and was studying an old picture of Mrs Thistlethwaite with her husband in full military uniform.

"She was clearly a well-travelled woman." I came to stand next to her and noticed images from all over the world. They appeared to be organised chronologically from left to right, as they started with a young Mrs Thistlethwaite in her wedding dress before the march of time progressed across the wall. "I suppose she accompanied her husband for his work."

"Africa, India, Australasia. They went all over the empire."

She marvelled at the range of countries on display before us as I concentrated on a few sparse dates that I could see stamped onto the images. She'd been in Burma in 1902, and British

Somaliland the following year, but anything else would require an element of guesswork.

"That's Tibet." I pointed to a photograph of a line of British diplomats with two Eastern gentlemen in long robes and a sole woman on one side. "In 1904, if I'm not mistaken."

Bella opened her eyes wider to question me. "How could you possibly know that?"

"Because as we've already established, I paid attention at school and specifically in Mrs Abbot's history class. I don't know why she was so interested, but she went into an inordinate amount of detail on the British expedition to Tibet. The man standing in front of Mrs Thistlethwaite is the man who led the mission. Lieutenant Colonel Younghusband brokered peace between the countries. The treaty was very much in Britain's favour and, if I remember correctly, it was signed on the seventh of September 1904."

"How very helpful. Perhaps we're looking for a disgruntled Tibetan." Bella laughed at her quip and walked off along the corridor. "I'm going to look for her bedroom. If she's anything like me, that's where we'll find her secrets."

"What secrets do you have that I don't already know?"

"Evidently none that I'm willing to share." She hurried up the stairs, and I went to the second door off the corridor, which looked a lot like a study and turned out to be just that.

The most remarkable thing about Mrs Thistlethwaite's house was just how tidy it was. Even after I'd tidied it, my own writer's room at home was a mess of papers and piled-up books. In contrast, Mrs Thistlethwaite's study looked as though no one had entered since it had first been decorated – except perhaps to dust and polish, as I couldn't find a speck of fluff or the hint of a smudge on any surface.

There were bookshelves on either side of a large sash window, in front of which stood a grand old desk. It is my philosophy as a detective that any investigation should begin with a good browse of a victim's book collection. This is not merely to have a sense of what kind of person the unfortunate soul was, but to judge them harshly if it turns out that they had poor taste in literature. This could not be said of Angelica Thistlethwaite entirely. In addition to her endless rows of romances with titles such as *The Rose that Would Never Flower* and *The Sheik of Hearts*, there was a small stack of mystery novels with my own at the very top.

I recognised several of my fellow writers' names, including such long-established authors as Livia Shipley and relative newcomer Emmeline Warwick. Two others I noticed fitted the descriptions that Jennifer had given of her aunt's previous targets. It was hard to feel much sympathy for the head of the Mystery and Detection Society whenever I thought of what she had done to my colleagues before me.

Putting this and my snobbish literary leanings aside, I opened drawers and rifled through boxes in the hope that I would catch the killer's scent, metaphorically at least. There were no important papers there, or even files relating to the society. The only thing that I found was a thin blue diary with various seemingly inconsequential notes.

If I'd been trying to find out when Mrs Thistlethwaite had met her bank manager or attended a tea morning at the local Women's Institute, it was a goldmine, but the only thing that interested me was a pair of letters marked in the margin of the page approximately once a week. I thought that "S.M." could refer to the days upon which she had a society meeting, though I would have to confirm the idea with her niece. Overall, I got the impression that Mrs Thistlethwaite knew to be careful, and I had almost given up altogether when I caught a glimpse of something in the light that streamed in through the window.

There was a large pad of paper fixed to the middle of the desk and, although it was blank, I could just make out the impression of words that had been written on pages that had now been removed.

I couldn't tell what they said at first, and so I took a pencil and, like a child doing a brass rubbing on an ancient gravestone, I revealed the secrets of the dead woman's hand. Much of what was there was hard to read, as words had been written one atop the other, thus cancelling one another out. The majority of the rest was of no interest to me; she had clearly written a letter to her secret lover, and there is no need to repeat any of the flowery phrases I found. However, there was one sentence in space at the very bottom of the page that stood out.

Augustus Black and his associate will arrive on the 2.40 train from Paddington. They will leave the next day at 3.25.

So Mrs Thistlethwaite knew about Black and that meant... What did it mean? His influence on the case kept circling my mind without settling in place. Was it possible that she had become involved with some terrible criminal organisation? Could it be that he was the manly lover she had described to Travers? I tried to overlook the approximately forty-year difference between them, but it seemed far-fetched to say the least. Black had looked so much like the stereotypical American gangster that I could never imagine prim and proper Mrs Thistlethwaite having anything to do with such a person. And yet his appearance did fit with one part of her personality. It occurred to me that—

"Marius!" Bella called down, and I was pulled from my hypothesising. "Marius, come quickly."

I left my rubbing on the desk for the police to see and followed my accomplice up to the first floor of the house.

"Where are you?" I asked when I'd poked my head through the first few doors and not found her.

The upstairs was just as well-furnished and carefully

presented as what I'd seen below. I must say that Mrs Thistlethwaite had good taste. I don't know what I'd expected, but her house was the definition of comfort. I could happily have lived in such a place myself – though, within a day or two of moving in, I am sure that it would have grown to resemble my own disordered flat in St James's.

Bella whistled, and I followed the sound along the carpeted corridor to the front of the house. She was in a small bedroom, busily poking away to her heart's content. I believe that the main reason we both enjoy being detectives so much is that we are singularly nosy individuals, and it gives us an excuse to indulge our instincts.

"What have you found?" I asked when she didn't immediately reveal her discovery. The décor in the room was rather light and youthful and I wondered whether these were the niece's quarters, rather than the aunt's.

"You won't believe it." She was standing beside a small, lacquered dressing table that looked as though it had been imported from the Far East. Atop its glossy surface were more framed photographs. Most of them were of a smiling middle-aged couple who I took to be Jennifer's parents. Her mother was the spit and image of her sister, as I had seen her in photographs in the entrance hall. Mrs Thistlethwaite herself featured in a few, and there was one that Bella must have moved as the photograph was now lying on its back. Something about the way she was waving a piece of paper in the air, as though she'd just received the results of an important exam, told me that the two items were linked.

"I found this letter hidden behind the back of the photograph."

"You clever thing." This may have sounded a little patronising, but I was genuinely impressed. "How did you think to look inside the frame?"

"Never mind that, just listen to what I found." She cleared her throat and began to read.

"My dearest Jennifer,

"I am sorry that I will never have the courage to send you this letter. I can only pray that you find where I've hidden it one day. The truth is that I have written it a hundred times and tried to tell you in person one hundred more.

"The first thing I must say is that, since your parents died, I have always treated you in a way that I felt was the most likely to produce a strong, capable young woman. I believe that I have achieved my aims in that respect, and I have no regrets for the distance that exists between us. I grew up in a very different time from yours, and the life I lived before you came along was one typified by order and self-control. When I look at the state of the world today, my own upbringing sometimes feels as though it happened many centuries ago.

"Now that this is clear, I can tell you the real purpose of this letter; I am writing to explain why I gave away my only daughter. I was forty-five when I fell pregnant. Oswald was still a serving officer, and I accompanied him on every trip that the British Army would allow. We had never wanted children, and none had come along. My foolishness and vanity led me to spend time with a young lieutenant who flattered and, I'm not too proud to say it, seduced me. I had thought myself too old to become a mother, but the world moves in mysterious ways and that is what happened.

"I could not risk my husband discovering that I had strayed. Oswald's complexion was so different from the young officer who had taken me abed that I was sure the baby, when it arrived, would betray my secret. The only way to hide my indiscretion was to travel home to Devon and give the child up for adoption. During those six months, I entrusted my secret to your mother, and she begged me to let her raise you as her own daughter.

That's correct, Jennifer; I am your natural mother, though my sister did a much better job than I ever could have.

"Soon after you were born, I returned to Oswald in Asia where he was then stationed. I saw you intermittently, and it was never easy to be in your presence. This was not just because you reminded me of the terrible sin I had committed, but because some part of my maternal instinct was irrepressible.

"I have loved you all your life as my niece, and I hope you can forgive me for never being your mother.

"With much sincerity and affection,

"Angelica Thistlethwaite"

I looked at the photograph on the dresser more closely. I looked at the mother holding the tiny baby, and it was impossible to say whether it was Mrs Thistlethwaite in the photograph or her sister.

EIGHTEEN

"We must tell Jennifer," Bella said as soon as she'd finished her reading. "This could change her life."

I was more hesitant. "It's not our place to interfere." I looked at the other photographs, still trying to make sense of what I saw there.

"Marius, this is Jennifer's room. Mrs Thistlethwaite clearly wanted her to know the truth, or she wouldn't have hidden the letter where she did."

"We should tell the police first. You're right that this could change Jennifer's life. It could also change the order of inheritance, and we mustn't do anything rash. Especially as this could end up having a bearing on the case we're investigating."

"How can you be so detached? The poor girl who is crying on our friend's shoulder at this very moment should know who her mother really was."

I stopped what I was doing to look at her. "Exactly. She is already upset at having lost her aunt. Imagine if we were to reveal that it was actually her neglectful mother who died."

Her perfect face froze and not a muscle twitched, nor an eyelash batted before she spoke again. "Very well, but she must be told in time. We can't just leave this letter here for her to discover when she's old and grey, if at all. She's lived her whole life believing a lie."

I decided to be just as dispassionate as she'd suggested. "I imagine it is more common than anyone knows, especially during wars and when men are off travelling the world playing soldiers and sailors."

Her expression became a touch more disapproving. "If you hadn't been a soldier yourself, that would sound quite unfeeling. Even then, I'm not sure why you would say it."

"I'm not criticising the men themselves. It's the kings and politicians moving the pieces around the board who are to blame." I cut this complaint short, as it could have gone on for a lot longer. "Now, unless you're desperate to hear more of my thoughts on the injustices of the world, I suggest we look for Mrs Thistlethwaite's bedroom."

I left Bella behind to inspect Jennifer's meagre quarters for a while longer and went back to the hall to follow it around to the front of the building. The white walls and rich green carpet put me in mind of a fairy tale for some reason, though I cannot tell you why or even which one. The four-poster bed, which dominated the master bedroom, would not have looked out of place in *Sleeping Beauty*. However, there was nothing particularly personal to find in Mrs Thistlethwaite's bedroom beyond more photographs of foreign climes. The ones in her bedroom featured few people among the incredible landscapes, and there were no secrets hidden in the frames, I checked. There were images of waterfalls and deserts, jungles and endless plains. It made my own trip around Europe look decidedly unadventurous.

It is an odd sensation to creep about a dead woman's house. Even though our accommodating friend Valentine had allowed us to search the place, I couldn't help but feel like a snooper. There was nothing of interest in her wardrobe and so I went over to the first bedside table, which had a run of small drawers on one side of it. I found another terrible romantic novel, a pair of reading glasses, and a few clean handkerchiefs. In a mystery like this one, the key piece of evidence that leads to the killer will often be something which at first seems inconsequential – something which the police might well overlook entirely until it falls to our brilliant detective to see through the culprit's stratagems. I toyed with the idea that Mrs Thistlethwaite's frothy reading material would end up being this clue but soon changed my mind.

What I did find, buried deep in the bottom drawer under several pairs of pyjamas, was a brand-new pair of platinum cufflinks. They were still in their bag from a London jeweller's, and I was overjoyed to find that each one had been inscribed with a sentence in tiny letters around the outside. I squinted to read the words: "To My Mystery Man". It sadly did not include any initials or a Christian name, but it did reinforce what Travers had told us.

In the drawers on the opposite side of the bed, I found a toothbrush, a pair of men's pyjamas and a book about the birth of the American military. All in all, I felt that a male visitor had probably left the items there, and I decided that I would ask Jennifer about it once we'd finished our search. As I could find nothing to tell me who the fellow might be, or any pointers to the culprit's identity, I soon returned downstairs to do just that.

"Do you know the identity of your aunt's gentleman friend?"

This question alone was enough to make the poor girl look worried. "Her gentleman friend?"

"Her..." I tried to find another euphemism. "Travers at the hotel told us that Mrs Thistlethwaite had a male admirer." This sounded worse. "I mean, that she had a boyfriend of some variety. I found several items in her bedside table which would suggest that was the case."

She had to blink a few times as she made sense of what I was telling her. "I suppose it is possible." She even shook her head a little. I could imagine how she was feeling. The thought of my mother finding love again is positively... Actually, I don't know what it is because I've never imagined such an eventuality before. "I go to see my cousin in Brixham once a week. She has a house overlooking the harbour, and I sleep there for a night so as to have a break from my life here. I'd never heard of Angelica spending time with one specific gentleman, but she had the opportunity to entertain here whenever I was away."

Lovebrook was standing by the window, looking out at the pretty garden, which was just as well-kept as everything we'd seen in the house. He was evidently paying close attention as he turned back to our witness at this moment and asked a question of his own. "Even if you weren't aware of such a connection between them, does anyone come to mind who could fit the profile of a potential... paramour?"

This was quite the silliest conversation to which I'd ever been party. Three grown adults were forced to find polite words to skirt over the issue. There was evidently a man who came to Mrs Thistlethwaite's house each week and stayed the night, but we had to discuss the matter as though referring to two children who, on occasion, would while away their time together playing with dolls and tin soldiers.

Down with euphemisms; up with plain speaking, that's what I say!

Jennifer was clutching the arms of her chair, as though she were afraid they might try to escape. "It's very difficult to say." She had a brief think before continuing. "I know there were certain men in the society who took a keen interest in her."

"That would fit with the idea of a mystery man," I said before realising that none of them had access to my thoughts and didn't know about the cufflinks. "I found an undelivered present in Angelica's bedside table. It was a pair of cufflinks with the engraving 'To My Mystery Man'. It would make a lot of sense if the person for whom they were purchased was in the Torquay Mystery and Detection Society."

"Or perhaps she just enjoyed the fact that only she knew his identity," Bella commented, and we all turned to Jennifer to see what she thought.

"If it were one of her acolytes, I can't say who would be the most likely candidate. As you may have worked out by now, half of the people in this town thought that my aunt was an angel and the rest believed that she should be locked away."

I looked at Lovebrook then to see if he had any strong feelings on the matter, but he was happy to listen for the moment and gave nothing away. It was hard to know sometimes whether his affable, perhaps even passive manner belied a fine mind, or he really was just a little bit dreamy.

"What about Black?" I asked when the silence had gone on for too long.

"I beg your pardon?" Jennifer certainly didn't appear to know what this name meant. I suppose that she could have been acting, but I believed her.

"Augustus Black." I paused to examine her reaction, but there wasn't one. "A man we saw causing trouble on the train yesterday and then several times at the hotel. He came into the swimming pool just after I discovered Mrs Thistlethwaite's body."

I don't know what she was thinking at that moment, but she peered from one to the next of us in turn. "I don't understand. If you have a suspect, why has no one arrested him?"

"Because he's disappeared," Lovebrook replied. "I've given instructions to the Torquay police to look out for a man of his description, and I've discussed the matter with Scotland Yard, but until we find him, there's nothing more we can do."

I thought it interesting that he held back the key fact that we had just learnt. Black didn't exist, and he hadn't told her.

"I don't know anyone by that name," Jennifer said in a low, worried voice. "I've certainly never heard my aunt talk of him."

"And yet," I began with a touch more excitement than I'd intended, "if you go next door to the study, you will find that Black's name has recently been written on the pad there."

It was at this point that sweet little Jennifer became more nervous. "I should probably have told you before that there are many things that my aunt kept secret. I always assumed that she didn't entirely trust me. Whenever she was planning some new piece of cruelty, she would become very quiet and cold. Perhaps she thought I would nip her nastiness in the bud."

I replied with a nice vague, "Hmm... I see."

"What about her estate?" Lovebrook tried a different approach. "You said that your uncle will inherit. Is it possible that he was there in the hotel last night and pushed her into the pool?"

She didn't hesitate for once but told us straight out. "Not unless he returned from Southern Rhodesia without anyone noticing. Angelica had been writing to him there recently. He is planning to visit in the spring. And if you're asking whether he could be the killer, he suffers from terrible arthritis, and I doubt he'd have had the strength. If anything, my aunt would have been the one to push him in the pool and claim his inheritance."

I couldn't help smiling at this, because I am a terrible person with a morbid sense of humour, but it stirred another question in me. "What about this house? Has it always been in the family?"

"No, she bought it three or four years ago." She looked down at her hands as they threaded into one another. "Angelica was one of those people who never talk about money but, when I first came to live with her, I know that her finances were in a bad way. Her husband was a gambler before he died and whatever money he had from his army career had long since dissolved. Much the same thing occurred with my parents' inheritance; she'd taken out loans to cover her debts and the money went to paying them. She never told me how things improved, but they did, and drastically, which is how she could afford this house."

This was just the kind of thing we needed to investigate, but I had no idea how we would go about it.

"And the society?" Bella chose to concentrate on the group at the centre of the case. "Did she make any money from that?"

Jennifer shook her head. "Not from what I saw, and I was responsible for looking after membership fees and recording expenses. We have an account at the bank on Torwood Street. Most of what comes in goes out again soon enough."

"And aside from your own contribution, was there anyone in particular who helped Mrs Thistlethwaite with the society?"

"Mr Travers was always willing to aid my aunt in any way that he possibly could. I used to joke that he... Oh, you don't think...?"

"No, we don't," Lovebrook intervened, which meant that no one had to say anything irritatingly discreet again. "He is the person who told us about your aunt's affair in the first place." Affair! That was a perfectly accurate and grown-up word. Why hadn't we been using it from the beginning?

"I see." Jennifer took a deep breath but released it ever so quickly. "Well, aside from Mr Travers, the main person who assists with the running of the society is Miss Elsbury. She's a dear old thing. She meets... or rather, she met my aunt once a week to discuss real cases of crime that she'd discovered in the newspaper or possible discussions we might organise."

"Were you present at these meetings?" Lovebrook asked, and I realised that all three of us had latched on to different threads and were pulling them at the same time. I couldn't imagine why he'd asked this, but then he probably wondered what a pair of cufflinks might have to do with anything.

"Normally, yes, unless I was away. I believe they met a few

days ago while I was in Brixham, for example, but I tended to be present."

This fitted with what I'd seen in the diary and, unless the dear sweet Miss Elsbury turned out to be a secret maniac, I couldn't imagine what good it would do us. In fact, the initially exciting interview had petered out without much to show for itself. Lovebrook thanked our witness, told the constable outside to let her stay in the lounge until his colleagues came to examine the house more thoroughly, and we left her with her thoughts.

"I think she's the killer," Bella said with great alacrity as soon as we'd reached the end of the path.

"Don't be ridiculous," I told her. "I've rarely met a more instantly likable human being than Jennifer Capshaw."

"All the more reason for her to think she can get away with it," Lovebrook replied, and I noticed him looking back towards the house where Jennifer was perched beside the window, gazing out at the world.

"Don't you start, too, Valentine." A note of shock had entered my voice. "Surely you can see just how much that poor creature is suffering?"

"Well..." he began again, and I doubted for a moment whether he would reveal what he was thinking. "She may be suffering, or she may be putting it on so that we won't suspect her. You have to admit that her timing was spot on; we entered the house, and she immediately fell into my arms in need of support."

"That's right!" Bella exclaimed a little too joyously and had to drop her voice again so as not to be overheard. "She made sure that the professional officer couldn't search the place, leaving two hobbyist sleuths who may or may not know where their elbows are located."

"This is insanity," I protested once more. "A dear girl like Jennifer loses her parents in an accident, and then the woman who took her in is murdered, and you think the worst of her."

"So what you're saying..." Bella allowed a theatrical pause, and I knew that she was about to put forward an even nastier theory. "...is that she may have killed her parents too?"

I turned away from them, as I didn't want to hear any more. "The world has gone mad."

"You must admit that she would benefit most from her aunt's death. Perhaps she discovered the letter in the picture frame, realised that Mrs Thistlethwaite was her real mother and believed that it would give her the evidence she needed to overturn the existing will. Perhaps she even knows what it says. There's most likely a copy in that house somewhere."

"Oh, that is interesting," Lovebrook practically purred at this moment. "So little blue-eyed Jenny was the secret daughter of the dragonish victim. I wouldn't blame the brat for killing the wicked woman."

"She's not a brat!" I might have said this a mite too vehemently. "She's a sweet and beautiful human being."

My words died away, leaving us in silence for approximately three seconds before Bella pushed us both along the road so that she was free to laugh at me.

"'A beautiful human being', Marius? Might it not be that you're just the tiniest bit under this girl's spell?"

Lovebrook was happy to join in with her goading. "I don't blame you one bit, old bean. She is certainly very pretty. But do be careful. If she killed her natural mother and adopted parents, there's nothing to say that you won't be next."

"She didn't kill—" I started to say before realising there was no point in finishing that sentence. "I can't believe that you—"

They laughed at me all the way to the bank. Quite literally, I hasten to add.

NINETEEN

"Why the bank?" I asked Lovebrook as the bell above the door rang, and we entered the fine old establishment. It was one of those particularly traditional places where every male attendant wears a tailcoat and is probably called Brooks, and every woman behind the tills has permanently waved hair and responds to the name Ethel. The counter was made of good strong wood, the doors had green leather padding and a man at the front of the shop, who initially looked like a sculpture, bowed deferentially as we drew level with him.

"Hello there, sir, sir, madam. How may I be of service?" It seemed rude to interrupt him, but we probably should have. "Are you opening a new account, perhaps? Or maybe you would like me to tell you about the very reasonable mortgages that are currently available?"

"No, nothing like that," Lovebrook bluntly replied. "My name is Detective Inspector Lovebrook. I'm from the Metropolitan Police and I'm here to look over the accounts of Mrs Thistlethwaite."

The fusty fellow frowned at us as though we'd tricked him. "Oh... Well... I suppose that, if you must do that sort of thing, this is the right place for it. Follow me, please, sir, sir, madam." He nodded to us once again, but this time there was no warmth in the gesture.

He led us to a back room and, after a short, dull knock on the padded door, we entered to meet the bank manager.

"Detective Inspector Lovebrook and his entourage are here to see you."

"Capital. That's just capital!" A short, skinny man behind a desk the size of the *Titanic* rose a really very short way in order to greet us. "I was expecting a visit before long."

"It's good of you to see us, Mr Dulwich." Lovebrook hadn't guessed the man's name. He'd read it on the door.

"Please, sit down." We did just that and waited for him to continue. "Now, what exactly would you like to know about poor Angelica?"

It was Lovebrook's turn to be a gentleman, and he motioned for Bella to answer this question.

"We'd like to know about her financial situation. We got the impression from one of our witnesses that Mrs Thistlethwaite once fell into dire straits, but from the look of her house at the time she died, it seems that her fortunes reversed."

Mr Dulwich remained jovial. "They certainly did. She was very fortunate to have such generous benefactors."

"Benefactors?" I parroted the word back to him. "What sort of benefactors?"

Instead of replying verbally, he rose from his seat and moved to a cabinet in one corner of the gloomy office. "If you give me a moment, I'll be able to tell you."

Lovebrook nodded his agreement, and we looked at one another as a frisson of excitement passed over us. Dulwich worked swiftly to flick through the files in one of the drawers and soon extracted what he needed.

"Here we are. Mrs Thistlethwaite was one of our most loyal customers and we greatly appreciated her business." Something about the way he said this suggested that he was so grateful to her that he had avoided asking too many questions about her sudden wealth – or perhaps I'm overly suspicious. "You can see from the regular donations over the last four years just how popular her society became."

He slid six neatly handwritten pages across the table to us. The starting amount was pitiful, whereas the money that Mrs Thistlethwaite had when she died made me feel a little sick.

"How did she...?" I uttered without meaning to make a sound.

Pointing across the table to the relevant information, Dulwich maintained his businesslike manner throughout. He was a short man, but he had an impressive wingspan. "If you look at the column for monies received, you will see some of the donations that Mrs Thistlethwaite elicited." I did just that and felt even worse.

Miss G. Cooper – £2,000
Mr S. Hale – £3,000
Mrs E. Laye – £1,600
Mrs D. Mills – £8,000
Mrs G. Snow – £1,200
Mr H. Snow – £2,500
C. Butt – £6,000
Lady K. Rollo – £11,295

I was so thunderstruck by the quantities of money that people had seen fit to donate to the Torquay Mystery and Detection Society that the names rather ran into one another. Of course, the presence of a titled lady on the list suggested that Mrs Thistlethwaite had sought and received favour from the great and good of the land.

"This money went into her private account, not that of the society?" Lovebrook was quick to ask.

"That's right." Dulwich blinked as though his eyes were especially sensitive to the light. "The society's account holds comparatively little. It is mainly used for day-to-day matters such as running costs and membership fees."

"Did she ever tell you why people were so eager to open their chequebooks?" Bella was the first to get us to the point, and Mr Dulwich leaned back in his chair to answer in that smooth, confident voice of his.

"I believe that things really took off when the society solved a murder that the police had been unable to fathom. You know they tracked down an actual killer, and the man was hanged for his crime. That's the kind of thing that really excites people."

I had another question for him. "Did anyone else have access to this account?"

"No, she was particularly cautious when it came to her finances. I don't think she particularly liked me knowing how much she had, but that's rather a condition of my trade. Miss Capshaw could access the society account, but she had nothing to do with her aunt's money."

Lovebrook was less interested in Mrs Thistlethwaite's habits so much as where the money ended up. "You do realise that, if Mrs Thistlethwaite was soliciting donations for the society and keeping the money for herself, that could be a criminal offence?"

Dulwich finally looked a little flustered. "You can't possibly think—" He took a second to gather his thoughts before his tone became more resolute. "It really depends on the circumstances. We can't say anything for certain." He straightened his tie and seemed quite happy with himself.

"No, that isn't how it works," Lovebrook began, but he wasn't in the mood to convince the man. "You'll have a visit from the local constables, and I would make sure that all of your files are in order if I were you." He sat flicking through the papers for a few more seconds and then rose without warning.

As I had assumed there would be more to the interrogation than this, I did not.

"Come along, Marius," Bella had entered into her role as a tough, uncompromising busy once again. "We have more important work to do."

"I'm sorry, miss," Dulwich called after her as she swept from the room with a knowing smile on her face. "I didn't catch your name."

I considered telling him that she was no miss, but a lady, but I thought it might sound smug, so I merely nodded my thanks and hurried after my friends.

"My goodness, that was a lot of fun." Bella certainly showed her enthusiasm as we stepped from the bank to the street once more. This was definitely the holiday from her everyday life that she needed. "What did you make of that?"

"It seems quite simple," Lovebrook replied, and I wondered how this could possibly be true. "She was stealing money from the society, someone found out, and in a fit of rage pushed her into the pool."

"Marvellous!" Bella clapped her dainty hands together before realising that this was inappropriate. "Or rather, what do you think we should we do next?"

I allowed the confident inspector to answer this one. "I must confirm what Jennifer told us about Mrs Thistlethwaite's will. It's all very well saying that her uncle will inherit the estate, but what if it isn't true? I'm going to find out who her solicitor was and check my facts."

"Ah, that sounds less fun."

"I'll see you both back at the hotel." He tipped his hat to us and hurried off towards the centre of town.

Bella turned to me next. "Marius, how about some lunch?"

I considered her suggestion for all of two seconds before my stomach objected. "After what I ate this morning at breakfast, I think I'd prefer to wait a while. Don't forget we have to meet that fellow from the society for afternoon tea."

She'd lost all her energy, and I felt that her own stomach was partly to blame. "That's probably a good idea. Perhaps we should return to the hotel directly to see Mr Milton."

"What time is it now?" I asked and searched about for a clock on the buildings around us. Looking along Torwood Street towards the sea, I could make out an elegant clocktower with the harbour beyond it.

"Five minutes past three," Bella answered before I could.

I'd already taken off down the road before issuing my plaintive reply. "Oh, why didn't I mention it to Lovebrook? He could have called us a car!"

"Marius?" she said after me. "Where on earth are you going?"

I was running backwards. It was not the fastest method. "There was too much to consider at Mrs Thistlethwaite's house, and I didn't have time to tell you."

"And why don't you have time now?" She began to run but really wasn't dressed for it, so I slowed down even more.

"Because the London train departs in twenty minutes' time."

She had one last question before I could get away. "Why is that important?"

I shouted back over my shoulder, though I can't say that she heard me. "Just meet me there as soon as you can."

I knew that I had just enough time to get to the railway station, but I would be cutting it fine before the train left. I'd been storing up so much important evidence in my head all day instead of making sure to discuss things in the order they occurred to me. The difference between this case and the others we'd investigated was that this one felt too loose. So far, we'd only identified a few suspects, and one of them was potentially about to get away from us for ever.

I shot along the seafront, past shops and cafés, tea rooms and orderly windows displaying ladies' fashions. I've always thought that I'm in fairly good shape when it comes to exercise, but that doesn't mean I'm cut out for long distance running – especially not in a woollen suit – and I soon found myself slowing down. I got beyond the pleasure gardens and around the hill. I could see the Grand Hotel in the distance, and that glimpse of white helped push me on, as I knew the station was just next to it.

I really did call upon every last ounce of energy I possessed. I'm sure I was red-faced and panting, so it was a little unnerving when Bella pulled up alongside me in a taxi, looking immaculate. Unnerving, but very much appreciated.

"Get in, Marius," she called through the open window. "If you'd told me the plan, I would have explained that there was a taxi rank a few minutes' walk away."

"Right... Yes... Good," I said between tortured breaths. "I must remember to... talk things over in advance."

I collapsed into the car and the same chirpy driver who had driven us the day before was there, smiling back at me from the front seat. I realised that it was the same car too. He'd merely removed the sign that had previously been stuck to the door.

"Don't you work for the hotel?" I managed to ask as he pulled away from the kerb.

"I've got to take work wherever I can get it, these days, sir. Sometimes I drive for the hotel. Sometimes I drive for the mayor. And sometimes, until last night that is, I even drove for Mrs Thistlethwaite. I suppose you've heard all about it? From what Irene the operator tells me, that society of hers must have turned against her."

This intrigued me more than I could say. "Why would she think such a thing?"

"Irene?" He peered back over his shoulder again. "Oh, Irene has opinions on everything. I don't always listen, but this was a bit out of the ordinary. Wouldn't you say? It's not every day we have a murder in Torquay. We did once have a man who went about stealing unmentionables from ladies' washing lines, but Sergeant Stainsbury had a word with him, and the vicar agreed to stop." He waited for a few seconds before bursting out laughing. "I'm only joking, sir. It wasn't really the vicar." There was another explosion of laughter which suddenly fell quiet, and the driver turned serious. "It was the verger."

He cleared his throat and didn't say another word until we'd pulled up at the station.

"Will you be requiring onward travel to your hotel?" he asked with that cheeky smile of his. He must have been in his fifties, and yet there was something terribly boyish about him.

Bella was paying the fare and answered for both of us. "I think we'll manage just fine, thank you."

The London train was already there on the other side of the station. I sped up the steps to the latticed footbridge before realising that there was no one on the far platform and the train was about to change tracks. I doubled back along the bridge with a station guard watching me as though I had lost a marble or two.

Platform One was heaving with travellers, but I couldn't see anyone I recognised.

"Who are we looking for anyway?" Bella was peering about the place just like me.

"For a man dressed as a gangster, of course. Augustus Black, or whoever he really is, had the return journey booked for today, according to the impressions on the pad of paper on Mrs Thistlethwaite's desk."

Bella seemed to accept this without further question, and we moved along the platform through the crowd. We soon diverged to cover the ground more efficiently. I walked beside the rails and Bella hugged the grey limestone wall. The station was a picturesque Victorian affair. The metal canopy roof above our heads was supported by barley twist columns in matching colours to the ornate cast-iron spandrels between them. I only mention this because I had to keep ducking around them and the masses of people who were pushing closer to the edge of the platform as the train performed its manoeuvre.

It wasn't until we reached the far end that any hope drained away. We suddenly came out into a large space beyond the station building. There was nothing to see but bare platform and low wooden barrels where, come the spring, flowers would grow.

"Perhaps he changed his ticket and went by bus," Bella suggested.

I turned around to look back the way we'd come. "Or perhaps he's standing over there, and he arrived after us."

Still low in energy from my earlier exertions, I ran back to the middle of the platform, where a man was leaning against the wall. He gazed down at the bag on the ground at his feet. He wasn't wearing the black suit or hat anymore, but I recognised him just the same.

"I've got one question for you," I stated as soon as I was in earshot.

"Oh my good grief," he exclaimed with a shrill whistle. "You're that maniac who chased me this morning. What do you want?"

I thought that what I'd already told him bore repeating. "I've got one question for you, Black. Are you an actor?"

TWENTY

The man was no gangster, but he was a nervous wreck. "I never thought anyone would get hurt. I assumed it would be like any other job. I came down here last year for the same thing, and I had a jolly good night away."

"What in heaven's name does any of that mean?" Bella asked in the uniquely nonplussed manner that is reserved for the upper classes.

"He's talking about the job that Mrs Thistlethwaite hired him to do. He was supposed to come here on the same train as us, make a scene so that we noticed him, and then turn up first thing this morning face down in the swimming pool."

"That's right," replied the man no longer dressed in black who was not wearing a pork-pie hat and whose name presumably wasn't Augustus. "One of the many talents I have is holding my breath. There was a cleaner stationed outside your room whose job it was to take the service lift down to the swimming pool as soon as she saw you leave and tell me to get in the pool. She was to go back after to slip a note under your door, saying it was your fault or some such. The only problem was that you woke up at a ridiculous time of the morning, and so I wasn't in place to pretend to be dead."

Bella was clearly still bemused by all this. "But why would you do any such thing in the first place?"

Mr Actor had produced a handkerchief and proceeded to trumpet into it, so I answered for him. "It was one of Mrs Thistlethwaite's schemes. She was testing me. I imagine that she'd invented a tortuous plot that involved any number of twists and turns, and it was my job to work out who the killer was to prove my mettle as a detective. That's why she so generously paid for me to come here for two nights rather than just one."

"It was all going to come to a head at the ball tonight," the still twitchety man in blue responded. "There were other characters in place to play out various scenes for you."

I can't say I totally understood his story. "But what would you have done when I dived into the pool to pull you out and discovered that you had a pulse?"

This seemed to cheer him somewhat, as it provided an opportunity to discuss the cunning plot of a story that was never told. "That was the clever part. The hotel manager would have been there to tell you I was dead. But, again, you got up too early and ruined everything. In my absence, he would have been the one to direct you to certain information. I'd prepared a police file with information about my devilish past. I came up with the name Augustus Black myself. Do you like it?"

"No, I don't," I lied, as I actually thought it was rather good. "You've clearly been watching too many American films."

He let out a breathy laugh and agreed. "You've got me there. I like nothing better than the dark of a matinee. My favourites are always the ones where—"

"Thank you, but that's not what we need to know."

"Tell us why you ran away," Bella demanded. "If you had nothing to hide, why did you get so nervous?"

Our fake hoodlum was still nervous but did his best to reply. "I'm not used to actual murders. I saw the body of the woman who had paid me to hoodwink you, and I was worried that the whole thing had been planned to make me look bad. That's the kind of thing that happens in the films I watch. There's always a poor sap who ends up taking the blame for the machinations of some scheming Machiavel. I ran as soon as I realised that Mrs Thistlethwaite was dead, and then you came haring after me and I thought the worst."

"The worst of what?" A clean-limbed, suntanned fellow had appeared from the other side of the platform. "Here, Jimmy, are these folk giving you trouble?"

"Ah, the man in red, if I'm not mistaken," I said, as I'd recognised something in his carefree manner. "I saw your little performance on the train yesterday."

"Guilty as charged, officer. It was my idea to give the conductor a penny to come in on the act. I thought that made it all the more convincing," the confident actor replied, and I felt that, had he been in his colleague's place, he wouldn't have run away at the sight of a corpse. He held his hand out and indulged me with a mischievous smile. "Albert Hammond's the name. Master of acting, stagecraft and the odd piece of subterfuge. As is my friend here, Mr Jimmy Biggleswade. I take it you were our victim on the 2:40 from Paddington?" He didn't wait for an answer but turned to his friend. "Come along, Jimmy, they're already boarding."

"Wait, I haven't finished," I told Jimmy before they could disappear. "Why were you arguing with Mr Travers in the hotel garden yesterday? You looked particularly angry."

He adopted that same furious mien. "That was about my room. The blighter had put me in little more than a broom cupboard and I told him how unhappy I was." He crossed his arms rather contentedly. "I was soon moved to a rather nice suite overlooking the bay."

The feeling that we might finally be getting somewhere was swiftly draining from me, and the second man looked at Bella as though waiting for permission to leave.

"Before you go anywhere, I need you both to show us some form of identification," she told them in her authoritative voice, which really had improved over the course of the day.

They had no choice but to obey. They took out their wallets to produce their driving licences, and their names were the same as the ones they'd given us. We had just made the acquaintance of Albert Hammond and James Biggleswade. I made a mental note of the addresses on their driving licences, just in case.

"When you get back to London, you must report to a police station and tell them of the part you played in the events here this weekend." I was still afraid that they knew more than they'd revealed and would never be seen again. "If you don't, I will make sure that the Metropolitan Police track you down and arrest you."

"Oh, please, Mr Overdramatic," Albert teased. "We're actors; you just have to poke your head into the Garrick Club of a lunchtime and you're bound to run us down. We rarely eat anywhere else."

"I have one last question," I said before they could jump aboard.

"You said that when you first appeared," Jimmy told me quite rightly.

"Well, that question was needed in order for me to know what else I wanted to— Do you know what? It doesn't matter. My question is, were any of the celebrities at the hotel connected to Mrs Thistlethwaite's plan?"

"Which celebrities?" Albert demanded of his friend. "Don't tell me I missed out on someone interesting because I accepted a supporting role in this drama. Don't tell me it was Gladys Cooper. She's positively my favourite actress!"

Jimmy became more animated at this moment. "As it happens, I spotted the cricketer Dicky Prowse having dinner. But best of all, Clemmie Symonds was there."

"Oh, I love Clemmie." Albert put one hand to his chest as though pledging allegiance to the famous singer. "That voice!"

"I know." Jimmy was equally moved. "And have you ever seen such a beautiful woman?" He evidently realised that this didn't reflect well on the beauty in front of him and fell quiet.

It was up to his friend to smooth things over. "The most beautiful *famous* person." He tapped Bella on the hand. "You're quite lovely, my dear, but we haven't a clue who you are."

She was not offended and seemed to be enjoying their humorous back and forth.

I was not so keen. "You haven't answered my question. Prowse, Symonds, Idris Levitt and Alexander Fraiser: were any of them involved in the spectacle that Mrs Thistlethwaite conceived to test me?"

Jimmy finally provided a direct answer. "Not that she told me. As far as I know, it was just Albert and me, and then she wrangled a few people to help, like the cleaner, the manager and what have you."

"And there was a local amateur who came to play the coroner," the more boisterous of the two added. "Travers turned him away when the old woman was killed. He did the same to me, and so I never got to perform my second scene."

I was probably a little short with them, but they kept focusing on entirely the wrong things. "So who would the killer have turned out to be in the fantastical murder I was supposed to solve?"

"Is this another of your final questions?" Albert asked before his friend told me what I needed to know.

For a moment, Jimmy looked more like the gangster he'd been playing. "Mrs Thistlethwaite herself fulfilled that role. She thought it would be amusing to make the evidence point towards the hotel manager, when the underlying facts of the case really showed that she was to blame. I wonder if you would have solved it. It's a shame we'll never know."

"Now, if you've exhausted all your final questions," Albert began, his smile once more in place, "the baggage has been loaded, and the train is about to leave."

They shook our hands and moved off across the platform. Albert was still talking. "The next time we do something like this, you spend the night in the tiny bed and breakfast run by a nosy old soldier with gout, and I'll stay in the fancy hotel."

Bella and I stayed right where we were, still trying to figure out how any of this fitted together with the nasty woman's death. I suppose that Jimmy must have taken pity on me, as with most of the passengers having already boarded, he pulled down the window of the nearest carriage to shout to us. "Marius, Miss I Don't Remember Your Name! I can't tell you much else, but I know that Mrs Thistlethwaite didn't invent that story on her own." The train juddered forward a few feet, then began to move more smoothly. "There was someone else from her club who helped. Maybe he can tell you what's really going on here."

TWENTY-ONE

There wasn't long to go until our meeting with Robert Milton, but I thought I should at least check to see that the group who'd accompanied us to the hotel were comfortable in our absence. I found my family getting ready for a steam bath in a room next to the swimming pool. They didn't seem to have heard anything about the murder, and I can only assume that the manager had done what he could to keep it quiet. It's one thing for guests to discover that an old lady had met her fate in the hotel swimming pool and quite another to learn that someone killed her.

"We're sorry for neglecting you, boy," Uncle Stan told me as he sat on a wooden slat bench waiting for the steam to have its effect.

"Yes, we're terribly sorry," Mother added. "But we've been having such a wonderful time that the day has got away from us."

"We'll find it in our hearts to forgive you," Bella told them wryly.

"And we'll meet you for dinner this evening." Auntie Elle had her eyes closed. To be honest, I could barely see her by now as the attendant had added a jugful of water to the hot coals or whatever it was that provided the steam. "I hear that there will be a ball."

They seemed perfectly happy where they were, so I didn't burden them with my problems but went off in search of my occasionally faithful hound. He wasn't in the room with the treadmills, or in one which looked like some kind of hospital ward. We found him in a larger space at the end of the corridor, where he was being encouraged around a circuit by his trainer for the afternoon. There were tunnels to run along, ramps to mount and descend, and hoops through which Percy could jump. Perhaps what was most impressive was the fact that his two little doggy friends stood obediently at the side, waiting for their turn.

Bella and I were so engrossed in the spectacle we viewed through the porthole window that we lost track of time. There was something soothing about watching the dear canines going round and round the room, one after another. I think that they had reached a point at which they didn't really need the instructor there to guide them. I very much doubted that Percy would do anything so athletic for me, though perhaps a trail of food might do the trick.

"It almost makes me wish I had a dog," Bella muttered to herself in wonder before I pulled her away to head to the restaurant.

"Believe me, they're more trouble than they look." I felt a pang of guilt then. I hadn't chosen Percy as my pet, but I was very fond of him. "Though I suppose they're worth the effort. You never feel alone with a dog at your side."

Afternoon tea was being served in the lounge area between the main restaurant and the foyer. It was a small but rather grand space with black stone sculptures beside a carved wooden fireplace that looked like something from a medieval castle. There was an ornate chimney breast with inlaid ornamental columns and abstract shapes that were rather heraldic. The other three walls had oaken panels with the same dark stain as the mantel, and there were five or six small tables surrounded by leather armchairs. It was a perfect little snug in which to while away the time with a book. Sadly, we had work to do. Robert Milton rose from his chair in the middle of the room and motioned for us to join him before immediately sitting back down.

"Thank you for coming." He spoke as though he had arranged the meeting. "I wouldn't want you having a bad impression of me after what you must have witnessed at the town hall. It's awful how quickly people turn savage in a crisis."

"We appreciate you finding the time to—" Before I could finish this sentence, a waiter appeared with a large silver tray that was piled with various delights. I believe that I was almost feeling hungry again after our sizable breakfast, as the sight of cakes, sandwiches and petits fours made my mouth water and my stomach tingle.

"I hope you don't mind," Milton smiled as he took in the treat for which he had already told us we would be paying. "I took the liberty of ordering Devonshire afternoon tea for four. I'm afraid that I assumed that Inspector Lovebrook would be with you."

"I very much doubt we'll have any problem making up for his absence," I told him as I helped myself to a plate, and Bella looked disapprovingly in my direction.

The waiter was a lively young man with an efficient air about him. "There's Devonshire cake, Devonshire pie, Devonshire tea with Devonshire cream and, if anyone wishes to sample the hotel's Devonshire cider, an optional supplement can be paid."

"I think we'll make do with what we have," Bella answered before I could, and she quickly returned us to the conversation as the waiter emptied the various plates and cups onto the table and hurried away. "Now, we'd like to know exactly why there is such a schism in the Mystery and Detection Society."

"I would not use such a word myself," Milton replied, smoothing his wiry brows with one finger as he did so. "It is true that there has been some... animosity towards me in the group, but I can assure you everything has been blown out of proportion. That's normally the way of things in small towns like Torquay."

"Very well," I cut in. "What brought about the schism that isn't a schism?"

He blew on his tea, then popped a tiny square of cake into his mouth. "Some people didn't like the direction in which Mrs Thistlethwaite was taking our society. You might say that I became their spokesperson."

He watched me as he spoke and seemed to take exception to the way I was preparing my first scone. I had put the jam and cream on as I always did but didn't dare eat it.

"Are you Cornish?" he demanded, apropos of seemingly nothing, but at least he explained himself. "In Devon, it goes scone, cream, jam – in that order. Our barbarian neighbours in Cornwall do things the wrong way around."

"Does it really make any difference?" I put to him, and then he smiled and seemed to relax.

"No, it does not, but it goes to show how easily people pick arguments. It is much the same in the society. For the most part, Angelica and I rubbed along very nicely together, but the louder voices in the group exacerbated the situation and set us against one another. Louder voices like that of *Mabel Grimage*." He said these last two words particularly slowly and clearly.

"Are you suggesting that she could be to blame for Mrs Thistlethwaite's death?" Bella did little more than nibble on a cucumber sandwich the whole time we were there – which, quite frankly, made me question her judgement. The scones were really ever so tasty, no matter the order in which I added the cream and jam. As for the Devonshire cake, I'd never had it before, but it was a real winner. It was rich with apples and cinnamon, raisins and honey. If I hadn't had to concentrate, I would have sat in contented silence, savouring every bite.

"I don't know who is to blame for the terrible violence that has befallen this town." Milton gave the first sign that he resented our line of questioning. "All I know is that I'm eager to get to the bottom of what happened."

"Let me state things more clearly." I mainly said this to give me enough time to finish my mouthful. "A room full of people accused you of killing—"

"Half a room, at most."

"Fine, half a room of people accused you of being responsible for your enemy's death and you say that it couldn't be you because you asked a few questions at the meeting to prompt Sergeant Stainsbury to get on with the job."

"That more or less sums up my position." He really did have a pompous manner for a man wolfing down whole pieces of cake between each response. "But there is one thing upon which you are already mistaken." Even his pauses were arrogant. "Angelica was not my enemy."

He brushed the crumbs from his pale grey trousers with a look of smug satisfaction.

"Saying that she wasn't your enemy is hardly evidence of your innocence," Bella told him, but it did nothing to dent his confidence.

"But it's true. Angelica Thistlethwaite was not my enemy. She was my lover."

This claim didn't exactly leave us with our mouths hanging open, but I did have to swallow a gulp of tea.

Milton clearly enjoyed our reaction and soon explained. "If the truth be told, I hadn't wished to mention anything about it. Angelica and I kept it secret because it was no one else's business. The fact is, our initial animosity towards one another ignited the flames of passion within us." He was evidently prone to such ostentatious enunciations and, for a moment, I wondered whether he was one of the amateur actors that Mrs Thistlethwaite had employed to trick me. "Our antagonism was the source of our love. We could fight like wild animals but, once a week, when we were alone together, we combined like—"

I was glad that I thought of something with which to interrupt him then. "Did she have a nickname for you?"

He looked surprised but answered, nonetheless. "Yes, she called me Snouty. I believe it's an old-fashioned word for arrogant, but she liked to say I made love to her like a pig snuffling for truffles." I must admit, this turn of phrase made me stop eating. "Snouty Milton, that's what she called me. And I called her my beloved terror."

This certainly suggested that the letters I'd seen in Mrs Thistlethwaite's diary were not S.M. for Society Meeting, as I'd assumed, but S.M. for Snouty Milton, of all things. It wasn't so far off a clue that I'd included in my first novel, and I should have considered it more carefully.

"Very well," I replied once more, and I couldn't think what to say next, so I said it again and hoped that Bella would fashion something more sensical. "Very well."

"If you were really Mrs Thistlethwaite's paramour, what did she keep in her bedside table?" She apparently didn't believe him, and I couldn't blame her.

Milton would not be caught out. "You mean to say, what did *I* keep in her bedside table? I have a toothbrush, a pair of pyjamas and a book. I should also have told you that she had two nicknames for me. At times, she would call me her 'mystery man', seeing as we met through the society, and she kept my identity a secret from everyone. You know, I don't believe that even her niece knew about us; Angelica kept dear Jennifer in the dark about a lot of things."

His comment intrigued me, but before I could ask anything more, Bella raised an important point.

"Of course, the fact that you were romantically entangled does not mean that you couldn't have killed her. If anything, such a connection makes it more likely than the fact that the two of you argued in a local society."

He finally looked a little apprehensive, and that grin disappeared. "You can think that if you like, but the truth is that I was – and still am – deeply in love with Angelica." When he spoke of the victim, he showed a sensitivity that was quite at odds with the rest of his character. "We both lost our spouses too young and had been alone for many years. We stayed late one night to plan activities for the society. One thing led to another, and we found ourselves rolling around in bed like two seal pups."

I take it all back; I'm a strong proponent of euphemisms and they should always be employed.

"Did the *time you spent together...*" This was a perfect example of one from Bella. "...change the way in which you interacted at the society?"

"If you are asking whether we continued to disagree, then the answer is no. I came to see just how unique and valuable a perspective Angelica had. That isn't to say that, in public, we lost any of the antagonism we had previously possessed." He laughed under his breath, as though thinking of a secret he had no intention of sharing. "The truth is, we might have overdone things a little. Our fellow members took it all too seriously and believed that we truly detested one another. You could see the result at the meeting this afternoon. I finally begged Angelica to tell everyone the truth, but she had a theatrical bent and would not give up the act."

Bella corrected his assumption. "I was thinking more of whether you were involved in organising the events that Mrs Thistlethwaite planned. Did you know about Marius's appearance here this weekend and what it would entail?"

"Yes. Yes, I did. Jennifer had read your books, Mr Quin, and Angelica invited you to come. I was involved in the plan to test your skills as a detective. We did something similar to another author last year, and it was a spectacular failure..." he paused for effect, "for the author, I mean. The fellow couldn't have detected rain in the rainforest, and we showed him up for the phony that he is."

This got under my skin, to say the least. "From where exactly did you get the idea that mystery authors are supposed to be great detectives? Would you expect Mary Shelley to know how to stitch bodies together? Or Bram Stoker to be an expert on vanquishing monsters?"

He didn't answer but gazed about the room. Only a few tables were occupied, and he nodded to the nearest group as he ate another sandwich.

"Don't just ignore me," I told him, because I don't mind being rude to rude people. "Please explain why your girlfriend thought it was acceptable to treat my colleagues so inhumanely."

"She said you were full of yourselves," he finally responded, and a shower of fine crumbs sprayed onto his plate. It was an unpleasant sight, but I could fully imagine why a contrary woman like Angelica Thistlethwaite would have been attracted to her foe. "She said that the whole idea of your books is to show off how clever you think you are when, in reality, the game is rigged from the beginning."

"That is quite interesting, actually." I should probably have kept the previous acid tone in my voice, but this idea tickled me. "Would you mind explaining what she meant?"

He looked at Bella, then back at me, perhaps wondering whether I was laying a trap. "If you must know, she felt that there was no fairness in mystery novels. You could easily write a book pointing to one particular killer and then, on the very last page, switch around the evidence so that it incriminates someone else."

It was my companion who would extract the most important detail from what he was saying. "And she didn't like that because of her experience with the police when her sister and brother-in-law died."

He didn't answer this time. He just gazed down at the plates of food like some waif who hadn't eaten for a month. This would not be enough to deter Bella, and she continued to outline her theory.

"I'm right, aren't I? Mrs Thistlethwaite hated the way she'd been treated. She was accused of murder and, even if nothing was proven, that must have affected her reputation around here. She set up her society in order to do a better job than private detectives, mystery writers and even the police." Bella's eyes caught the light as she looked at him, and I could tell how happy she was to have a real understanding of our victim's actions. "She was a bitter woman, wasn't she, Robert?"

Yet again, he provided no response, but he did look straight at her as he took a handful of petits fours and inserted them one by one into his mouth.

As much as I enjoyed seeing Bella put a suspect through the wringer, such an approach with Milton wouldn't work, and so I changed the topic. "What about Jennifer? Did she know anything about your plan with the fake gangsters on the train and the body in the swimming pool?"

Milton stopped eating for a moment, and I got the impression that he hadn't expected us to discover as much as we had. In time, he swallowed and, thankfully taking a napkin this time, cleaned his mouth before replying. "She knew that her aunt was planning something, but Angelica never trusted her not to intervene."

"Was anyone else involved? Any other members of the society, for instance?"

I don't think he gave a single answer without considering what he wanted to say first. "Not the society itself, but Travers generally knew what was going on. She had him wrapped around her little finger. You know, she once told me that he was in love with her. Perhaps he couldn't take the pain any longer and bumped her off. Have you considered how easy it would be for the manager of the hotel where she was murdered to hide evidence and twist facts?"

I smiled ever so innocently. "Yes, thank you, Mr Milton. We have considered that because, as I believe you've already discovered, we're rather good at our jobs."

He watched me in the same way as he had Bella a moment before. "Jolly good. It's nice to know that someone around here is making an effort to find the killer."

Bella leaned forward in her chair and dropped her voice a little lower. "Are you implying that Sergeant Stainsbury isn't up to the job?"

"I'm saying that I doubt his commitment to finding the culprit, because he and my darling Angelica no longer saw eye to eye."

"But they had once?"

Milton clicked his fingers and pointed at her. "They had indeed. He even lent a hand to the society in the early days – how else could we have obtained the police files that we used for our investigations? Of course, after our success at solving crimes outstripped his own, he became terribly jealous and would barely speak to her."

I had a feeling that one of us should have said, *So what you're saying is that he had a reason to want her dead*, but that would have been rather obvious.

To my surprise, Milton suddenly seemed to lose his arrogance. I don't know what particular thought had caused it, but he stared into the middle distance and two lone tears rolled down his cheek. He had become so emotional that he had to pause the interview. A stoic smile returned as he noticed someone watching him from another table, but I still leaned forward to pass him a spare napkin.

"Thank you, Mr Quin," he said quite sincerely. "I'm so used to playing the part of a *mauvais sujet* that I sometimes forget I'm far nicer than many people believe. You see, I loved my Angelica. The world will never know it, but I loved her deeply, and the thought of continuing my life without her is hard to bear." He carefully dried his eyes, took a deep breath and attempted to regain his composure.

I turned to Bella, who no longer looked so comfortable directing her attacks at him, so I took charge. I must say that I was torn between accusing the man of faking this display of sorrow and sympathising with him for his loss. He was either a far better actor than the pair we'd met earlier, or he felt the loss just as much as he claimed. Unable to make my mind up, I focused on the questions we still had.

"What do you know about Mrs Thistlethwaite's financial situation? We heard that she was on the edge of bankruptcy a few years ago, but then she bought a mansion and had enough money to buy you platinum cufflinks."

"She never gave me any cufflinks." He looked confused for a moment but must have remembered that we'd been snooping around her house. "But she was certainly generous, and this coming Friday would have been the anniversary of the first time we joined in physical union." I wondered at this moment whether, as a private detective, it would be unprofessional of me to stick my fingers in my ears and sing the national anthem. "I remember that first time as if it was yesterday. We connected like two—"

"Thank you so much." I apparently wasn't the only one who felt he was going into too much detail, as it was Bella who interrupted him. "Could you answer the earlier question now?"

He nodded and was quick to do as he'd been asked. "I never

knew Angelica to be short of money. Perhaps that was before our time together."

I looked at Bella and she looked at me. I didn't know what to take from her expression, but I nodded anyway and pretended that I did.

"We don't know a great deal about you yet," she said, but instead of forming a clear question, she let the words linger. "I mean to say, we know about your relationship with Angelica, but little about who you really are."

"I don't think there's much to tell. I spend a lot of time reading – largely history books, as it happens. I was previously an artist and sign painter, but my first love has always been history."

I remembered the book I'd seen in his drawer at Mrs Thistlethwaite's house and couldn't imagine what this might mean for his ability to drown a woman.

"Do you have children?" Bella continued, and he seemed hesitant to answer, as though he felt it unnecessary to reveal anything so private.

"No. My wife and I were not blessed with offspring. That is the way of things sometimes."

There were probably a hundred questions still to answer. The problem was that I couldn't imagine him being able to help us with a single one of them. Aside from their rivalry within the society and the romance that followed, we hadn't discovered much to suggest that Robert Milton had a motive for murdering the woman he claimed to love.

"I must thank you for coming," I said to bring the conversation to a close. He looked down at the table as though he were reluctant to abandon the remains of our tea. I considered leaving just so that he could make the most of it, but he must have got the message that we intended to remain, as he took a sandwich and rose to standing.

Bella still had one more point to make. "I suppose that now

Mrs Thistlethwaite is dead, you'll be the person to take over the running of the society."

"That is a possibility." Milton looked worried for a moment, but then his fear subsided. "However, there are so many people who would object to my appointment that they are just as likely to find someone else. Jennifer herself would be a more acceptable option all around." He waved goodbye to his friends at the other table and moved to leave. "Thank you for the refreshments, Mr Quin, Lady Isabella. I have very much enjoyed our time together, and I hope our paths cross again in future."

"And you," Bella said with suspicion still in her voice. Perhaps this is what made Milton stop as he was about to leave and issue a small plea.

"I know that you've no reason to believe me, but I really did adore her." A previously unexpected level of sensitivity emerged from within him whenever he spoke of the victim. "Please find whoever killed her. I will certainly sleep more soundly when I know that the killer is behind bars."

TWENTY-TWO

"Is it enough?" Bella put to me after we'd dissected the conversation we'd just conducted. "He comes across as exceedingly arrogant, but beyond the chance to run a provincial society of meddlers and nosey parkers, what would he gain from Mrs Thistlethwaite's death?"

I couldn't respond immediately because this very question had been lodged in my head for some time and the answer was beyond my reach.

"Nothing," I eventually told her. "He has no financial motive that we can see. He clearly was intimate with her, and we've no reason to think that the relationship had soured if the present she bought him was for their imminent anniversary."

A silence followed, and I could read Bella's thoughts on her ever so expressive face. "We both know that nothing is fair in love and war. The very fact that they were enamoured sends him to the top of our suspect list."

"I thought you said that Jennifer was the likely killer?"

"I wasn't entirely serious, Marius." She leaned across the wreckage of baked goods to place her slender hand on my lapel. At first, she didn't say anything, and so I had a moment to gaze into those emerald eyes of hers. "I'm sorry to be cruel, but little Jenny is so sweet that she's almost too good to be true. That doesn't change the fact that Milton is a more likely suspect than anyone else we've considered. He and Mrs Thistlethwaite might have had a lovers' tiff that got out of hand."

I couldn't agree with her entirely. "Or perhaps he's simply more honest than anyone else we've considered. He hasn't hidden his real character from us, and I have to say I begrudgingly respect that. He has the manners of a pickpocket, the charm of a lizard and the warmth of a brick. It's easy not to like him, but that doesn't make him a killer. If anything, that could explain why he and Mrs Thistlethwaite got on so well; birds of a feather tend to flock together, after all."

"So where does that leave us?"

This was a question I'd put off asking. The truth was that, while we now understood our victim better than we had earlier that morning, we had very little idea of who would have wanted to kill her or why. Jennifer might be her daughter, and thus a potential heir, but there was nothing to say that she knew of her true parentage.

"Travers," Bella declared out of the blue, and before she could explain what she meant, the manager himself appeared in the entrance to the cosy tearoom. He was holding a pile of newspapers and looked quite shocked to be addressed.

"Yes, Lady Isabella? How may I help you?"

She clearly hadn't meant to get his attention and stumbled for a response. "I... You know, I was just saying that—"

"We could do with a newspaper," I said to come to her aid. "I don't suppose you have *The Times*?"

He had picked up a few old copies that were folded on chairs and now flicked through the fresh pile to select the right one. "Here you go, Mr Quin. It's a pleasure to be of service." He smiled that same artificial smile that I'd seen so many times from him and set about his task once more.

"Travers is another good option," Bella said in a far softer voice than before as I looked through the paper. "Perhaps even more likely than the man who loved Angelica Thistlethwaite is the man who loved her and lost her." She watched him waddling away through the foyer, back to his desk.

I was more than happy to explore the possibility. "And he lied to us."

"When?"

"He said that he didn't know anyone by the name of Augustus Black, and yet he was in on Mrs Thistlethwaite's plan. We might never have understood what she'd been up to if it hadn't been for our run-in with the actors at the train station."

She bit her lip as she considered this. "Yes, that is very interesting... though, I suppose Travers might just have been following his beloved's wishes to the last. Perhaps he thought he should go along with the plan to give her the send-off she would have wanted."

"It's possible," I agreed, losing my impulse once more. "Though I think it's far more likely that he was protecting his own back. He was probably scared that any connection to the dead woman's cruel plans could suggest involvement in the crime itself."

"That could explain it." She sounded just as frustrated as I felt and released a long, weary breath.

The newspaper that Travers had handed me was not *The Times* of London but the *Torquay Times* (*and South Devon Advertiser*). I'd looked it through from front to back and saw nothing to interest me until I closed it once more and a notice on the cover caught my attention. I'd barely looked at it at first, surrounded as it was by wedding announcements, notices about church meetings and cinema listings. But when I gave it due attention, I instantly gasped.

"What is it?" Bella shot forward in her chair.

"Look there." I gave the newspaper a good whack with the back of my hand, which apparently wasn't clear enough.

"Charlie Chaplin is in *The Circus* at the Pavilion Picture House. I've heard it's very good, but it's not starting until next week. We'll be long gone." Her brows knitted together as she presumably considered the possibility that we would be no closer to the truth by then. "Or at least, I hope we will."

"Not the cinema, Bella. The theatre." I pointed straight at the article that interested me and read it aloud. "'*The Rising Generation* by Wyn Weaver and Laura Leycester, as played at the Garrick and Wyndham's Theatres in London. Cast to include the brilliant actress, Mrs Georgiana Snow.'"

She remained quite unmoved. "Whether it's a film or a play, Marius, we will not have time to watch anything while we're here."

"You're missing my point, Bella. Look at the name of the actress!"

She took a moment to do just that. "Yes, Marius. Georgiana Snow is at the top of her game. I saw her in the play that her husband directed. It was with your friend Tallulah Alanson at the Lyceum. Now what was it called?"

"Bella, you're still missing my point."

She really wasn't listening to me. "Now that I think of it, I'm uncertain whether Georgiana and Henry Snow are still married. Wasn't there some kind of terrible bust-up? I believe there was a scandal connected to it, but I don't remember the—"

"Yes, yes. The actress Mrs G. Snow was previously married to the actor-director Mr H. Snow."

Her expression told me I was talking nonsense, and then her mouth did the same. "Marius, you're talking nonsense. Why would I be interested in such gossip in the first place?"

Perhaps I was expecting too much of her, so I gave in and connected up my thoughts more clearly. "The names we saw in the bank today. Do you remember any of them?"

She cast her eyes up to the plaster ceiling where a very modern glass light fitting stretched down towards us in tiers. "I believe there was someone called Cooper, and perhaps a Mills. To be perfectly honest, I was so amazed by the sums there that the names seemed of secondary importance."

"I had the same thought, but I still made a mental note of them. You're right that there was a Cooper: G. Cooper. It's a common enough name, but the G might well stand for Gladys. I also saw an S. Hale. S for Sonnie, perhaps? And then there was a Mrs E. Laye. Well, I think that must be Evelyn."

"Why would—? My goodness. Gladys Cooper, Sonnie Hale and Evelyn Laye are all actors!"

"As are Mr H. and Mrs G. Snow."

Reality was sinking in at last, and Bella spoke with more confidence. "There was a Mrs D. Mills on the list, but I don't know of any actor by that name. It must surely be the novelist, Dorothy Mills."

"And don't forget the penultimate name we saw. There are few classical singers more accomplished than Clara Butt. And I believe that the last name was Rollo. If I'm not mistaken, Lady Rollo and her husband are well known for their artistic patronage."

"So all of Mrs Thistlethwaite's benefactors were involved in the arts, but what does that mean for the killing?"

I stared down at the paper and tried to figure it out. "I still can't say, but I bet they've all passed through Torquay over the last couple of years. And I know someone who might be able to help us."

I pushed back my chair and hurried through the archway out to the foyer. I didn't wait for Bella but ran to the reception, flung up the wooden counter and seized the telephone.

"Excuse me," Travers complained from his back room. "This is not a public line." I kept dialling and so he soon gave up. "Really! Why do I bother?"

"Hello, Irene?" I asked the operator, which was a mistake as the chatty young woman assumed I knew her personally.

"Hullo? 'Oo's that? It's not Mike from the garage, is it? You're not putting on airs and graces for me, are ya, Mike Rutherford?" When I didn't know how to answer, she thought a bit more. "Wait a minute. What are you doin' at the Grand? You ain't going to that ball tonight, are ya? You're not ringing to invite me, are ya, Mike?"

"My apologies, Irene. This isn't Mike, from the garage or otherwise. My name is Marius Quin and I have an important call to make."

She immediately cleared her throat and switched to her telephone voice. "Yes, Mr Quin. Of course, Mr Quin. To whom may I connect you?"

"I'd like to get through to Christopher Prentiss at Cranley Hall in Surrey. That's Cranley L-E-Y, not L-E-I-G-H."

She didn't say anything for a moment, by which time I realised that Bella was standing next to me and the woman sitting behind the reception desk was regarding us with some suspicion.

"Christopher Prentiss?" Bella had evidently caught the gist of my request. "That's Lord Edgington's nephew, isn't it?"

"No, his grandson."

"Very well, his grandson. But how he can he help us with any of this?"

The line crackled and Irene spoke again. "I'm connecting you now, sir. Have a wonderful evening."

"You too, Irene." I spoke fast before she became occupied with another call. "Irene? I do hope that Mike calls and you get to go to the ball."

A girlish giggle reverberated down the line to me before someone picked up at the other end.

"Good afternoon, Cranley Hall?"

I recognised the voice of Lord Edgington's right-hand man. "Todd, is that you, old boy?"

"Marius Quin?" He was a dear chap and injected any amount of excitement into these two words.

"That's right. It's been far too long. We really must meet in the city for a drink sometime if your master ever gives you a day off."

"I'd like that very much, Marius. You can call me here at the house whenever you're free."

Bella nudged me, as I was apparently taking too long for her liking, so I jumped ahead a little way. "I'm sorry to be in such a rush, but I must speak to Chrissy. Would he happen to be home?"

"Yes, of course, Marius. I'll get him at once."

There was some noise in the background, and then a new voice came on the phone. It was not the youthful apprentice, but the aged detective who now spoke. "Mr Quin, how nice it is to hear from you. Are you looking to include my grandson in some variety of high jinks?"

To be quite frank, I was more than a little terrified of Lord Edgington after I'd been a suspect in one of his cases. "No, my lord. Nothing like that." I suddenly remembered his insistence on good grammar and tried to rephrase this in a full sentence. "Or rather, I am not involved in any high jinks. In fact, my friend Isabella Montague and I are investigating a nasty murder."

"That's superb!" He sounded most pleased for us. "Well, not the murder. That's terrible, of course, but I know Lady Isabella's father. We used to fish together." I believe that he would have happily chatted away for some time, but it was at that moment that a door opened nearby, and I heard muffled voices down the line. "Christopher has just arrived, so I will hand you over to him. Though before you go, I should tell you that Chief Inspector Darrington from Scotland Yard told me about your detective work, and I must say that I thoroughly approve."

"Thank you, sir. I appreciate that."

Lovebrook had popped up at some point and was curious about what was happening. "Is that Lord Edgington on the line? Ask him if he recalls the time I—"

"Hello, Marius," Chrissy muttered with his usual shy charm. "This is Christopher Prentiss. Perhaps you remember me from the case we investigated at Daly's Theatre?"

"Of course I remember you, Chrissy. I just called this number to speak to you."

He made a sort of humming noise that sounded both happy and uncertain. "To speak to me? Are you sure my grandfather isn't the one you want?"

"Not unless he struck up a friendship with the cricketer Dicky Prowse." He had no answer for this, so I pressed on. "Am I right in thinking that Prowse was one of your suspects? You told me all about him that night at the Savoy."

"That's right." He became a little more excited. "He and I met on our case at... at... To tell the truth, I don't remember the name of the house. We investigate so many murders and the majority of them take place in large stately homes. One tends to run into any other."

"I know just what you mean. I've only carried out a few brief investigations, but I already get them muddled."

Bella prodded me with her foot to get on with it just as Lord Edgington whispered something to Chrissy.

"Grandfather tells me that the name of the house was Mistletoe Hall. I knew you were better off talking to him. Was that all you needed to know, or shall I pass the phone back now?"

He was a dear, kind boy but prone to thinking too little of himself, even though I'd once seen him solve a most taxing case when no one else could.

"No, Chrissy, I've told you. It's you I need. Now listen, I'd like you to get a message to Prowse. Please tell him that I was the man who spoke to him at dinner last night at the Grand Hotel. Tell him that he's not in any trouble and that he can trust me. If you don't mind, that is."

"No, that will be absolutely fine. I'll ring him straight away."

"Thank you, dear boy. Please ask him to call me at the hotel. And tell him that Angelica Thistlethwaite is dead. I don't know if that will mean anything to him, but it might just make the difference."

"So you're hunting for a killer? Did you catch the detecting bug from Grandfather?"

I laughed. "Yes, something like that."

"In which case, I hope we'll be able to investigate a murder together sometime." There was some more indistinct mumbling. "Sorry, Grandfather just told me that I'm babbling and must finish the call."

I glanced across at Bella and realised just how much in common she had with Chrissy's august forebear.

"Thank you, Christopher," I told him as I pulled back to look at the phone. "You can call me on Torquay 2234 if you need to get in touch. You're a great help, and I really appreciate it."

We said goodbye, and I hung up the telephone on its hook. The receptionist was still looking suspiciously in my direction, and my friends were gathered around expectantly.

"So?" Bella prodded me with her words this time. "What are you thinking?"

"I'm not totally sure, but with all these sightings of famous people about the place, I decided that we should get the help of a celebrity of our own."

TWENTY-THREE

It would be a waiting game, but that didn't mean we had time to kill. As soon as I was off the phone, a constable appeared to summon Lovebrook to the scene of another crime.

"Is it a body?" I asked, but the man was giving nothing away.

"I had a call from the sergeant instructing me to fetch you. He didn't tell me anything else."

I didn't believe this was entirely true, but Bella and I followed Lovebrook out of the hotel and, as the inspector's car could barely fit a driver, we piled into the taxi once more. Even then, it was a tight squeeze with three of us on the back seat.

"Afternoon all," the driver said with his usual enthusiasm. "I hadn't expected to see you so soon."

Bella was happy to see him and joined in with his repartee. "We really should get better acquainted if we're going to spend time together," she joked, which was the cue for our loyal chauffeur to tell us all about himself.

It wasn't the moment for such levity, but he was an accomplished storyteller and helped the journey to pass more swiftly. I couldn't resist a smirk at his most colourful anecdotes.

"And that, my new friends, is how I nearly lost an eye but found a farthing," the driver, whose name we now knew was Sylvester, concluded as he pulled to a stop in front of a small terrace house on the far side of town.

We three passengers looked at one another, as we didn't know who should pay.

"I don't have any coins left," Bella revealed, and Lovebrook just shrugged, so it fell to me to take out my wallet.

"Would you like me to wait here, guv?" our driver asked.

I paid him the fare and opened the door. "That's very decent of you."

"Oh, I'm not in any hurry. There are too many people in the world rushing to get somewhere without knowing where they need to go. I'll be fine right here."

"Thank you, Sylvester." I patted him on the shoulder and climbed out of the taxi. "It's been a pleasure."

There was yet another constable guarding the door to number 487 Babbacombe Road, and I realised just how well staffed the Torquay police department was.

Stainsbury stuck his head out of a ground-floor window. "In here, folks, and watch where you walk."

I didn't know what to expect as we entered the house and saw the first signs of chaos. There were blood spots on the worn carpet beside a boot stand, and a few more next to the door to the front parlour. They'd been circled with chalk, and we carefully stepped over them. I braced myself for the worst but, when we walked into the neighbouring room, there was no body for us to see, just Stainsbury crouched down on the floor looking at a halo of blood.

"Whose house is this?" Lovebrook asked, and the sergeant hesitated before answering in his usual reluctant tone.

"A young man called Paul Turbot's. He works—"

"On the front desk at the Grand Hotel," I said, as a memory

came back to me. "I had a conversation with him before bed last night."

"Is that why he was murdered?" Bella's voice was so sad just then I barely recognised it. "He saw the killer and had to die?"

"He's not dead, but he's in a bad way," Stainsbury said, as though we were terribly dim. "His mother found him about an hour ago. He was taken to hospital, but it looks as if he was lying unconscious here for most of the day."

"When did he finish work this morning?" I asked, as this would surely give us an idea of the time he was attacked.

"Just before the body was discovered. He works the night shift at the hotel. His mother would have found him earlier, but she started her job in the bakery just before he was due home."

"That doesn't help us rule out any suspects, then. He could have been attacked at any time today." Bella walked across the room to stand beside the sergeant and examine the blood. "Is it dry?"

"Totally." He looked a mite more approving than he had a minute before. "I think that the victim was knocked out by the door and then dragged in here so that no one noticed him."

Lovebrook was the next to have a crack at a hypothesis. "Is it possible that the killer attacked him for some other reason that is not immediately apparent? Might it not be the case that someone heard of Mrs Thistlethwaite's death and came to kill Paul, knowing that the two crimes would be connected?"

"Anything's possible." Stainsbury shrugged, as if it wasn't his concern. "But I very much doubt that'll turn out to be the situation here. The fact is that Paul and his mother only recently moved to town, and the boy doesn't seem to have made any firm friends or enemies since they arrived. Which is hardly surprising if he sleeps during the day and works at night."

I looked about the room and noticed that the shelves on either side of the chimney breast had been emptied of their ornaments. Shattered porcelain figures lay on the carpet beneath, and a few cushions had been thrown from the sofas.

"Whoever attacked him evidently wanted us to think that this was a robbery of some sort, but they didn't do a particularly good job."

"That's right." Stainsbury stood up. I think I'd forgotten just how tall he was. He had a thuggish air about him that would have lent itself to an occupation on the other side of the law. "His mother is in the kitchen with one of my officers. She says that nothing of any value is missing, though I doubt there is a great deal here that would interest a professional thief."

It didn't appear that there was much more to say on the matter. The motive was apparent; he had been silenced so as not to reveal the identity of Mrs Thistlethwaite's killer. Standing in that small lounge would do little to help us, and it made me wonder why the sergeant had called us there.

Lovebrook must have realised that we were far from the verge of a great discovery and made a suggestion. "Bella, perhaps you could accompany me as I interview Paul's mother. We may not reveal anything important, but it's worth a second try."

Stainsbury did not appear to appreciate this intervention, but he did nothing to stop them. And then we were alone together.

"Do you smoke, Quin?" the big man asked, and he had such a gruff manner that I was uncertain what the best answer would be.

"No, I'm afraid I don't."

"Excellent. I've only got one cigarette left. Come with me."

His footsteps shook the house as we walked back through the front door, past the constable and outside. Dear Sylvester gave us a wave and so Stainsbury kept walking until we reached the corner of the street, where he leaned against the red post box and lit his cigarette with a match.

"I don't like it," he said and, while my instinct was to ask what it was he didn't like, I managed to keep my mouth shut for long enough for him to explain. "I don't like any of it. I don't like the murder, or what's happened to young Paul. I don't like Scotland Yard poking around here, and I don't like what's going on in my town."

"What about Mrs Thistlethwaite? Did you like her?"

He cast his stern gaze on me, which would have been enough to put me in my place, even without the subsequent response. "She was not an easy person to like, but we had an understanding."

"I had assumed as much. I couldn't imagine her getting away with all she did without some awareness of her escapades on your part. Did you assist in her programme of torture?"

"Torture? That's going a bit far, isn't it? She had a bee in her bonnet on any number of matters, but I wouldn't say she tortured anyone."

"You didn't answer the question."

He looked away as a rather grand Armstrong Siddeley drove past. "I knew what she was up to, and I turned a blind eye to some of her less hospitable behaviour. The fact is that no one made a formal complaint against her, so there was no reason for me to get in her way."

As reluctant as he was to answer my questions, I felt that he wanted to get something off his chest. I was fairly certain that was why he'd invited us there in the first place, so I kept prodding for more. "And what about her? Did Mrs Thistlethwaite like you?"

"We got on fine... for the most part."

"I've heard that suspicion fell upon her after the death of Jennifer's parents. As a general rule, Mrs Thistlethwaite didn't like detectives, so what made you different?"

"All that stuff was before my time." He rounded his shoulders again and snorted in derision. "She may not have liked me at first, but I could see how much influence she had around here and made sure to win her over."

So Stainsbury was a relative newcomer to the town. I should have considered the fact that his accent was far more City of London than town of Torquay.

"You won her over by lending the society unsolved police files and ignoring her eccentricities." He had nothing to say to this, so I kept talking. "Do you think she was to blame for her sister and brother-in-law's deaths? Faulty brakes and a flight off a cliff into the sea – wasn't that how they met their maker?"

"Something like that, but as I said, it was before my time."

I was tired of his reticence and raised my voice. "Come along, man. You must have an opinion. Mrs Thistlethwaite was practically the mayoress of Torquay. She had a flock of followers and, from what I can tell, could order any one of them to do her bidding. I don't believe for one second that you could resist peeking at the files, especially as her family finances were in dire straits when she inherited her sister's wealth."

"All I know is that Angelica kicked up a fuss when the allegations were made. She said she was being victimised and that the sergeant at the time had it in for her. She threatened to sue him and used the money she'd inherited to do just that. Sadly for her, the case was thrown out of court, and after she'd paid off the debts her husband had left her, there was little money remaining."

"Was that all it was? She didn't have any lavish habits of her own? I know she came close to bankruptcy before her society found its feet."

He ruffled his moustache and shifted his weight off the post box. "I don't know anything about that, but it's Jennifer who deserves our sympathy. Not only did she get nothing from her parents' outdated will, she was walking on the beach when they met their end. Can you imagine what witnessing such a horrific scene would do to a young girl?"

I'd detected a contradiction in his behaviour. I felt that he'd pulled me outside to share a secret but was unwilling to say what it was. He was a shifty character at the best of times, and there was a definite layer of guilt simmering beneath the surface of his surly exterior.

"Whatever you want to tell me, you can. I'm not going to run to Lovebrook and get you in trouble if that's what's worrying you." I waited for a moment to show that I was serious. "All I wish to know is who killed the woman I found in the swimming pool this morning and who attacked the receptionist from the hotel."

He looked as though he wanted to strangle me. "I'm not protecting anyone, if that's what you think."

"Oh, come on, Stainsbury. You clearly have a guilty conscience, so tell me why."

He stepped forward and stared down his nose at me. "I've read about you, Quin. I know about the murders you solved, and I was willing to talk to you as equals, but I've just changed my mind. You should learn not to stick your nose in other people's business, especially when it's a case for the police."

He fixed his eyes on mine and wouldn't look away for what felt like hours. I don't mind telling you that I was the first to blink. He smiled, knowing that, in this small, insignificant contest at least, he was the victor.

"Toodle-oo, Marius. I'm sure I'll see you around." He stubbed his cigarette out with great force on the post box, and I was frankly rather glad he hadn't done it on the top of my head.

TWENTY-FOUR

Paul Turbot's mother, it turned out, would not be the person to unlock the secrets of Mrs Thistlethwaite's violent death. I'm sure that Bella was terribly compassionate and Lovebrook showed just the right level of sympathy, but we left the quiet suburban street knowing very little more than when we'd arrived.

There was a sense of defeat in the taxi on the way back to the hotel, and I believe that even Sylvester felt it, as the few comments he did make were soft and subdued.

"What about the will?" I suddenly remembered to ask the inspector. I'd been distracted by a telephone call to a legendary detective (and his grandfather), and then we'd heard the news about Paul. It was really no wonder that Lovebrook's mission to the local solicitor had slipped my mind.

"It's just as Jennifer said, I'm afraid. The house and most of the money goes to Mrs Thistlethwaite's brother in Southern Rhodesia. All she gets is a monthly stipend of fourteen pounds and seven shillings, and that was only thanks to a codicil that her aunt added."

"Mrs Thistlethwaite wasn't exactly generous, was she?"

Bella replied, before dropping her voice to a whisper so that the driver couldn't hear. "She left her daughter practically penniless."

I thought of a potential solution to this sad scenario. "Let's hope that the uncle is more munificent. If he's living in Africa, he'll surely let Jennifer remain in the house where she lives."

"If he's anything like his sister, I could see him selling it instead." I couldn't blame Bella for this reaction. Every new thing that we learnt about the dead woman made me like her less.

"Will you check the ports and that sort of thing to make sure that Mrs Thistlethwaite's brother didn't slip into the country and kill her for the inheritance?" I put to Lovebrook, but he was well ahead of me.

"There's no need. I've already telegrammed the British South Africa Police in Salisbury. They've promised to send officers to confirm that Donald Shepherd is at home."

"Impressive stuff, Lovebrook," I told him. "You're not just a pretty face after all."

"I've always thought that my hands were my best feature." He smiled and held them out before him to show this was just a quip.

This helped to lighten the mood a touch and, when we reached the hotel, I paid Sylvester for his services.

"Will you need a car at any other time during your stay, sir?" He appeared to be sad to lose us, though perhaps it was our custom that he was most fond of rather than our company.

"I'll tell you what, Sylvester, if we manage to leave tomorrow, you can drive us to the station."

"For that, sir, I'll put on my hat." As promised, he jammed his chauffeur's cap on his head.

"What a nice fellow," Bella commented as we strolled up the steps to the hotel.

"He has a noble soul," I replied. "If there were more people like Sylvester in the world, there would be far fewer murders."

"Of course, that might not be the best outcome for either of us," Lovebrook said as he walked alongside us. "If there were no more murders, I'd be out of a job, and you'd have nothing to inspire you."

Bella shook her head at this, and I opened the door to the hotel before the commissionaire could rush over and do the honour.

"Excuse me..." I waited for him to tell me his name.

"Burton, sir."

"Yes, Burton. Can you tell me what time you finished work last night?"

He bowed his head as though to show how sorry he was that he hadn't been on duty to save Mrs Thistlethwaite. "I finished my shift at eleven. I'm afraid I was long gone by the time..." He was simply too discreet to finish this statement, and his chin fell closer to his chest.

"Thank you, Burton. It was worth a try."

We were approaching the reception when something occurred to Bella. "Surely the fact that Paul was attacked after his shift ended suggests that Travers couldn't have done it. He's been at the hotel the whole morning. Perhaps that clears him of any involvement in Mrs Thistlethwaite's death, too."

It was odd to be having this discussion within sight of the manager. Travers sat at his desk, staring gloomily at us across the entrance hall.

Sadly, Bella's theory was less than watertight, and I told her just that. "While I'd like that to be true, there are several reasons why your idea isn't sound. For one thing, Travers could have a car of his own parked outside and sped off to Paul's house on a break to knock him unconscious. He surely knew when his own employee left the hotel and could have timed it to be there just as he got home, long before Paul could tell anyone what he saw last night."

She was silenced by my uncompromising response, whereas Travers at least tried to smile as we approached.

"Lady Bella, gentlemen," he sang, and I could see just how much effort it took to force the muscles in his face to take on that shape. "Will you be joining us for the October ball this evening? It's an annual event and we always have a lovely time."

I looked at Bella and spoke in a slightly more cordial tone. "It would be a shame not to go." Of course, what I was really thinking was that it would be a wonderful opportunity to watch the townspeople and several of our suspects mingling together. If we had to get dressed up to the nines to do that, it was a sacrifice I was willing to make.

"Splendid, splendid." Travers clapped his hands together in delight. "And I will reserve our very best table for your dinner. Miss Clemmie Symonds is staying at the hotel, and I have a great hope that she may sing for us this evening." He winked at us each in turn in a theatrical manner, and I got the sense that he already knew that his hope would be realised.

"I actually have a question for you, old chap," I said in my most cloying voice. I sounded rather like him for a moment. "I was wondering why you hid the truth from us."

"I beg your pardon?" He glanced to his right to check that his colleague at the next desk wasn't listening and that there were no guests around to overhear him. This wasn't enough, and so he walked us over to the fountain in the middle of the foyer where the sound of the falling water could drown out the conversation.

"You heard me, Travers. Why didn't you tell us about Mr Black? You knew what he was doing here, and yet you claimed not to know the man."

He dangled helplessly before me like a fish on a hook. His excuse, when it came, was suitably desperate.

"Because I started lying and didn't know when to stop." He put his hand to his mouth, as if he wanted to stop himself from saying anything more. "I didn't know what had happened to Angelica and so I went along with the story she'd made us rehearse. When I realised that everything had gone wrong and she was dead, it was too late. Black had got away, and I couldn't risk incriminating myself with talk of fake murder victims and actors playing criminals."

"That's a feeble explanation and you know it."

He screwed up his face and seemed to beg me for understanding with a flash of the eyes and his rising tone of voice. "It might sound crazy, but it's true. I thought that I would be the obvious suspect, and I was scared that Stainsbury would arrest me. After all, I was the victim's spurned admirer. I have no alibi and easy access to the hotel. To be quite frank, I'm amazed I'm still free."

"I can imagine how hard all that must have been for you." It was Bella who finally took pity on him. "But the best way to stay out of prison is to help us find the real killer." The tenderness she showed him reminded me why we work so well together on our cases – and why we should never swap roles again.

Travers was instantly charmed by her. "Of course, Lady Isabella. I'll do whatever it takes to assist you."

I maintained my same insistent tone. "You can start by telling us what created the division in Mrs Thistlethwaite's mystery society. Plenty of people take exception to Mr Milton, but we haven't discovered the reason for it."

"There's a very good reason: that man is not to be trusted." Bearing in mind that it was Travers who had pointed us in Milton's direction in the first place, this was hardly damning evidence.

Lovebrook gave it a go next, and I had to hope that his cut-glass diction might encourage the man to reveal more. "Yes, but what caused the rift between him and Angelica in the first place?"

Travers's manner at this point was quite different from his usual public persona. He suddenly seemed more fragile, and I felt we were getting a glimpse of the real person behind the façade. "It started over something very petty. I believe it was the choice of a crime that the group discussed one week a little over a year ago. Angelica took exception to just how vocal he was and the more she tried to control him, the angrier he became. It all turned rather personal between them." *More than you know!* I thought but didn't say. "She seemed to take great pleasure in riling him."

I was once more disappointed that a potential avenue of investigation had led really not so far at all. "Well, thank you for your honesty, Mr Travers. We appreciate your assistance."

Lovebrook managed to sound a little chirpier in reply. "Yes, thank you, Mr Travers. You've been a great help."

"I mean it," he exclaimed more loudly again when it was clear that we were unmoved by his argument. "Robert Milton is not to be trusted. Week in, week out, for the last year, he and Angelica fought like dogs. I'm not the only person who thinks he must be to blame."

There was so much in what he was saying that tickled me, but I had to keep a straight face throughout. "Of course, Mr Travers. This is just the kind of thing we need to hear. I can't thank you enough."

I believe this was an exceptional piece of acting on my part, and he certainly looked cheered by my words. He nodded gratefully, and we turned away from the reception. We made it to the lift, told the attendant which floors we required, and then each of us let out a disheartened sigh.

"I really hoped that Milton was the kind of person who would take bloody revenge on his enemies," I said to myself as much as to my companions, and Newbury, the lift assistant, couldn't hide a fraction of a smile.

"As did I," Bella responded, "but the worst thing we can say about him is that he's terribly mean when it comes to paying for afternoon tea."

I was tempted to put forward the theory that Travers was still acting. Perhaps he had found out about the relationship between Milton and his amour and set out to kill one and frame the other for murder. It was a dark and depressing scenario, but one which barely left my mind for the rest of the evening.

"At least there's dinner to enjoy," Lovebrook said to cheer us. He was good at setting people back on their feet after a fall, which was one of the many things I liked about him.

"And dancing," Bella continued ever so morosely, and it didn't have the same effect.

The lift dinged for my floor, but the others stayed behind to travel one level above mine. All the way back to my room, I wondered whether another threatening message would have been left for me or I'd find the dead man that the note that morning had mentioned. Of course, that warning had been a fake left there by a cleaner who'd been instructed to watch my room. This knowledge didn't calm the uneasy feeling I had as I put my key into the lock and slowly turned it.

There was nothing out of the ordinary inside. The suite was perfectly still and there was no sign that anyone had been in there to place evidence that might incriminate me. I had a quick look in the airing cupboard just in case some unfortunate hotel worker or murdered guest had been stuffed in there, but I'm happy to say that I found little more than a pile of fresh towels.

It is at moments like this that it's nice to have a dog. I would have liked nothing better than to sit in my comfortable lounge overlooking the bay with my hound at my side and a glass of something strong in my hand. Sadly, Percy was busy elsewhere, and I didn't have any whisky, so I did the next best thing.

I hadn't had time for a shower that morning after my dip in the pool. Other things had taken precedence but, with my black evening suit laid out ready to wear, now would be the perfect time. The shower tap looked like a control lever on a ship's bridge. It was all glistening chromed steel and seemed to only have one option, on or off. This meant that, as soon as I climbed inside the bathtub, I was shot in the chest with the force of a firehose, and I can't say I minded it one bit. There's really nothing worse – well, there is, but I like a bit of hyperbole from time to time – than a weak shower, and this was the opposite. I turned around so that the steaming hot water massaged my back and, for a minute or two, all my worries were forgotten.

Of course, it wasn't long before an apparently infinite number of interpretations of a very strange case invaded my thoughts. It wasn't the murder itself that was unusual, nor the choice of victim. From everything I knew about her, Mrs Thistlethwaite was perfectly horrible and half of Torquay and beyond clearly took issue with her arrogance and casual cruelty. No, what struck me as odd was the lack of a front-runner in the race to be crowned culprit.

We weren't exactly short of suspects. In addition to Travers down in his den at the entrance to the hotel, Milton was a grumpy, self-interested sort. Far-from-upstanding Sergeant Stainsbury was in with a chance, too. And it was easy to see why Lovebrook and Bella were so suspicious of Jennifer Capshaw and her show of emotion at her aunt's house. They thought that what we saw there were crocodile tears, but I wouldn't believe it. Jenny's exquisite softness of character, although it probably goes against every rule to which a detective is supposed to adhere, made me believe in her innocence. The fact is that, if she was aware that Mrs Thistlethwaite was her real mother, it would have made it harder for her to kill. And if she didn't, then she wouldn't benefit from the death in the first place.

As the room filled with steam, and I totally forgot about washing my hair, I realised that I was lying to myself. I was happily overlooking evidence for the simple reason that Jennifer Capshaw had angelic eyes that would draw crowds to a museum. I thought back to the night before, when her aunt had been berating her in front of everyone, and I knew that removing Angelica Thistlethwaite from her life would have made it a great deal better. Blood may be thicker than water, but it's not thick enough to help anyone tolerate such unkindness.

So where did any of that leave us?

Back to the beginning was one way of looking at it, but I had to hope that the balls we'd set in motion would reach their destination before long... Whatever that might mean.

You'll be happy to know that I did locate the soap and wash my hair. And when that was done, I wrapped myself up in the fluffiest white towel ever created to get dry. All that was left to do was to shave, get dressed in the very best suit I own – I almost lost my flat in order to purchase the thing, so it was nice to get some more use out of it – and then leave my suite feeling, if not ready to face the world, then at least ready for dinner.

TWENTY-FIVE

I sat on a bench in the foyer until Bella arrived, and it was definitely worth the wait. She appeared on the landing in a scarlet ballgown as though she'd been magically transported there. She was always going to take the stairs. The lift would have offered a far less dramatic entrance, and her skirt might have got caught in the doors. It trailed a little way behind her as I watched her move towards me. Her eyes were so bright, and the smile on her face so full of life and good humour, that I was instantly put in mind of the girl I'd fallen in love with when I was just a boy. We were a great deal closer to thirty than thirteen now, but she still had all the youthful exuberance that she'd ever possessed. Even when nothing else could that day, she had the power to make me forget everything else around me.

"Mr Quin, don't you look dashing!" she declared as she reached the last few steps, and I held my hand out to help her down.

"I don't know. Do I?" I hadn't meant for this to sound like a joke, or, in fact, say these words out loud, but she laughed all the same.

"You know you do. Now it's your turn to compliment me."

Ooh, this was dangerous. What could I possibly say about her? That her hair was like obsidian glittering in the sun? That her eyes were as green as a Welsh valley in the summer? Nothing so charming would jump from my lips because my tongue had somehow become disconnected from my brain. All I managed was a Neanderthal mumble of "Red, pretty, nice you." Luckily, Lovebrook arrived at that moment to distract her.

She put one arm through each of ours... Wait, no. That would suggest she had four arms. I'll try that again. Bella linked arms with us and, with that same radiant smile on her lips, we walked to the restaurant. My family were already there waiting for us, and I was amazed to discover that my uncle, who was normally found in flour-covered trousers and grubby shirt-sleeves, possessed an evening jacket.

"My goodness, Stan, you look like a real person!"

He was not the type to take offence and punched me on the arm for the trouble. "Thank you very much, Marius. I thought I should make an effort."

Mother examined the three of us in a row, but rather than continuing the seemingly inevitable chain of compliments, she said, "We all look wonderful, and so does the food."

Dinner was no simple affair. Chicken and brie vol-au-vents were followed by an *appetiser* of crimped cod and oyster sauce. The first course was a perch water-souchy with red mullet. The main was braised beef à la Flamande and by the time dessert arrived I didn't want to look at another crumb. I did consume a small portion of suédoise of strawberry, but it was very much under protest.

"I haven't eaten this well since I left home for the police," Lovebrook declared as he finished his last spoonful. He resisted licking the traces of sweetened cream from his ramekin, which surely demonstrated his good breeding.

"Where is home?" Bella asked, and I thought we might finally get the story of who our friend really was.

"Somewhere not so exciting," he replied in typically evasive fashion.

"Are your parents still wherever it was you grew up?" Auntie Elle enquired with some tact.

"They are indeed." Lovebrook looked at the ceiling as though he were gazing at the stars. "There's no budging some people. They barely ever leave Oxfordshire, if the truth be told."

So, Valentine Lovebrook was from Oxfordshire! I was learning more about him by the hour and was eager to enquire into his family background, but there was a commotion behind us, and the same famous figure we'd seen as we were leaving the night before entered the room. In terms of sartorial elegance, Alexander Fraiser put Lovebrook and me to shame. It's not all about the cut of a suit or the quality of the fabric, though. Sometimes, it's the way that a man wears his clothes that really marks him out in a crowd. Fraiser had that *je ne sais quoi* in abundance.

The future husband of Deidre Peppers (the expatriated American heiress to the Peppers' plastic fortune) looked as though he'd already had a fair bit to drink before coming down to dinner, but he went straight up to the bar, nonetheless. I watched as he slammed a few coins on the counter and pointed at one of the bottles on the shelf behind the white-suited waiters.

It caused a stir in the restaurant, but it was still early, and people went back to their conversations before long. There was a jazz quartet playing ever so softly in the corner of the room, but a larger group of musicians was getting things ready on a stage in front of a run of windows that overlooked the swimming pool and the bay beyond. No one was dancing yet, but I was impressed by the show of chic attire at the tables surrounding our own. The great and good of Torquay had come out in force, and it looked as though we had quite the evening ahead of us.

When the first band's soft background hum reached its conclusion, their more prominent colleagues took over.

"Ladies and gentlemen," a man in a white dinner jacket with black lapels announced in what I took to be a New York accent, "we are the Jules Laverne Orchestra, and I am your bandleader for the evening, Jules Laverne. The dance floor looks awfully lonely, so if anyone wishes to be the first brave soul to step onto it, my colleagues and I will start you off with a nice easy foxtrot."

"Come along, Marius," Bella demanded before I had time to duck beneath the table. She grabbed hold of my arm and pulled me from my seat, practically knocking it over in the process.

"Thank you to the beautiful young lady and her very lucky partner," Jules Laverne announced through the microphone, a few bars into the performance.

"If I didn't know how to foxtrot," I whispered to Bella as we took our positions, "I would be very angry with you now."

To my genuine horror, no other couples followed us onto the floor. We moved in a circle in the centre of the room with every last eye trained upon us, and I don't believe I'd ever been quite so aware of my own clumsiness. Even a simple sidestep seemed to drag and stutter. My arms were heavy, my legs weak. If Bella hadn't been holding me, I believe that my muscles would have slackened and I would have collapsed to the floor.

"You dance beautifully, Mr Quin," she told me, and I realised for the second time that weekend just how different our perceptions of the world around us tended to be.

"I don't believe you, but I appreciate your vote of confidence." I'd chosen just the right word, as, on hearing what she had to say, I suddenly felt more sure of myself. My movements became smoother, and I glided about just a little more deftly. I even risked spinning her under my arm in a twirl that sent the skirt of her glossy red dress billowing out like a parachute.

What I hadn't noticed until now was the fact that the music was getting faster with every phrase that passed. It had started at a leisurely pace but had turned quite brisk.

"You know that half the people here are staring at you wondering how any woman could look so beautiful?" I said in a voice that was not my own.

She looked at me through the corner of one eye as we danced. "And the rest?"

"Half of *those* are wondering why you would ever be seen in the presence of an oaf like me, and the final quarter are from Mrs Thistlethwaite's society and they're only watching in the hope that we'll fall flat on our faces."

She laughed without making a sound. You might think that's impossible, but Bella could do anything. "You are too hard on yourself, Marius. I've said it a thousand times."

I believe that the audience had come to realise what the band was doing as there were a few whoops and cheers as I released Bella's hand, opened up our bodies and then closed them again all whilst staying in time with the vigorous beat of the bass and snare. There was even some laughter as the bandleader turned to the audience and, rather than waving his skinny white baton at the musicians, he pointed it at us.

"Aren't they doing well, folks? It's just like a wedding."

I intended to find him after his work for the evening was complete and throw that damn stick of his into the sea, but for the moment, I did my best to meet the challenge he'd set.

"I never knew you had it in you, Marius." If Bella was incredulous, she wasn't the only one. I was surprised that I possessed the energy to dance for so long, let alone the coordination.

By this point, the spectators around the edge of the room had set down their cutlery to clap. I'm not sure whether it helped us keep time or merely heaped on more pressure, but I stuck with them. I tried my best to lead Bella into a few steps beyond the basic slow, quick quick, slow that every beginner learns, but it was becoming increasingly difficult.

At some point, I realised that the bandleader was doing this for the laughs he'd inspired rather than any expectation that we would be able to make it to the end of the piece of music. He didn't know Bella the way that I did, though – no matter how fast the orchestra played, she would have dragged me around after her until she'd won.

I was almost out of breath when the music reached its peak and the improbably named Jules Laverne raised his stick to bring a halt to proceedings. The resultant applause made it very nearly worthwhile; the smile on Bella's face made up the difference. I stood at her side as she curtseyed and some people – my uncle foremost among them – got to their feet to pound their hands together in recognition. If I'd been the kind of person who enjoyed such attention, I would have raised my hand and bowed, but I was happy for Bella to have every last bit of it.

She rose from that humble final pose and stood before me once more as our eyes met. "That was heavenly, Marius. Thank you so much."

Her hand at her waist squeezed mine, and then she said something that every boy who has ever fallen in love with a girl (only to lose sight of her for ten years, find her again in the dead of winter in the biggest city in the world and open a detective agency with her) longs to hear. "I just wish that Gilbert had been here to enjoy it."

TWENTY-SIX

"My goodness, boy," my mother called when we were still ten feet away. "Where did you learn to dance like that?"

"Shouldn't you be asking Bella? I am nowhere near as good as she is."

"That goes without saying," Stan replied and then explained the thinking of the table, "but we would expect a fine young lady like Bella to be a good dancer."

"Whereas you'd expect me to have three left feet?" No one answered, but I kept talking to show that I took no offence. "I was taught to dance during the war. Between death-defying raids over the top and the endless shelling, there isn't a great deal to do on the front line. There was a soldier called Tommy Flank, who was the size of a small building. He had legs like grain silos but the lightest feet of any man I've met. Tommy was a champion dancer and so, to kill time, he taught us a few simple steps. When I was living in Paris, I had the chance to put them to use and, by the end of my time in Europe, I was a half-decent dancer."

"Well, I never." Lovebrook gave another brief clap for my story. Such praise would eventually go to my head, so it was lucky that, as the dance floor became more crowded with various couples hoping to emulate our success, an unexpected visitor arrived.

Jennifer Capshaw's appearance at the entrance to the restaurant did not go unnoticed. Every last person who knew her stopped what they were doing to look. I can imagine what her aunt's acolytes must have thought as she walked towards the bar in a simple blue gown. They were judging her for not mourning her deceased relative. I suppose they might also have been thinking how pretty she looked with her wispy and wavy brown hair loose around her shoulders, but the consensus, based upon the downturned mouths and wrinkled brows, was one of disapproval.

"That poor girl," Mother said, and my heart broke just a little for Jennifer as she stood all alone beside the back wall. "Marius, make sure that she's all right. She has suffered enough already."

It was good to know that my family had caught up on that day's gossip, but I didn't think about this at the time. I have no memory of getting to my feet. I barely remember how I crossed the room, but I can picture with great clarity Jennifer's expression when I held my hand out to her. It appeared that she hadn't noticed my approach, as she reacted with a startled look.

"Marius... I didn't know you'd be here."

"Nor I, you." This sounded a bit too medieval, so I cleared my throat and tried again. "My mother thought you looked lonely and sent me over to check." This was no great improvement.

"I wasn't going to come." She held her bare wrist with her other hand as though the near-sleeveless dress she wore left her cold. "But I was on my own in that big house, and I felt so lonely that I couldn't bear it any longer." Her voice was brittle, and she spoke faster with each sentence. "I bought the ticket for my birthday last week. I'd hoped that the lift boy, Ian

Newbury, would invite me, but he had a shift tonight, so here I am on my own." She gave a nervous laugh, and it made me a little cross that the poor creature could find herself in such a situation.

"I think you meant to say, here you are with me, my friends and my family," I told her, and a shy smile lit up her face.

"Thank you, Marius. I don't know why you're so nice to me."

"I don't know why anyone wouldn't be." I also didn't know whether I should throw her into the deep end (if you'll excuse the inappropriate pun) by introducing her to my rabble right now, or I should give her a chance to recover her nerves first. I went with the second option. "Would you care to dance?"

She nodded with great trepidation, and I held out my hand again. This time, she took it. Don't worry, I did not plan to spend the whole evening on my feet. I promise this is the last time I will have to describe two people throwing themselves around a restaurant in time with a lively jazz band.

I'm happy to say that the waltz that was then playing started slow and remained that way throughout. There really is no better dance for shuffling about the place without too much effort! Jennifer was not the type to take charge of a dance floor as Bella had, so I was happy to be afforded some small shred of anonymity.

"I thought that I would have a very different life by the time I was twenty-four," she whispered sadly in my ear as we moved around the clock. "I thought that, after almost a quarter of a century, I would understand more about the world and have made something of myself." She was looking at the closest pairs of dancers just as they were looking at us.

"I'm five years older than you," I replied, "and I still don't feel as though I know a great deal about anything."

She shook her head. "That's nice of you to say, but you've published books and been to war. You've achieved something.

I'm a soon-to-be-homeless secretary with no family, and now I'm suspected of murdering the woman who kept me."

She looked so deeply into my eyes then that I considered telling her that no one thought so badly of her. It wouldn't have been true, but I was desperate to reassure her. "You can concentrate on the negatives if that's what you want, but I promise you this: every person who you think has got their head screwed on the right way is just as lost and uncertain as you are. If there really are people in this world who have all the answers, I have yet to meet them."

This made her a little more cheerful, though I don't know whether she believed me. "You seem to have some answers. You certainly know what to say to make me feel better."

"I suppose I'm a good enough improviser." Despite this claim, I had to think for a moment to know what it was that I actually thought. "Human existence is all about pretending. The most successful people are the ones who feign competence better than everyone else."

I was relieved when this strangely abstract conversation was interrupted by an elderly couple who came to dance alongside us.

"It might have been a controversial opinion," the grey-haired gentleman told us as he held his partner on the spot to say his piece, "but I thought your books were jolly entertaining."

I mouthed a "Thank you", and the pair of them spun around so that the lady was now facing us.

"I felt quite the same way. It's a tragedy about Mrs Thistlethwaite, but she did tend to see the worst in everyone. I don't see why we can't solve mysteries and still give people the benefit of the doubt."

They whooshed away without another word, but the fact that they'd spoken to us gave a pair of their friends permission to do the same.

"Good evening, Mr Quin, Miss Capshaw," began a haughty

lady dressed all in lilac with enormously tall hair. "I was curious to know whether you have considered the possibility that Mrs Thistlethwaite's shepherding of our society is the reason she was killed?"

"As it happens—" I tried to say, but she talked right over me.

"Surely it's possible that one of the people into whom our amateur investigations probed paid someone to kill her, either as revenge or to prevent her discovering some terrible secret. Don't you think that Robert Milton is the likely suspect?"

She didn't wait for an answer but moved to the centre of the room with her partner.

"My goodness, they are an eccentric lot," Jennifer said, and her voice had recovered its usual warmth.

It wasn't long before the next interested party had shimmied up to present some new facet of the case.

"Smugglers!" the neatly attired gent exclaimed.

"I beg your pardon, Mr Thomas?" was all my partner could say in response.

"I said, smugglers! This area has a long history of smuggling, and you can't deny that Mrs T met a watery end. My money is on smugglers."

"Oh, come along, Harold," the rather bored-looking lady he was holding complained. "You promised me a dance, not a conversation."

She pulled him away, which meant that another couple could take their place. This continued with barely a break in the long line of dancing detectives until Jenny was laughing so much that we had to sit down. She came to a stop before we reached the table and took me by the hands.

"Thank you, Marius."

"You've already said that."

"Yes, but I really mean it. Thank you for making me feel better. I don't think I've been so entirely lost since I was eighteen and my..." She couldn't finish that sentence but found another to replace it. "I don't think anyone has shown me such kindness in a long time, and I truly appreciate it."

"You haven't met my family yet. There's still time to change your mind."

I gave her my arm and escorted her over to the table. I hadn't expected Bella to be the first of the group to address us, but that's what happened. "Jennifer, you dance exquisitely. You even made Marius look proficient."

"That's very droll, my dear," I told her, "but I believe you were a little more complimentary just a short time ago."

"Oh, very well. You were both very good." She nudged me in the ribs to concede that she was teasing. "Now, what would you like to drink?"

Lovebrook had taken a chair from a recently vacated table and presented it to the new arrival, who accepted it with a brief smile. After that, my mother decided to make a fuss of Jennifer, and we all did our bit through the course of the evening. Lovebrook also took a few turns around the room with her, and the two seemed to enjoy themselves.

I tried to make the most of my time there by observing the carousers as though every last one of them was a potential killer. I don't think it got me very far. For one thing, the only confirmed suspects present were Jennifer and Sergeant Stainsbury, whom I barely recognised out of uniform. I should probably stress that he was not naked, but in civilian clothes and looked a different person altogether. He was quite handsome in his navy-blue blazer as he danced with a woman whom I took to be his wife.

After some time without incident, the bandleader interrupted the music to make an announcement.

"Ladies and gentlemen, I am sorry to tell you that we have reached the end of our solo performance for the evening." This drew a disappointed groan from those most keen to continue dancing. "But that just means that we will now be accompanied by the dulcet tones of none other than the Nightingale herself, Miss Clemmie Symonds."

There was a real eruption of cheering and clapping as he said this, and the young lady I had already spotted three times that weekend took to the stage. She was wearing a glimmering silver ankle-length dress that moved like mercury under the lights. She had all the grace of a ballerina and seemed to glide over to her spot before the microphone.

"Thank you, everybody," she said in the breathy whisper I'd heard broadcast so many times from the Savoy Hotel. "It's a real pleasure to be here."

She looked at Jules Laverne, who nodded, then raised his baton before the excellent band began its next piece. Clemmie tapped her thigh to keep time and, after a few bars of introduction, she launched into the song.

"I can't say why I love you, but I do.
I can't say why I love you, but it's true.
I can't say why I feel the way I do tonight,
But the stars are out and the moon is bright.
I can't say why I love you, but I do."

There was such emotion in her voice that it was easy to imagine she meant every word she sang and was directing each of them just to me. Well, that's what I thought at first, but then one of the lines caught in her throat and I realised that I wasn't the man she'd fixed her gaze upon. I had the definite sense that her eyes had become attached to someone just a little way behind me at the bar.

Alexander Fraiser stood in space with one hand in his pocket and the other holding the dying end of a cigarette. He was staring straight back at the singer and looked like a man with any number of troubles.

"I can't find the words I wish to say,
I can't say how you make me feel so gay.
I can't describe the way you turn the night to day,
You make light from grey, scare my woes away,
I can't find the words I wish to say."

As the music built towards the chorus and you could almost see the musical notes swirling around the room to lift the dancers' feet, I noticed a look of sheer misery on the exquisite singer's face. She opened her mouth to continue, but no sound would emerge.

Seeing the very thing that I had, the bandleader urged the orchestra on and signalled for it to vamp the current bar. This time, when her cue came back around, and with a smile on her face to cover her feelings, Clemmie managed to start the chorus.

"I only wish we were together all the time.
I only long to say that you are truly mine.
If only there was somewhere I could be alone with you
Where you'd hold me tight, and I could say that I'm in love with—"

This was as far as she got before her sobs distorted the words of the song and, instead of concluding the pretty ballad, she wailed in apparent agony.

Fraiser had been watching her throughout but turned away as soon as the music stopped. He walked back to the bar, swallowed down the remains of his drink and slammed it on the counter before leaving the room. Clemmie stared after him even after he'd disappeared. Her tears fell to the stage, as large as any raindrops, and it would be up to the band to comfort her as Jules Laverne returned to the microphone to address the crowd.

"I'm terribly sorry, ladies and gentlemen. Miss Symonds wasn't feeling well before coming out here tonight, but she didn't want to let anyone down. She still deserves our applause, of course, and we're all very appreciative of the effort she's made."

He clapped as she was helped from the stage, and the audience responded without a great deal of enthusiasm. When even this ripple of support had faded, Laverne stepped closer to the microphone.

"We've got the lyrics written up on paper if anyone here fancies taking a whack at them."

At this announcement, little Jennifer flinched, and Bella immediately turned to face the stage. I could imagine what they were thinking. To one of them, the idea of getting up there was appalling, and to the other a dream come true.

I didn't wait to find out what would happen but left the room when no one was paying attention.

TWENTY-SEVEN

I checked with the reception that there'd been no calls from Christopher Prentiss or Dicky Prowse, but nothing had come through to the hotel. I'd assumed that someone would have relayed any message to me, so this came as no surprise. I was about to return to the restaurant when I noticed that the door to the library was open and there was a man in a smart black suit smoking just within it.

I recognised Alexander Fraiser even from twenty yards away and went to see what he'd make of my presence there.

"Good evening," I said as I took a seat some distance from his.

"Is it?" he snapped, his breathing laboured, as though he were trying to calm himself down but couldn't. "I'm sorry. That was uncalled for. I'm sure everyone else is having a perfectly lovely time." Even this he said with a dose of cynicism in his voice.

"Don't you wish to be here? Is there somewhere else you'd prefer?" I looked around the room as if appraising it for the first time.

"No, no..." He turned to look at the fireplace. The two brass griffins remained in stasis on the guard, looking just as unhappy to be there as before. There was silence for twenty seconds, and I was doubtful that he would have anything more to say to me, but then his head turned in my direction. "Have you ever found the life you've always dreamed of having, only for it to be denied to you? Have you ever seen perfection that is just out of reach?"

I don't believe he really cared about my opinion. The fact that he was talking at all told me that he needed to get his thoughts out, and a perfect stranger was the only person he could tell. Of course, that didn't stop me from answering honestly. "If you have to ask, then you evidently didn't see me dancing earlier this evening. That's exactly how I've felt for the best part of a year."

For a moment he looked a little frightened, as though he'd picked the wrong Joe to engage in conversation. I don't know what he saw in my face, but it must have reassured him somewhat and he soon continued. "You're talking about a woman, I imagine."

I just laughed.

"It's always a woman." He stubbed out his cork-tipped Virginia in a purple glass ashtray on the table and immediately lit another. He leaned forward to offer me one across the room, and I was tempted to accept just to ingratiate myself with him, but I hate the feel of smoke in my lungs – when you've experienced it in a war zone it really loses its charm.

"That's very kind, but no, thank you."

He didn't seem offended and returned to his previous thought. "It's *always* a woman... I don't understand why God didn't just make us all want the same thing. It would have made life so much easier."

"I don't think humankind would have achieved a great deal

if that were the case," I replied. "Imagine a world where we all have what we're looking for and are thoroughly content with our lot. We'd never have progressed as a species."

"You know, that sounds just perfect right now." He leaned back in his chair and looked nostalgically up at the ceiling. "I wish I was the kind of man who was happy with what I'd been given. The problem is that my once fine family had fallen on hard times, and I grew up poor and hungry. I fought to become someone who could sit in a building like this one and not feel out of place."

There were plenty of conclusions to draw from this. I just couldn't do so out loud. Remember, this is the man who was engaged to a rich American heiress and who had presumably just made one of the most beloved and beautiful singers in Great Britain break down in tears in the middle of a performance. It really wasn't so difficult to fill in the gaps in his story.

When I didn't say anything, his gaze dropped, and he muttered to himself. "Maybe I'm my own worst enemy. Maybe I should learn how to change."

"I know exactly what you mean." My fingers drummed on the armrest, as if working of their own accord. "It's another design flaw. Humans aren't built to complete our objectives with ease. Worry, doubt and insecurity are the default settings for the ridiculous machines in our heads."

Perhaps things had turned a little too personal as, rather than heartily agreeing with me as I was sure he would, he remained quiet, and I was worried for a moment that I'd overstepped the mark. A man in the public eye would have to be careful whom he trusted, and I should probably have been a little subtler in what I said to him; I might have at least taken my time to win his trust instead of babbling. The problem was that I agreed with much of what he'd said, and it sparked numerous thoughts of my own.

"You sound like a sensible man, Mr...?"

"Quin. Marius Quin." As comfortable as I was in my armchair, I moved closer to his table and stopped to shake his hand on the way.

He looked puzzled as he accepted it. "Marius... I know that name from somewhere."

"I'm an author. I write mystery novels. That's why I'm here this weekend. I gave a talk last night to a local society."

This last piece of information turned his face oddly blank. "I see. Mysteries." He held his head with one hand, so that his index finger touched his right temple. "Then shouldn't you be the one with the answers?" He was the second person that night to imply such a thing. "I thought your type were supposed to be experts on the human mind – able to work out every enigma going."

"No, that's our detectives. I don't know why people get confused when they're fictional characters and we're real. Perhaps Conan Doyle likes to claim he is as great a genius as Sherlock Holmes – I really can't say. Personally, I'm more of a stage magician than a savant. If my books fool anyone, that means I've pulled off a good illusion."

"Ah, so you're a practitioner of smoke and mirrors? Could you possibly tell me how to disappear from this building without anyone noticing?"

We'd moved away from the topic that most interested me, but this was a curious phrase and I wanted him to tell me more. "Literary smoke and mirrors don't count for much in the real world, I'm afraid. What makes you want to get away from your get-a-way so desperately?"

I believe that he at least considered answering the question, but then he shook his head and had second thoughts. "No, I'm no quitter, and I'm not scared of anyone." I would have certainly liked to dissect this strange declaration, but it would have only put him on edge. "I didn't get to where I am in the world by giving up. There's a solution to every problem; I just have to find it."

I wanted to know more but kept my response suitably ambiguous. "If you need to discuss the situation, I can be as objective as you like."

He sighed and a puff of smoke filled the space between us. I had to wonder how long he'd been holding it in as, for a moment, I was a bird flying through thick clouds.

"It's kind of you, fella, but I think this might even be beyond a man of your talents."

"You know, you're probably right." I was losing him and I knew it. Rather than prodding him for more, I decided to share something of my own experience. "I can't say that I'm the best judge of... well, anything really. I had the life I wanted on a plate, and I took that plate, smashed it to pieces and then jumped on it for a good long while."

"All because of a woman." He seemed to grip his skull rather violently then. "It's always a woman."

The discussion was probably doing me just as much good as it did him, and I found myself exploring a topic of which I hadn't spoken even to my closest friends.

"Not just any woman, a princess among paupers, a goddess among... goats or something, I don't know."

Despite my very poor metaphor, he licked his lips and was clearly desperate to know more. "Pretty, is she?"

"There is no adequate response to that question, so I won't even try," I said with a wink. "But it's not just her beauty. Bella and I grew up together, and I think I was in love from the first moment I saw her. By the time we were seventeen, she felt the same way. I was all ready to ask her to marry me when my call-up came and..."

He leaned forward in his chair like a child glued to his

favourite weekly programme on the wireless. "What happened?"

"I funked out. I was so scared of dying that I couldn't ask her. And now I live with the image of her disappointment like a flash of light burnt onto my retina."

He clapped his hands together in frustration. "But after the war? You made it through alive. Why couldn't you rekindle love's young flame?"

"I should have. Of course I should have, but I felt so guilty for everything I'd done that it was impossible. By the time we saw one another again, it was too late."

"Another man?" He scoffed to himself bitterly. "There's always another man."

"Indeed."

This was as far as I would go. I couldn't talk about Gilbert or the way I felt about Bella now. I could barely admit to myself how I still pined for her, so how was I going to say it out loud to a fellow who, I had the creeping suspicion, was not my kind of person at all? There was something too brash and coxy about him for that.

"If you don't mind my saying, from what I know about you, Mr Fraiser, it already seems as if you have most things pretty well organised in life. What's distressed you so much that you're in here alone, filling your lungs with smoke, when you could be having a good time at the ball?"

He stilled every muscle in his body, and I knew I'd made a mistake. I should never have revealed that I knew who he was, but it had seemed like the right option at the time.

"It's been nice talking to you. Tell whoever sent you that I won't be intimidated."

As he shot up from his seat, I did my best to recover. "I'm sorry, you misunderstood me. No one sent me. I just came out of the restaurant and saw you here."

He stopped in the doorway. "Exactly. You pretended that you were here by chance when, in truth, you only came in because you recognised me. You lied, and so now I'm going to bid you farewell, Mr..." Despite his promise, he didn't leave the room immediately. "Wait, Marius Quin! You're the detective I read about in the paper. I knew that I'd heard that name before." He closed his eyes for the count of three before walking away.

"*Zut!*" If I'd had anything to hand, I would have thrown it across the room in frustration.

I felt simultaneously so close and so far from solving the case. Whether the presence of a slew of celebrities had anything to do with Mrs Thistlethwaite's death or not, I was determined to find out what they were all doing at the hotel. Both Clemmie Symonds and the man I took to be her lover were scared of something, but as the one hope I'd previously had was refusing to call me back, and I'd now scared off Fraiser, I didn't see what else I could do.

I was tempted to return to my room or fetch my dog and go for a walk but, as I left the library, Robert Milton appeared through the front door, and I had the definite sense that something had upset him. He was not dressed for the ball but still wore the same casual attire as when we'd met him that afternoon.

"Hello, Marius," he said, hurrying towards me. "Have you seen Sergeant Stainsbury? I need to talk to him." He was quite out of breath and his gaze was oddly intense.

"What's the matter, Robert? Please tell me there hasn't been another attack."

Still flustered, he shook his head. "No, nothing like that, but I've remembered something that I believe could be important. I must speak to the sergeant."

"What is it?"

He looked over his shoulder at the deserted foyer, then pulled me towards the restaurant and the noise of the orchestra so that we would not be overheard. "I suppose it does no harm to tell you. I should have remembered before, but it only occurred to me when I got home this evening. You see, I was sitting in my lounge with a glass of Scotch, reminiscing over the short time Angelica and I shared together, when I remembered the last night I spent at her house. You see, she wasn't herself. She wouldn't tell me her problems, but she was definitely frightened."

"You think that she knew she was in danger?"

"I do indeed." Frightened was the word for him just then, too. He put one hand on my sleeve to impress his words upon me. "I begged her to tell me what was wrong, but all that she would say was that a man by the name of Fraiser was causing her trouble. She said that she wished to handle it on her own."

"She didn't say how she knew him or what business they had together?"

Milton shook his head. "No, and it was strange because she normally trusted me with what was happening in her life. We would talk about every last detail – the good and the bad – but this was the first thing that she refused to divulge."

"Fraiser," I muttered, casting a glance back towards the room where I had been speaking to him just minutes before. "Did she mention his first name? There's an Alexander Fraiser at the hotel this weekend. He's one of those men about town you read of in the papers."

He took a moment to think before confirming what I felt that I already knew. "Alexander Fraiser. That's the chap. I saw his name on a letter she was writing the next morning, and I asked her again, but all she would say was that she'd made a mistake." He stopped himself then, as though to make sure he recalled the conversation accurately. "She said that he was not the kind of person that one crosses. She refused my help, and I can only wish now that I'd been more insistent."

"You mustn't blame yourself," I said to reassure him, then

gave him a few moments to regain his composure before asking what I needed to know. "What day did this happen?"

When I'd first met Milton, he'd seemed like the type who would never show emotion in public, but he really did look distressed at this moment. "It was yesterday morning – less than twenty-four hours before she was killed."

TWENTY-EIGHT

I couldn't be sure where to turn next. An already nebulous case had only become more complex, and yet I thought I could see a path to the truth. I just needed to know how to take the first step.

I returned to the restaurant where my family and friends were still whiling away a pleasant evening. Lovebrook and Bella had apparently forgotten that we were investigating a murder, and I couldn't entirely blame them for wanting a break from such a gloomy pastime. The inspector was performing what looked very much like a Charleston with my mother, and Bella was regaling young Jennifer with stories. I had a feeling that they were probably about me when I was a boy, but I suppose that was better than her getting up on stage to replace Clemmie Symonds. It was bad enough that my most competitive childhood friend was good at simply everything she did. I was uncertain how I felt about the idea of the ball being her springboard to a career as an internationally admired singer.

"You know, Jenny's actually very sweet. I can see why you like her," she confided in me once our group had broken up into a few different conversations, and Stan was telling our guest about the wonders of yeast. "The poor creature seems a little heartbroken because the hotel lift attendant couldn't accompany her tonight, but she's been very good company nonetheless."

I didn't have much to say to this. Jennifer was in love with Newbury from the lift, and there was nothing I could do about that, but I did have a question for her.

"Jennifer, did you say you turned twenty-four tonight?" I said out of the blue, and the chatter around the table suddenly stopped. I suppose this must have sounded rude, as my two keenest judges (my mother and my former girlfriend) both screwed up their faces in discontent.

Jennifer looked uncertain whether to answer but finally did so. "Not tonight. My birthday was over a week ago now."

"Twenty-four! That's nearly a quarter of a century," Stan responded with a disbelieving shake of his head, as though no one had ever reached such an age before. "Why didn't you tell us? We shall order more wine to celebrate!"

I don't think he needed an excuse to enjoy the party more, but he had certainly found one. And as the group lavished Jennifer Capshaw with attention, I whispered my excuses to Bella and returned to the reception. I had to make a telephone call to confirm what I thought I already knew.

"Has anyone called for me?" I asked the gaunt man at the desk, who was presumably covering the injured receptionist's shift.

"No, sir, not in the short period since you last asked," he replied in a slow, local drawl.

"Very well. You must find me if they do. My room is number 216. If I'm not in the ball, you'll find me there."

He nodded, and I signalled that I needed to use the telephone before realising that there was a public one on the other side of the entrance hall. I thanked him for his help and walked across to it.

"Hello, Irene. Are you still hard at it?" I said to the operator, as she was apparently yet to clock off. "What time do you finish?"

"Not until eleven, Mr Quin," she replied with a giggle. "Why? Are you inviting Cinderella to the ball?"

It was not an offer I'd been planning to make, but I replied in similar good spirits. "I'll tell you what: if that fool Mike Rutherford from the mechanic's doesn't call you, there's a seat at my table with your name on it."

"Do you really mean it?" She gasped in excitement. "I'll run home and put on my glad rags just as soon as I finish here." She became a little formal then. "Now, how can I help you, sir?"

I cleared my throat. "I'd like you to connect me to the same number as earlier this evening in Cranley, Surrey."

"Cranley Hall, wasn't that it?"

"That's right."

"Very good, sir. I'm trying that number now." She fell silent for a few moments and the line crackled warmly like a log in a fire. "I'm sorry, Mr Quin. There's no answer. It is past ten thirty, though. Perhaps the household has gone to bed."

"I suppose you're right. Thank you, Irene."

"No, Mr Quin. Thank *you*. I'll see you at the hotel shortly."

I was making women happy left, right and centre that night. It certainly made a change from my normal interactions with them.

"Actually, I have one more call to make. Can you put me in touch with my publisher, Bertrand Price-Lewis, at Sloane 1772? I know he'll still be up at this time of night."

"Of course, sir." She set about her task and, a few moments later, a familiar voice came down the line.

"Good evening. Who's calling?"

"It's me, Bertie. It's Marius."

"Oh, how nice to hear from you, my boy. How's the third book coming along?"

That really wasn't what I wanted to discuss. "It's... coming. But that's not why I'm calling. I need to tell you that if anyone from the Torquay Mystery and Detection Society ever calls to invite your authors to speak at their events, you're only to allow it if they ask for Carmine Fortescue. They really put me through the wringer, and I don't like the thought of someone of a fragile disposition suffering as I have."

"Whereas Carmine deserves to be taken down a peg or two?"

"Something like that, yes."

He laughed down the line at me. "Is that really why you're calling at this time on a Saturday night? Margery thought there must be something wrong."

I scratched my, for once, stubble-less cheek. "Well, she's right. The woman who invited me down here has been murdered."

"Not the nice young lady who called here?" he asked with dismay. "She telephoned asking for a photograph of you."

"No, not Jennifer. She's fine. It was her aunt; the woman who ran the society."

"Oh, the poor creature."

"No, she wasn't poor at all – not by any definition of the word. She was a rotter, but I believe I've just identified her killer. And the woman responsible may be even more despicable than she was."

I don't think that dear Bertie knew how to take this news. "Well, that's... wonderful and awful at the same time. Good luck with your endeavours, Marius, and do try to stay safe. You seem to have a habit of placing yourself in danger."

"Don't worry, old friend. Bella is here to look after me, and the police are doing what they can."

He breathed a little more easily after that. "I can't tell you how much better that makes me feel. Lady Isabella will screw your head back on if it ever gets too loose."

I would have told him that she'd been responsible for just as many reckless acts as I had over the last year, but it wasn't the moment to argue. "Thanks, Bertie. I'll see you back in London very soon."

"Yes, we should probably meet to discuss—" I didn't hear what he said next, as I'd hung up the telephone. I doubt he would be too offended. Editors tend to have thick skin.

I considered going back to the table until what I had an inkling might happen came to pass, but instead I paused in the doorway and watched my family and friends enjoying themselves. If my suppositions were correct, the motive for Mrs Thistlethwaite's death and the attack on Paul Turbot were selfish and mercenary, and I doubted that I would be anything but bad company if I returned to my party. So, instead, I went to linger in the cool air of the hotel terrace and feel bad about the world.

I stood beside the railing and gazed out towards the sea once more. It was hard to comprehend that the distance from me to the horizon beyond the bay was actually very short and that the sea itself extended thousands of times further than human sight could gauge. For a moment, I felt very small indeed when considering that Tor Bay, within the English Channel in the Atlantic, was really just one name of one piece of water that was connected to all the oceans and most of the seas in the world.

I was just exploring these highly irrelevant thoughts when I realised that I wasn't alone. I couldn't see who was sitting at a table in the darkness, but I could make out the glow of a cigarette and the occasional puff of smoke.

"I'm sorry, I didn't mean to disturb you," I said and was about to go back inside when a voice cut through the still night.

"It's a free country… to an extent." The breathy words came back to me, and I knew exactly who it was.

I didn't see any other way to approach her, and so I did

something that I had already avoided once that night. "I don't suppose that you have a spare cigarette? I left mine up in my room."

She didn't say no, and so I walked closer. The table where she sat had a parasol protruding from it, and she was sitting in its shade. All the other oversized umbrellas around the terrace were closed, and I had to wonder whether she'd raised it in order to be that little bit more hidden. By the time I reached her, she was holding out her slim case and a matchbook from the hotel.

"I'm sorry you weren't feeling well," I told her as I lit my chosen tube of lung misery – as no one calls cigarettes.

"I doubt that you or anyone else in that room believes that I'm really ill. It was nice of the boys from the band to try to protect me, but I made a spectacle of myself." Clemmie Symonds looked back through the windows at the dimmed lights of the restaurant where her colleagues were still entertaining their audience.

"That may be true but look on the bright side; only three or possibly four people here know why you cried."

She dropped the gold case to the table, and it made a brief, loud clatter. "So that's who you are," she said a little cryptically. "I did wonder."

I was quick to set her right. "No, Miss Symonds. It's not what you think. If anything, I believe I can help you."

"You won't be surprised when I tell you that I've heard that before."

Her attitude in person was very different from the impression she gave on the radio. She presented herself as a wide-eyed ingénue, but there was a world-weariness to her that I hadn't expected. Even in the darkness, her big brown eyes shone, and it was hard not to be distracted by her beauty – which, now that I come to think of it, is a common failing on my part.

"I'm not trying to take advantage of you. I swear I'm not.

When I tell you who I am, I will fully understand if you don't trust me, but maybe that will change in time."

"In time?" She whistled out a breath through her teeth. "I'm leaving here at the very first opportunity I get."

I seized the closest iron chair and pulled it next to hers. "That's just it. I saw you for the first time last night. You've looked out of sorts ever since, and yet you're still here. In fact, I don't think you can leave until someone gives you permission."

She regarded me with suspicious eyes, but did nothing to contradict my theory, so I started from the beginning.

"Now, I know this sounds far-fetched, but it happens to be the truth. My name is Marius Quin, and I'm a mystery novelist and a private detective." Saying the words out loud to a total stranger made them all the less believable. "With our associate from Scotland Yard, my friend and I have been investigating Mrs Thistlethwaite's death."

I watched her expression change at the mention of the victim's name, but she denied any knowledge of that supremely manipulative person. "I'm afraid I haven't been keeping up with the news recently. I wasn't aware that anyone had been killed."

At least this response meant that she didn't dismiss me as a fantasist. After all, who's ever heard of a novelist who solves crimes? The very idea is implausible.

"*Peu importe*," I muttered to myself, because sometimes nonchalance can only truly be expressed in French. "The point I'm trying to make is that I know why you came here. I spoke to your friend Alexander Fraiser and, while he wouldn't confirm it, I understand from what I've seen that the pair of you are being blackmailed."

She looked at me for a few seconds and took her time to formulate the right response. "That's preposterous. There's nothing so interesting in my life that someone could use it to extort money. I eat, I sleep, and I sing."

"It's the sleeping part that presumably caught your blackmailer's attention." I didn't want to be gauche, but I could see that she wasn't taking me seriously enough. The gamble failed.

"Goodbye, Mr... I don't even remember your name." She dropped the cigarette to the ground so that a trail of sparks fired across the flagstones. "Goodbye."

I spoke again before she could get too far. "I'm not asking you to tell me anything about your connection to Mr Fraiser. I have no desire to get you into trouble, and I certainly don't wish to exploit you. I swear that I'm trying to help you out of your predicament, and all you have to do is tell me that I'm not a thousand miles from the truth."

She stopped near the glass door to the restaurant, half in shadow, half in light, and I knew that she would listen to what I had to say.

"I don't know all the details, of course, but I believe that Mrs Thistlethwaite was blackmailing various famous people. She received large sums of money from some very prominent names. I imagine that she invited you to the hotel, placed you in compromising situations and then demanded payment in exchange for her silence. For whatever reason, you couldn't pay, which is why you remained at the hotel, though it kills you to be here."

She didn't turn around. She kept her eyes fixed on the door and put her hand to the handle to leave but, at the last second, she gave the tiniest nod. It was really little more than a flinch, but it was enough to tell me that I was on the right track.

TWENTY-NINE

I returned to my party feeling rather sure of myself for once. Our suspects were all present as well, but I imagine you'll be glad to know that I didn't get up on the stage to accuse them of anything. I wasn't looking to make a scene, and there were still a few pieces that had to fall into place before I could tie the case up in a bow for the police. So, instead, I sat and watched the dancers who had been spinning around the room for hours by now. It was fun to imagine that the same forty or so pairs hadn't stopped all night.

I noticed that Travers was particularly busy, as he rushed from table to table, checking that his guests were enjoying themselves and that each person had exactly what was needed. The expression on his face made him look like a man crossing a high wire over a live volcano, and while it was true that this had been the case for much of the day, there was an added awkwardness to him that was noticeable even from across the room.

"Is everyone..." he began when he reached our table. "That is to say... isn't the entertainment wonderful tonight and... Well, it's good to see that you are all having a grand time here at the Grand Hotel." He had to grit his teeth as he said this, and I could tell he had used the line one or ten times too often that night.

I doubt that Sergeant Stainsbury was any cheerier, even though he spent much of the time dancing with his wife. He kept looking across at me, which presumably caused him to lose concentration and, judging from his partner's reaction, step on her foot. He kept his distance from our table, too, and there would be no occasion for conversation.

Someone who did seem very chatty, though, was Robert Milton. He'd stayed to enjoy the music after delivering his message to the apparently unconcerned sergeant. I saw him work his way around the room, much like Travers, but between his brief conversations at each table, he would apprehensively peer over at ours for a moment. He reminded me of a politician, canvassing his voters for support, and it occurred to me once more that he could have killed his secret lover just to gain control of the society. I'm glad to say that this would not turn out to be the case, but the very idea of such a petty motive for violence stuck in my craw and turned my stomach.

The would-be future husband of Britain's most eligible American expatriate was back at the bar, drowning his sorrows. Alexander Fraiser had passed through the open, chatty stage of drunkenness in which I'd found him in the library, and now sat staring into his tumbler of... whichever drink he'd ordered. His shoulders were hunched, and he held the glass tightly in both hands. I was rather glad that I didn't have to talk to him at that moment, as I believe that one wrong word in his ear could have led to a fight.

Our suspects weren't the only ones watching me. Bella's expression betrayed her concern, and she soon nudged me to check that everything was all right.

"Are you quite yourself, Marius? You look terribly ponderous, as though you're composing a sonnet."

"With imagery like that, Bella, perhaps you should be a writer in my place."

I'd expected a roll of the eyes or perhaps a brief sigh, but she smiled and put one hand on my shoulder. "I hope you still know how to enjoy yourself. I'm well aware that we have other things on our minds tonight, but you're not going to solve the case from this table, so you might as well let your hair down."

I turned to look at her, face on. "This is as low as my hair is physically capable of going, and you'll be happy to know that I'm having a wonderful time. I might even say that I haven't a care in the world. Only one thing could improve my evening and I hope that will come in time."

She bit her lip to stifle her response just as the band stopped playing between songs. "You've done it, haven't you? You know who the killer is."

I said nothing. I didn't need to, as she already knew the answer. I watched as her gaze raced around the room in search of the culprit. It stopped off at every obvious point before coming back to our table. "It isn't...?" She asked the question with her eyes.

"All I'll tell you is that Mrs Thistlethwaite was a blackmailer. That's why there were so many famous faces here this weekend and why the great and good of Britain had supported her society – or at least, transferred large sums into her bank account. Oh, and it may strike you as interesting that Jennifer was born almost exactly twenty-four years ago."

She ran through these facts in her head, and I have no doubt that she would have contested my decision to say no more, but I was distracted by the arrival of someone I hadn't seen there before. She was a tall, rather broad girl with a lot of make-up and peroxide-blonde hair. Jennifer spotted her and called her to our table, but first she had to go through the rigmarole of a greeting from Milton before a few other Torquay luminaries shook her hand. She was rather like a celebrity, or at least a big fish in a small pond.

"Everyone, allow me to introduce my friend Irene Adams," Jennifer said when we finally had the newcomer to ourselves.

"Irene and I know each other well," I told her and rose to receive an unexpected kiss on each cheek.

"Oh, Mr Quin," the excitable young lady said as she gripped my hand. "I can't tell you how much I appreciate your inviting me down here. I would surely have stayed at home on my own and cried into my pillow if I hadn't come."

"You are very welcome, Irene. I'm only sorry that your young man didn't make the effort himself."

For a moment, she looked disgruntled. "Mike Rutherford is not my young man." A smile soon returned to her bright red lips. "Though now that I'm here, I may have to find one to take his place." She giggled and I couldn't help copying her.

Lovebrook had performed his usual gentlemanly duty and found a chair which Irene now occupied. She spent the next ten minutes chattering away without letting anyone else say a word. As the local operator, she had evidently found her perfect vocation.

Bella and the inspector were fascinated by the young woman and listened with great interest, much as anthropologists will study a subject in some far-flung foreign land. This process was only interrupted by Robert Milton, who had finally completed his circle of the room and looked set to leave for the night.

"Everyone is still very shaken by the news, of course," he told us before changing to a more hopeful tone. A pout shaped his lips, and he seemed almost beatifically at peace with the world. "However, I can't help feeling that this was the right day for something sad to happen. A ball, such as this one, has the power to lift up the community and bring us together at difficult times."

His eyes were on Jennifer as he spoke, and I watched for some sign that she might know of his dalliance with the dead woman. If she was aware of it, she gave nothing away and merely nodded her thanks for his considerate words.

With his part said, Milton closed his eyes and smiled. His attitude had changed even since we'd spoken an hour before. I didn't like the man, and there was something particularly disagreeable about him at that moment. I felt he wanted us to know just how good and righteous he was, and he was willing to wait there until we'd acknowledged it. I suppose such busybodies are common in smaller towns, but he was even less tolerable than most. He reminded me of the vain and frankly rather creepy Mr Collins from *Pride and Prejudice*. He was just that kind of person and I couldn't wait until he'd gone.

His loud, overblown proclamations caught the attention of Fraiser at the bar, who glowered in our direction as Milton bowed and backed away.

I turned to face the dance floor, where Stainsbury was standing looking uncomfortable, as though his suit were too tight. He must have known that I was looking at him, as our eyes locked on to one another's, and I realised that the moment had arrived.

"Bella, Valentine, everything's in place. I need you to come with me." I waved at the sergeant to do the same, and my friends followed me out to the foyer. When we got there, Milton and Travers were in the middle of a furious argument, and before I could give the instruction to arrest the killer, Travers punched him in the mouth.

THIRTY

"You saw what he did!" Milton was enraged as he lay on the floor in the middle of the entrance hall, nursing a bloody nose. "You're all my witnesses. Sergeant Stainsbury, arrest that man."

"You deserved it, you swine!" Travers was in a real paroxysm and stood over his victim, still brandishing his fists.

"To be fair, he did deserve it," I conceded, and Stainsbury didn't know whether to arrest the hotel manager or pat him on the back.

"Marius, do stop being so cryptic and tell us what you know." It was Lovebrook who said this, but it might just as well have been Bella.

"Milton killed his lover, Angelica Thistlethwaite. I can only assume that Travers worked that out and punched him accordingly." This would end up being the one conclusion I got wrong that night, and the revelation made Travers quite wild.

"You nauseating rat! I should have stabbed you instead of punching you!" He looked as though he might stomp on the man's head, so Lovebrook stepped forward to control the scene.

"Now, hold on just one moment," Stainsbury said with two hands out in front of him as though trying to prevent a train from rolling off the tracks. "What evidence have you got that Mr Milton murdered Mrs Thistlethwaite?"

"Where do I start?" This was more than a rhetorical question. I really wished that someone else had worked it all out, so that I didn't have to do the job. Happily, Bella had made a good go of it and did the honours.

"We discovered that Mrs Thistlethwaite came close to bankruptcy some years ago but died very rich and so we visited her bank in the centre of town. Mr Dulwich there told us about the large sums that several extremely well-known persons had paid her over the last few years to support the society – or at least, that was what Mrs Thistlethwaite had told her bank manager, though the money enabled her to buy a grand house and made little impact on the group she founded."

"That's terrible." Still on the floor, Milton was acting shocked. "But if she was a criminal, why are you blaming me for anything?"

"Oh, hush," I snapped, because the man had rubbed me the wrong way ever since we'd first met. The fact that I'd had to pay for the murderer's afternoon tea probably didn't help. "Please, Bella, continue."

She looked surprised that I sounded so grumpy, but she soon did as I'd requested. "Well... we knew of the lengths to which Mrs Thistlethwaite and the society had gone to make their guests feel unwelcome, and this made us even more dubious about the payments. When we worked out exactly who had been paying her, we were put in mind of the various celebrities we'd seen here this weekend. Marius decided to call Lord Edgington's grandson, who is a friend of the cricketer, Dicky Prowse. We'd seen Dicky here last night and—"

She stopped speaking then because of the shrill sound of the telephone. Timothy Travers, who was now cradling his hand in the crook of his arm after its impact with Milton's nose, walked to the counter and reached over to pick up the receiver.

"Hello, the Grand Hotel. This is the manager Timothy Travers speaking. How may I help you?" There was a brief silence. "Yes... That's right... Would you like to talk to him now?" He pulled his mouth away from the phone to address me. "Mr Quin, Christopher Prentiss is calling. He says he's been trying to get hold of you."

"Send my apologies and tell him that I will call him back forthwith."

"Very good." He spoke into the phone again in the same overly polite manner in which he did most things. "We greatly appreciate your call, Mr Prentiss, but Mr Quin is occupied just now... That's correct. He has identified the killer... As a matter of fact, the blighter's lying on the floor after I socked him in the mouth... Thank you, sir. You really are too—"

"Travers!" Stainsbury barked. "Would you please come back here so that we can finish this?"

The manager made his apologies to Chrissy once more and scurried back across the room.

"Thank you." The sergeant huffed out an irritated breath. "Now, Lady Isabella, you are free to continue whenever you are ready."

Apparently less sure of herself than she had been, Bella looked nervous. "Marius tried to contact Dicky Prowse through Christopher Prentiss, who just rang, but... Well, it was only this evening that Marius realised that—" This was as far as she'd got in her deduction, and I knew that I would have to take over the task. "As he didn't hear back from Christopher, I don't quite understand how he uncovered the rest of the story."

Everyone turned to me then, so I sat down on the bench beside the public telephone and started from a more obvious place. "You locals knew when we arrived here that I was in for a rough time of it. Mrs Thistlethwaite did not set up her society to celebrate the work of the police or detective writers. She despised anyone who believed himself capable of solving complex mysteries because of the suspicion that had fallen upon her when her sister and brother-in-law met their untimely deaths some six or seven years ago. Whether they died in an accident, and she was angry at the false accusation against her, or she really did tamper with their car to kill them, I cannot say. But one thing is clear: Mrs Thistlethwaite was prone to unscrupulous schemes.

"Her attempt to humiliate me during my talk last night did not go far enough for her liking, though at least I was not subjected to the physical discomfort through which she put some of my fellow writers. She planned the first scenes of the piece of theatre she had directed to occur on the train on our way from London. We caught sight of two men dressed very much like American gangsters, whose job it was to tempt me into a fictional murder investigation which she predicted I would be unable to solve. I should have realised that she was behind it from the beginning, as she'd been very particular in her letter about the importance of my confirming my travel arrangements in advance – a demand which was repeated by Jennifer on the telephone."

Milton had had enough. He pushed himself up on his elbows and launched another complaint my way. "What has any of this got to do with me?"

"It goes toward motive, your honour," Lovebrook quipped. "Objection overruled."

"Thank you." I gave my loyal friend an appreciative wink and continued my account. "When the time came this morning for me to find the fake dead body in the pool, there was only one problem. I woke up early to walk my dog who didn't need walking and so, by the time I got downstairs, the actor who called himself Augustus Black wasn't ready to pretend to be dead. In his place I found Mrs Angelica Thistlethwaite."

The only sounds in the foyer just then were the tinkling of the water in the ornamental fountain and the strains of music that floated over from the restaurant. Those listening to me looked hungry for every last detail, but I was trying to keep the story concise.

"You know much of the next part. Black happened upon me with Mrs Thistlethwaite's body and immediately scarpered. It was only later this afternoon that I felt confident he hadn't had anything to do with the killing and had run off because his connection to the dead woman might have incriminated him. But then, he wasn't the only person involved in the dubious plan."

I turned to the manager. "You've confessed to your part in it, Travers, and you should have known better than to interfere in people's lives and play with emotions as you did. If you'd come clean about what you knew early on, we might have caught the killer more swiftly. You were so afraid of the white lies you'd told getting you into trouble that you had to keep lying. Whether you've committed any prosecutable offence is debatable, and I'll leave that up to the sergeant to decide."

Stainsbury nodded, but his expression was as steely as ever. Whether the good sergeant himself had committed any prosecutable offence would, equally, remain to be seen.

"One person who had little knowledge of the details of her aunt's machinations is Jennifer. I did assume early on that, as the dead woman's secretary, she would be the first to know, but her aunt apparently didn't trust her with such information until it was too late to do anything about it."

"This is all just smoke and nonsense," Stainsbury said to mangle or perhaps coin a phrase. "What of actual crimes?"

"Very well, you're right. The fact Mrs Thistlethwaite hired a few actors, and put obstacles in my way to bamboozle me, is not relevant in itself, but it spoke to the lengths to which she was willing to go. And so, when I discovered the money that any number of well-known and respectable people in Britain had paid her, it made me wonder whether she had developed a taste for such manipulation and turned it to her advantage. I believe she discovered the secrets of these famous personalities, brought them here to the hotel and blackmailed them with what she knew. I would have been able to confirm this sooner if I had been able to speak to Mr Prowse, but I found another means by which to do so. There are more people here at the hotel who suffered Mrs Thistlethwaite's scheming."

Milton still wasn't giving up. "There you go then. One of them must have taken exception to what she did and killed her. It sounds as though every single person here had more of a reason to do it than I did." Figuring that no one would punch him with two police officers there to protect him, he climbed slowly and theatrically to his feet. He was not the best actor and rubbed his back exaggeratedly to show us the hidden damage of Travers's attack. "Let's say that Angelica threatened to expose an actor, singer or what have you as a cheat, an embezzler or an alcoholic. If he didn't have the money, he might have decided to push her in the swimming pool and watch her drown. I already told the sergeant what she said to me about Alexander Fraiser."

"Very well, but that's not what happened." I knew he wouldn't listen to me, and he didn't.

Instead, he moved around the foyer to look at his fellow suspects. "If it wasn't one of the people she blackmailed, what about Travers? He loved her and failed to win her love. That's a far more likely reason to want her dead than anything you can say about me. Heck! Even the sergeant here didn't get along with her." He walked straight up to the man and looked him in the eye. "She had you under her thumb and you were too scared of the power she wielded. Isn't that right, Stainsbury?"

"No. It's not," I answered to prevent the already tetchy sergeant from losing his rag. As Milton was determined to continue with the charade, I sat back on the bench and waited. I did consider calling Chrissy to see what he had to say, but I decided that I should at least listen to Milton's balderdash to make sure no one believed it.

"Of course, my money is on the sweet little niece. It's no secret that she didn't get along with her aunt. My dear Angelica was forever belittling the girl. It's hardly surprising that she ended up snapping."

"Except that she didn't," I complained, but he still wouldn't listen.

He clapped his hands together and pointed at Lovebrook. "That's it! I've solved the case for you. I've always been a major contributor to our society, and I'm proud to have wrapped up another mystery and tied a bow on top of it. Angelica was murdered by her niece, Jennifer Capshaw. After all, she's the one who will benefit most from the death."

I would love to have picked apart his case against her, but it would have to wait. "No, nay, nope, not at all," I very nearly shouted, standing up from my comfortable seat. "That's not how it happened, because you really are the killer. I'm fairly confident that, by seducing the woman you claim to love, you discovered that she'd been blackmailing people and set your sights on a share of the spoils. I know for a fact that someone has continued to threaten her subjects since Mrs Thistlethwaite died, and the only thing I can imagine is that you used her death to apply more pressure on two people in this hotel whose names need not be dragged into the proceedings."

I walked right up to him to utter the key words. "From the look of sheer terror that I've seen several times on their faces, I believe you told them that if they didn't pay the money that your girlfriend had demanded, they would end up just like her."

THIRTY-ONE

Like a clown with only one joke, Robert Milton kept trying the same old routine.

"Now, listen... All of you, listen. I'm no killer. I loved Angelica. I loved her from the bottom of my heart to the very top of it." The difference this time was that even he didn't believe what he was saying. "You know me, Dennis." It took me a moment to realise that this comment was addressed to the sergeant, and I had to question why it was that I never tried to find out police officers' first names. "You know me. You know I wouldn't hurt Angelica."

I was surprised to see a look of disgust form on Stainsbury's face. "I know you fought like devils in every meeting you attended. I know you never had a good word to say about each other."

"But that was all a pretence. Quin here will tell you about the evidence he found at her house. We were lovers, but Angelica preferred to keep her private life private." Things were getting desperate for Milton and, for some reason I've never quite understood, desperate men often turn to the nearest woman in the hope that the font of human kindness that they assume resides in each of them will spill forth in their favour. "Lady Isabella, have you actually heard any solid evidence to prove that I am a killer?"

To be fair to the man's judgement, Bella did waver for half a moment. Her lip trembled, as if she wished to say something but wasn't sure whether she should. In the end, she looked to me for help, and so I told her exactly why the murderous Robert Milton could not be trusted.

"I can't say for sure, but I believe you only ever seduced your enemy to see what you could get from her. You saw the success she had – the money she'd made and the influence she could exert – and you wanted some of it for yourself. You won her trust and found out the mechanics of her plan, but that wasn't enough. She could buy you presents, and you could stay at her sumptuous house once a week, but it wasn't the same. You needed to transfer the enterprise into your own name, and the only way to do that was to kill off the competition."

Now Milton was the one who was trembling. I don't think he'd imagined for one second when I'd first accused him of murder that I knew so much of what he'd done – to be perfectly honest, a few bits came to me as I went along, but a large part of the case had been built on good old-fashioned detective work.

He held his breath for a moment, and I thought he might be ready to admit defeat. Then, in a high, panicky voice, he gave it one more go. "But this is ludicrous. I could never have done the things you've suggested. I don't know anything about the rich and famous. I'm a humble man and wouldn't know where to begin."

I do like it when suspects phrase things in a way that enables me to deliver the perfect rejoinder. "That's right, which is where your accomplice came in."

I spoke quietly to Lovebrook so as not to give the game away, and he moved off towards the restaurant. Sadly, I realised at the last moment that I'd left off a key instruction. "But don't tell her the real reason we want her here," I called after him, and he nodded and continued on his way.

The only problem now was that I had to fill time until he got back. I considered launching myself into the accusation once more, treading over old ground and mainly just scaring him so that he didn't start whining, but luckily Travers had a question for his rival, who stood in the middle of the hotel foyer, not knowing which way to look.

"I will never understand why Angelica opted for you over me. She chose a brutal, selfish man over someone who truly loved her. How could you hurt her even then?"

Milton began to cry. Tears sprang from his eyes, and I knew that he felt so hard done by that he couldn't comprehend the path before him. He would spend a night at the local police station and appear before a magistrate in the morning to be remanded at the nearest prison. He would be given no bail before the trial and, by the time he had his day in court, the case against him would be so strong that there was only one verdict that the jury could possibly give.

Robert Milton would hang before the year was out.

And as I looked at that cruel and callous creature, some far too forgiving part of me wished that I was playing a trick, and the real killer was about to make her appearance. I almost wanted to alleviate the pain he was feeling, but there would have been no justice in that. And when Lovebrook returned and everyone was amazed to see the woman standing next to him, I explained the final part of Milton's plot.

"You said that you could never have found out so much about the celebrities who stayed here, and the same was true for Mrs Thistlethwaite. The size of the deposits in her bank accounts told me that she really had discovered her victims' secrets, but how could she have done so without the capacity to listen in to their most private conversations?"

I turned to her possibly unwitting, possibly naïve, or

perhaps even willing accomplice. "That's where Irene came in. As an operator with an ear for gossip here in Torquay, she must have heard all sorts of scandalous information that I have no doubt Mrs Thistlethwaite charmed out of her."

Irene immediately joined her fellow blackmailer in a state of tears. "I never knew what she was doing with it. I thought she just liked a chinwag. We all like a chinwag, don't we? We all like a bit of a natter from time to time." She touched her hair then to check that it was not out of place but could do nothing for the lines of black makeup that were running from her eyes.

"Of course, Irene. But you broke the trust of your position. You listened in to conversations that weren't meant for your ears. And when Mrs Thistlethwaite died, Milton here made you do even worse, isn't that right?" I honestly couldn't decide how critical I should be of her. She'd broken rules, but I somehow doubted she knew what her supposed friends were doing with the information that she gave them.

"I didn't think nothing of it." She would need a moment to compose herself before saying anything more. "He asked me to listen out for information on the case and told me to tell him as soon as I heard anything."

"Lies!" Milton bellowed, but his act was fooling no one.

"Far from it," I replied. "In fact, it's proof that you were giving Irene her orders. Soon after I rang Cranley Hall in order to contact a celebrity whom I'd identified as one of Mrs Thistlethwaite's victims, you appeared and told me of an imagined threat she'd received from Alexander Fraiser. I have no doubt that Irene rang to inform you of what she'd overheard and, in turn, you told her not to let any calls from Christopher Prentiss or Dicky Prowse reach the hotel."

He opened his mouth to defend himself, but I hadn't finished. "And then, the last time I spoke to Irene on the phone tonight, I had a sense of her involvement. I rang my publisher for no other reason than to tell him I had identified the killer and that it was a woman. I knew that, as you were not at home, Irene would come here to tell you what she'd heard. You were the first person who she talked to when she arrived, and I saw your demeanour change in a second. When you came to speak to us, you couldn't hide how happy you were because you thought you were off the hook. You must have believed that we'd picked Jennifer as the killer, which is what you wanted all along."

"No." His eyes were wild and didn't know where to rest. He touched the pure white hair at the side of his head and straightened his tie as though that would be enough to fix everything. "I was just relieved that the right person had been caught. Miss Capshaw is the one you need. She is the one who would gain the most from her aunt's death."

"That's the second time you've made such a claim, but how would you know? Did you have romantic late-night conversations with Angelica about her will? Or did you perhaps forge a letter in your lover's hand which claimed that she was Jennifer's real mother?" Nothing but silence came back to me. It made a nice change. "You were a sign-writer, were you not? That presumably gave you some skill with an ink pen. The mistake you made was the choice of evidence you concocted. If you'd written a letter from Mrs Thistlethwaite confessing that she killed Jennifer's parents, it would have given her niece the perfect motive. Instead, you went for an implausible story that was easily disproven."

This was the moment when he knew that the game was up. He no longer searched around for sympathy, but stared at one spot on the wall and seemed to shake as though an earthquake was passing through him. His fists were tightly clenched at his side, and he had no excuses left to give.

"You see, in the funny little story you wrote..." Perhaps I sounded smug, but if you can't be a trifle superior when describing the despicable acts of a murderer, when can you be?

"...you suggested that Angelica had left her husband for six months to hide the fact she was pregnant. But Jennifer recently turned twenty-four, which means that she was born in—"

"—October 1904," Bella interrupted, her voice full of excitement now that she finally understood the clues I'd given her. "That was just a month after Angelica was photographed with her husband on an expedition to Tibet. She couldn't very well be hiding her pregnancy whilst standing beside the man from whom she was hiding it."

"Precisely. There is a photograph from September 1904 on the wall of her entrance hall. It would have taken weeks to get back here, and she would have been in no state to travel if she was about to give birth. All you had to do was look at the photographs all over her house to realise that your plan would come to naught. You made yourself very at home there, and it really is a shame that you didn't take the time to check your facts."

"You make me sick," Travers interjected, whereas the recipient of this bitter observation could find no words to respond.

It was just then that I noticed someone standing beside the fountain in the middle of the foyer. Jennifer had left my family behind in the restaurant to find out why so many of us had already gone. She must have heard what I'd just explained and worked out the rest. She looked at Milton and shook her head in dismay. Perhaps she hadn't loved her aunt. Perhaps she hadn't even liked her, but as I'd believed since we'd first met, Jennifer Capshaw had a good heart and lacked the fury and loose morals that it took to murder another person.

After this stalemate continued for a few moments longer, Inspector Lovebrook decided that the time had come to arrest the killer. He had a pair of handcuffs in the inside pocket of his dinner jacket – which rather impressed me, as it hadn't spoilt the line of his outfit one bit.

He clamped them on our culprit's wrists and announced

the charges against him. "Robert Milton, you are under arrest for the murder of Angelica Thistlethwaite." This was as much as he got out before Stainsbury grabbed the man by the shoulder and led him away.

"You've made a terrible..." Milton began, but the sergeant pushed him forward a little more roughly and he wouldn't make another sound.

THIRTY-TWO

There's nothing quite like a bed in a nice hotel. It seems to enfold and embrace you as you dive into it. I certainly enjoyed mine that night, though I must admit, my suite was rather too big for me on my own, so I fetched Percy from the lower floor so that he could sleep on my feet. Despite the fun he'd been having with his fellow canines and their pack of well-trained assistants, he actually seemed happy to see me, which definitely made a change from his normal behaviour.

I slept like a mummy in a tomb and, just for once, Percy didn't wake me up at a ridiculous hour to demand a walk. I could only think that his exertions on the treadmill, running circuit and on regular walks around the hotel had tired him out. I finally woke at nine with his slobbery jowls on my pillow, but that was a small price to pay for a proper night's sleep.

I still had some questions about the case, but I didn't know who to ask and I wasn't sure they'd be answerable in the first place. It occurred to me that both Irene Adams and Timothy Travers had come very close to breaking the law and had perhaps stepped over that line. There were a few things that I had chosen not to mention about them the night before, as I couldn't decide whether I thought them terrible people who deserved to be in prison, or unfortunate souls who were taken in by a manipulative criminal (or two, in Irene's case).

Though I'd painted her as a gossip and an eavesdropper, she'd definitely done worse by not connecting my call to Cranley Hall and stopping Chrissy's call from reaching me until her shift was finished and someone else took over. It made me wonder whether first Mrs Thistlethwaite and then Milton had paid for her assistance, but I was willing to give her the benefit of the doubt, or at least leave it to the local police to determine the part she had played in proceedings. Either way, I heard that the Torquay telephone exchange was about to be automated, so she would be out of a job soon enough.

Of course, there was nothing to say that Stainsbury would investigate the situation with any great fervour. I could only assume that he'd had a similar arrangement with Mrs Thistlethwaite to the one Irene had. Whether he'd accepted money to turn a blind eye to her schemes or merely indulged her bad behaviour and found himself within her grip ever after, it was difficult to say. I'd had the feeling since our conversation outside Paul Turbot's house that the sergeant was a good man caught in a difficult situation, but sometimes, that's what turns men bad in the first place. I saw him once more before I left Torquay, and I considered encouraging him to avoid any such grey areas in the future, but I believe he already knew how lucky he'd been to avoid suspicion himself.

As for the injured receptionist, we heard the day after the attack that he was awake, and the doctors hoped he would make a full recovery. The very fact he'd been targeted should have helped us to eliminate a few different suspects. Travers, for one, had never denied staying late at the hotel, so killing his colleague wouldn't have helped his case. It was Robert Milton who had gone home early and must have been caught sneaking back in for his tête-à-tête with Mrs Thistlethwaite. The swimming pool was a romantic enough spot for two lovers to meet, but such things are only obvious in hindsight.

At breakfast before we left, none of us overindulged. This was the first positive thing to come out of it, but I was also happy to see a smile on Clemmie Symonds' face. What she was doing mixed up with an engaged man like Alexander Fraiser, I will never know. But at least I'd managed to keep her name out of the investigation. I had no doubt he would eventually marry for money, not love; he was that kind of person. But for an hour or so, he and his secret paramour looked comparatively cheerful, sitting at neighbouring tables with their backs to one another.

"Mr Quin," a soft voice called as I brought my bag down to the reception, and there was Jennifer Capshaw looking as fresh and innocent as when I'd met her two days before. Which, I suppose, isn't saying too much. If she aged horribly in the space of forty-three hours, that would be something worth remarking.

"What did I tell you about calling me Marius?" I asked her, but she'd thrown her arms around me to say thank you and presumably didn't hear.

"I don't know how I can ever repay you." She held me tight, and I didn't necessarily want her to let go.

"There's nothing to repay. I'm just happy that the right person was punished." I had a grey area of my own to discuss. I almost felt guilty for suggesting it, but I'm a private detective, not a police officer, and I don't always have to be whiter than white. "There's a letter hidden behind a photograph of you and your mother in your bedroom. I don't know if the police seized it or put it back where it was, but if you were interested in contesting your aunt's will, it might give you the evidence you need. I doubt that Sergeant Stainsbury would stand in your way."

She looked up at me and I caught the slightest hint of mischief in her that I hadn't seen before. "I don't think that will be necessary. My uncle isn't as mean as Angelica was. He'll make sure I'm looked after. And besides, he's not a well man, and he doesn't have any other heirs. The money will come to me in the end."

I crossed my arms and tipped back my head, feeling both impressed and just a touch gulled. "Oh, will it really? You didn't tell us that when we interviewed you."

She put the toe of one red shoe on its point and swivelled it from one side to the other. "How careless of me. I suppose I was just overcome with the emotion of the whole thing and wasn't thinking straight."

"Oh, yes, that must be it." I reluctantly pulled away from her then, though, as I imagine you've already worked out, I found her rather lovely. "Well, if you ever get in trouble again, you know where to find me."

"I'll be certain to call, Detective." She curtseyed and looked just as sweet as she really was.

I peered over her shoulder at a young man who was lingering in the doorway. I barely recognised him without his lift attendant's uniform, but his red hair shone in the dull morning light.

"Newbury is taking me out to the pictures." She blushed then and her gaze travelled to the reception. "To make up for not coming to the ball last night. You know, he was very jealous to hear that I danced with another man."

I laughed at the idea of someone being envious of me... though perhaps she was talking about Lovebrook. "I'm glad to see he's treating you well."

She was already walking away, and as there was nothing more I could do, I just waved.

"Thank you, Marius." She backed through the foyer and

almost bumped into the commissionaire by the door. "I'll never forget you."

I'm not sure I totally believed her, but it was nice to hear, nonetheless. Bella came to stand beside me and watched her leave, but she said nothing... at first.

"Fine, I was wrong about her. But I still think my conclusions were sound enough."

"Oh, yes, they were exceptional," I replied as Percy sniffed one of the departing dogs and looked just as sad to say goodbye to the pretty King Charles spaniel as I was to leave a place with limitless breakfasts and two swimming pools. "This case was your finest hour."

She would probably have kneed, kicked or poked me then for being cheeky, but her need for information apparently outweighed her desire for petty revenge.

"Did you manage to speak to Christopher Prentiss?"

"I did."

She gave a flustered huff. "Well? What did he say? Was your hypothesis about Prowse and Levitt correct?"

I laughed at her, because she really was too easy to tease. "It was indeed. Chrissy spoke to the cricketer, who told him in the strictest confidence that both he and Miss Levitt were offered a free stay at the hotel. Ostensibly, they would have to provide positive quotes on their time here for a newspaper advertisement, but in reality, this was just the first step in Mrs Thistlethwaite's plan to blackmail them."

Rather than asking another question, clever old Bella put the pieces together. "So she intended to get them down here, photograph them in a compromising situation or what have you and then demand money in exchange for the evidence."

"That's the long and the short of it. Levitt was recently married to a very old, very rich lord, and while he might not have a problem with her extra-marital dalliances, it isn't the kind of thing any of them would wish to see published in the press. Luckily for them, they had a bad feeling from the beginning and escaped from the hotel as soon as I made the connection between them."

"But how would Mrs Thistlethwaite have known about them in the first place? Or Symonds and Fraiser for that matter?"

I was happy to solve another brief mystery. "Prowse wondered the very same thing, though after all we've discovered about Mrs Thistlethwaite's operation, I think I know."

She thought for a moment. "Irene!"

"That's right. Levitt was down here six months ago for a race and called Prowse at home. I remember reading something about Alexander Fraiser having family in Devon, too, so perhaps he did the same thing with Clemmie Symonds."

"How remarkable." She took a moment to marvel at the underhand scheme before turning towards the exit. "It goes to show that you can never be sure who's listening."

I didn't reply because my mother called out just then to get our attention.

"Wait for us," she shouted as though we would leave without them, and I noticed my aunt and uncle were following close behind.

"Don't worry, folks," I told them. "There's plenty of time before the train leaves. We'll see you there."

Bella and I walked out to our trusty taxi, where our bags were already waiting.

"My favourite honeymooners," Sylvester declared as he packed the boot and then rummaged inside in search of his cap.

Neither of us had the heart to tell him we were not really a couple, let alone married. So instead, we spent the next three minutes discussing the beautiful wedding we'd had at St Paul's Cathedral.

"It was a Friday, not a Thursday," Bella insisted, because she likes arguing with me even over fictional events. "You wore a blue suit and your club tie, and the photo that appeared in *The Tatler* did me no justice whatsoever."

"Oh, my darling Bella," I told her in my most saccharine voice, "you always look lovely to me."

"You may only be teasing," our wise chauffeur commented from the front seat, "but I know real love when I see it."

So then neither of us said a word to one another until we were halfway back to London. My family made up for this, and it was a jolly journey in most respects, but I couldn't help feeling a tug on the heartstrings as the train skirted the coast at Dawlish before pulling sharply away from the sea. The storm that had been on the horizon for much of the weekend had never made landfall, which only added to my impression that Torquay was a magical place to spend a holiday, even if it did have the odd eccentric inhabitant.

When we arrived back in the city, we hired three separate taxis, and only Mother and my dog accompanied me home.

"Thank you, Marius," Bella told me before she could slip into her car, not to be seen again until another exciting case presented itself. "You may think me quite mad, but this weekend was just what I needed."

"Oh, Bella." I bit my lip as I looked at her. "You're right. I know few people as lunatical as you are."

She tutted and tapped me with the pair of leather gloves that she held in one hand. "You can say what you like, but I'll thank you anyway." She smiled, and I knew she cared. "I feel totally refreshed and up for whatever the world throws my way, and it's all because of you."

I put my hands on the door that separated us and moved a fraction closer. "Any time, old friend. Whenever you need me, I am just a phone call away."

She didn't say anything more but gave a brief, contented nod and got into the taxi. I stood back on the pavement to watch it drive away, and then it was my turn to go. I thought about the weekend we'd spent away from London all the way back home. I thought that I might just be able to live with the fact that Bella had chosen someone to marry over me, just as long as she really was happy.

"I have to apologise for neglecting you this weekend," I told my mother as I put my key in the lock and opened the front door. "I promise that people aren't generally killed wherever I go, and I hope you still had a nice time."

She put her hand on my jacket to stop me. "Marius, I had a simply wondrous time. I don't think I can imagine a nicer holiday."

I looked at the dear woman for a moment and had to give her a kiss on the forehead because I loved her so much. "Then that is all that matters, and we'll have to do it again soon."

This evidently pleased her, as she rushed into the house, chattering away about all the things she'd enjoyed at the Grand Hotel.

"Of course, nothing compares to a swim in a pool, and we were unlucky on that score. Although I can't say I would have wanted to go anywhere near it after they'd found a body in the water. We found plenty of other ways to unwind. I'd never realised before that steam could be so refreshing. I assumed that Scandinavians were quite mad to cook themselves like that, but I must apologise to a whole region of people and confess that I have rarely enjoyed myself so much."

As she was talking, I approached my writing room and found a calling card that I'd never seen before lying on the threshold. I couldn't imagine how it got there until I picked it up and my blood, though it may not have run cold, certainly dropped a degree or two.

All it said was, Courtesy of Lucien Pike.

I'd been so distracted by the appearance of this foreign object in my locked house that I hadn't so much as glanced around the room. It was only then that I saw Bella's fiancé sitting in my chair. One of Gilbert's arms was splayed out across the desk, and he was bent over as though writing a letter, but that was all too clearly not the case.

"Mother," I yelled as soon as reality hit me. "It looks like I'll have to take back what I said about not finding bodies wherever I go."

A LETTER FROM THE AUTHOR

Many thanks for reading *A Body at the Grand Hotel*. I hope you were glued to the book as Marius and Bella unpicked this thorny mystery. If you'd like to join other readers in accessing free novellas and hearing all about my new releases, you can sign up to my readers' club.

benedictbrown.net/benedict-brown-readers-club

If you enjoyed this book and could spare a few moments to leave a review, that would be hugely appreciated. Even a short comment can make all the difference in encouraging a reader to discover my books for the first time.

Becoming a writer was my dream for two decades as I scribbled away without an audience, so to be able to do this as my job is out of this world. One of my favourite things about my work is hearing from you lovely people who all approach my books in different ways, so feel free to get in touch via my website.

Thanks again for being part of my story – Marius, Bella and I have so many more adventures still to come.

Benedict

benedictbrown.net

facebook.com/benedictbrownauthor

ABOUT THIS BOOK

This is one of the few books I've written having spent a good bit of time in the location where it's set. I went for a weekend to Hinwick House, the setting for my Lord Edginton mystery *Blood on the Banisters*, but that was after I'd written the book. I've made flying visits to various houses and areas that have featured in my three different series, but I got to spend three whole nights at the Grand Hotel in Torquay, and, as there was no body in the swimming pool, we had a lovely time.

The hotel now has over one hundred rooms, but when it was built in 1881, there were only twelve. It was initially called the Great Western Hotel, after the railway line that arrived at the station next door, but the name was changed when the hotel was sold and expanded at the end of the century. This happened again in the twenties, at which point it became one of the first hotels in Britain with central heating – though I've no idea if the pool was heated! We swam in that elegant, kidney-shaped pool, but my wife complained it was too cold.

As it happens, we stayed in room 216, which is known as the Agatha Christie suite, and matches Marius's room rather closely. I'd booked it on an almost suspiciously affordable app and, though the photographs matched the one I wanted, I didn't believe it was the room where a young Christie had spent her (first) honeymoon until we got there. We watched the sunrise from the lounge and enjoyed a very sunny day at the Queen of Crime's nearby home of Greenway, before the rain began and we spent most of the next six days of our trip to the south-west of England in waterproof clothing.

Despite, or perhaps because of, the bad weather, I really fell in love with the lush green countryside in Devon and Dorset and knew before we left that I would set a book there. To complete our trio of Christie visits (and crown our poor luck), we also went to Burgh Island Hotel for afternoon tea, but we popped a tyre on the way and had to change it in the rain after we discovered that the motorway rescue service would take two hours to get there. Burgh Island inspired Christie to write *And Then There Were None*, just as the Grand Hotel inspired this book... obviously.

I am an obsessive holiday planner and will spend days searching for the hotel of my dreams, before normally booking the very first one I looked at. Torquay has two large classic hotels that were there in the twenties, but I felt that the Grand offered the kind of communal experience that hotels of the day provided. It might not have formal dances and my imaginary pet service anymore, but I loved eating breakfast in that massive room, dining in the restaurant and taking tea in the library.

Though my Edgington books have passed through the Ritz and the Savoy, I'd wanted to write a full-on hotel book for some time, and the idea I'd landed on had always featured a suspicious society. I wonder whether any of my readers noticed the perhaps unlikely influence of Roald Dahl's *The Witches*, because that was definitely in my mind when I came up with Mrs Thistlethwaite and her gang of slavish devotees.

I loved the book but had nightmares about the film from 1990 with Anjelica Huston – which is also set in a grand hotel in the south-west of England. I remember watching it at the cinema with my family and pretending I'd dropped a pound coin beneath my seat in order to have an excuse not to look at the screen when the convention of old-lady witches remove their skin. It might well be the scariest kids' film ever made. There was another film that is referenced in the book, and I think anyone who's seen it will know what it is – though read on to confirm the name. I should have held off until a Christmas book to introduce Sylvester the taxi driver, but he fits perfectly here.

One of the reasons that I wanted to write this book was to focus more on Marius as a writer, which is a theme that will continue in the next book as he looks into a famous criminal case from years earlier. I think that readers – myself included before I became one – have ideas of writers that don't match up to reality. There's a gap between me as a writer and my readers, as I make no in-person public appearances. Though I try to reply to every email I receive and host the odd Facebook stream, I've only actually met two of my readers at this point. As an independent writer (and father of two young kids), a book tour wouldn't do me much good, and I'm unlikely to win a literary prize any time soon, but the more traditional relationship between writers and the public interests me.

In the previous book in the series, Marius's unimpressive literary award was already mentioned, largely for comic effect. With the gala thrown in his honour, I wanted to turn his expectations on their head and challenge the image of him as a great novelist. I do love a good baddy, and though ostensibly the victim, Mrs Thistlethwaite is a great foil to Marius, even after she's dead. I must say that "Thistlethwaite" is one of the hardest words I've ever come across to type on a keyboard – I think it's something to do with the arrangement of the letters and the repeated TH. Up to this point, it appears two hundred and eleven times in this book. After about the hundredth time of failing to type it correctly, I started calling her the far easier to type "Pox", and then replaced every instance of Pox with the right word when I'd finished the first draft. In future, I'm going to stick to simpler names!

This is the first Marius in which characters from the Lord Edgington novels appear (except of course for Lovebrook and Marius himself, who were each introduced in books before this series began). I really enjoyed seeing Chrissy and his grandfather from another perspective, and readers with good memories will realise that Dicky Prowse, Idris Levitt, and Georgiana and Henry Snow have all featured in previous mysteries – though I made sure to avoid too many spoilers. I should also reveal that Inspector Lovebrook's name was chosen by readers of my newsletter. I had over 250 replies and the most popular choices were Lionel and Sebastian, but I wanted a name that he would find embarrassing, so I went for the third-place Valentine. I actually think Valentine Lovebrook sounds pretty cool, but it's not the kind of name you'd want for yourself.

I had an unexpected companion as I wrote this book. It was not just my son Osian, who'd just started walking on his own, having taken his first solo steps six months earlier and deciding that it wasn't for him. Every morning, as I sat writing, Osian would toddle into my room, steal the phone from its holder, make me give him the dancing Wall-E toy on my desk and then toddle off again. Outside my window, there was a similarly frequent visitor as, for only the second year since I've lived in my village in the north of Spain, a pair of storks have been nesting. One of the immense white birds would fly across the field behind our house several times each morning in search of sticks and food, and then swoop past my window on the way back to their home on the top of the bell tower in the centre of the village. I did try waving, but they just ignored me.

I could tell you all the interesting things I learnt about these incredible birds who fly up to see us from Africa each year, but I think I'll leave that until the next chapter.

HISTORICAL RESEARCH

I believe that online newspaper archives are one of the most brilliant resources a writer could have. I didn't initially take out a subscription to the British Newspaper Archive, as I was worried just how long I would spend reading articles on it, but I'm so glad that I eventually did. It is an incredible tool for research. I use it for checking whether words and expressions were in use at the time of writing – and often find evidence of terms prior to their inclusion in the Oxford English Dictionary. But it is also useful for adding rich details to my books and there were several elements in this book which were shaped by my findings in contemporary papers.

A good example of this is the advertisement for a play that Marius spots in the local paper. The text I have used is a direct quote from a large notice just below the masthead of the *Torquay Times* from the very day that this book is set. It is the kind of thing you would ignore as it is surrounded by other, smaller announcements, church notices and items for sale on the front page, whereas the news itself starts (to some extent) on page two. I was looking up something entirely different when I saw the advert and decided to use it as a key piece of evidence –

though I do wonder whether readers who are very familiar with celebrities from the 1920s would realise the significance of the list of names earlier.

Speaking of celebrities, I had to look up exactly what meaning the term held in the twenties and I was surprised by my findings. Magazines from the era like *The Tatler* and *The Bystander* were not so different from modern magazines like *HELLO!* in that they tended to focus on the lives of the rich and famous. However, the celebrities of the 1920s were a very different bunch to the kind we get today. In fact, there was a weekly column in the *Daily Mirror* called simply "Celebrities" which not only went into the lives of such glamorous personalities as the Bishop of Gloucester, the Duchess of Sutherland and the wife of the director of the Bank of England, but even posed questions on the nature of fame. One quote ponders, "What is fame? To be celebrated does not follow that you are of any value to your country. Charles Peace (the robber/murderer who has been mentioned in these pages before) was, I suppose, the most celebrated man of his period, yet he did not exactly add to the lustre of his country's glory."

Famous people who were considered to add lustre to their day include classical musicians like Clara Butt, authors like H.G. Wells and Rudyard Kipling, the songwriter Ivor Novello, the actress Gladys Cooper along with husband-and-wife thespians Sonnie Hale and Evelyn Laye – many of whom made it onto the list of Mrs Thistlethwaite's benefactors. A nice little coincidence that I didn't realise until now was that Gladys Cooper – who was a major actress of her day – would later feature as the wealthy benefactor to David Niven's character in the film *The Bishop's Wife*, which just so happens to feature a friendly taxi driver called Sylvester. Perhaps the least exciting celebrity story I came across was an article from 1925 which described the shocking encounter between Lord Oxford and a wasp! The peer ended up with a swollen arm and was told to rest indoors. The paper gave no mention of the health of the wasp.

I also looked in the papers of the day to check what dog shows consisted of in the 1920s and, while they were popular, they did not feature the athleticism that is a key element of them today. Such events like agility and flyball were introduced towards the end of the century. This didn't stop me from giving Percy and his friends their own obstacle course, but I was interested to read about Crufts and its founder. Mr Charles Cruft worked for a dog biscuit manufacturer and visited various shows for his work before establishing his own in 1886. Crufts became notable for being the first to admit all breeds of dog and, in 1891, won royal patronage with Queen Victoria's famous Pomeranians (also mentioned in previous books) winning joint first prize.

By 1928, there were ten thousand applicants for the show, three and a half thousand dogs on display on three miles of benches, and exhibitors included the future king Edward VIII (then Prince of Wales) with his Alsatians, along with any number of dukes, duchesses, viscounts, baronesses and ladies. The Best in Show award was introduced that same year, and it was won by a greyhound called Primley Sceptre who... wait for another of those brilliant coincidences that I love... belonged to the owner of Paignton Zoo, which is a mere three miles away from Torquay's Grand Hotel.

The dog's owner was an eccentric animal-lover who inherited a fortune from his brewer father and devoted his life to studying and breeding animals. He seems like a principled chap as, having set up his first zoo in Paignton in 1923, he soon closed it again when the council tried to impose an entertainment tax on his visitors. He refused and was taken to court, at which point he used the defence that the centre was there for the purposes of education. It is hard to imagine any zoo owner today deciding that he "does not intend to defraud the public by charging tax where no entertainment exists". He lost the case, but, clearly a man of principle, would have the same argument with the council eleven years later. Interestingly, when the Second World War broke out, all the animals from Chessington Zoo were evacuated to Paignton, along with its model steam train and full, working circus and all its staff. Clearly there was no room for clowns in the British Army.

Newspapers are also very useful for looking up images, and (this is going to sound a bit weird) I spent a long time looking at bathing costumes. Such clothing at the time really was very different from today, and I came across some fascinating examples of bathing capes, beach pyjamas and hand-embroidered Parisian one-pieces. I did originally have Marius running about the place topless, but I thought I'd better put a vest on him to make sure he wouldn't face imprisonment.

I also found some funny stories about them. Even in the first twenty results of my search looking at the years 1920 to 1929, I found two cases of women having bathing costumes stolen, and the story of a man who was charged five pounds for swimming without one on "to the annoyance of lady bathers". Another man was sent to prison for a month for stealing one from an open car, while a chap in Glasgow was sent down for forty-two days for accepting a bet to wear a woman's costume in a hailstorm in the centre of the city.

Meanwhile, actress Miss Winnie Wager was banned from Wallasey Municipal Swimming Baths in 1928 for her "American style" costume, which consisted of a thick woollen bodice and red knickers with a skirt. As scandalous as this no doubt already sounds, her biggest mistake was that the bodice was white, of all colours! The officials told her that, if it had been yellow, she would have been fine.

In the same year, Folkestone Pier hosted a bathing costume parade for girls, and as the men were feeling left out, they added a laughing competition. Perhaps my favourite article though is also in Folkestone but in a totally different paper and five years earlier. In the *Sevenoaks Chronicle* from 1923, an ex-councillor with a penchant for complaining about things compares women's "immodest" tennis attire to bathing costumes. The grump goes into great detail, complaining about "audaciously low-cut jumpers" and the "lawless freedom of scanty skirts". I faithfully reproduce the best bit here for your enjoyment...

"We all like to see newspaper photographs of pretty women, and it is an indisputable fact that the camera cannot lie; but these postures and antics of lady lawn tennis players are so glaring that their reproduction in the Press would bring a blush of shame to the cheeks of the players thus portrayed." Councillor Clark turned from the Folkestone Tennis Courts with an air of sadness. "Unseemly antics," he murmured; "unwomanly abandon," shaking his head.

Whenever I write about trains, I spend far too long researching them. The service from Paddington to Torquay really did have Pullman dining, and it really did take three hours and forty minutes to arrive – which is not much slower than the service that runs today. I probably spent a couple of hours reading old newspaper articles about the region's railways, but these were the most pertinent facts I discovered. Presumably, the service would have been less regular in winter, as most of the articles I found were talking of the daily summer services that were laid on, but I'm fairly confident that there was a Friday out and Monday return train throughout the year for people to spend the weekend breathing the fresh sea air.

The Pullman company, which is still associated with the very finest train carriages, brought over the concept of train-based dining from the States. Its owner, George Mortimer Pullman, designed train hotels which were even frequented by the American presidents of the day. The first public dining carriage in the UK was introduced on 1st November 1879, and by 1931 there were two hundred of them running daily from just one of the big four rail companies. Standards were very high during this period, with real crockery and cutlery, six-course meals and even undercover restaurant inspectors whose job it was to check that everything was up to scratch.

Like much of British cuisine, dining cars suffered massively through the Second World War and rationing and, when they were reintroduced in the forties, they were far simpler than before. Happily, many of the classic and beautifully decorated carriages have been preserved and there are special train services all over Britain where you can still eat in such luxury – if you have £200–£700 to shell out for a day trip with meals. Look up Belmond's "British Pullman" train for some of the most exquisite carriages which influenced the one in this book. You can even pay to be part of a "Moving Murder Mystery". Or you could take this book on a normal train and save a few quid.

Sticking with the elegance of the past, I was glad to write about dancing again. Before we had children, my wife Marion and I took three years of ballroom classes and, despite the fact we're still good friends with our dance teacher, I'm sad to say we have forgotten most of what we learnt. One basic step I can still remember, though, is the foxtrot. Growing up with a dance-mad mother who sent my brother and me to contemporary dance classes, I always thought of the foxtrot as a quintessentially English dance, but I was wrong. There are a few different explanations for its origin, but it is likely to have come from African American dance clubs at the turn of the twentieth century. It was made famous by another type of celebrity that is less common these days, a husband-and-wife dancing duo by the name of Vernon and Irene Castle, who added their own look to the dance. One of the reasons it stayed popular throughout the century was that, unlike the waltz, it is danced to a 4/4 beat, and so continued to be performed when rock and roll and pop music came into fashion.

Time for some bullet points...

- I found a clipping from the *Western Mail* which simply says... "Dead On Line. Missing from a Paddington to Torquay train, Arthur Benjamin Simpson, of Cambridge-street, S.W., was afterwards found dead on the line near Dawlish." Which sounds to me like a mystery that is worth investigating... or perhaps writing a book about.
- The word cakewalk has meant a number of things. I knew it as an attraction at a fair which might today be known as a fun house, with moving obstacles and spinning tunnels – there are references to this dating back to 1908. It was also an African American dance move, originating on slave plantations. According to the OED, it was named because dancers would have to do the most amusing walk and the winner would receive a cake. This then figuratively came to mean "A task or role which is easily accomplished or performed" – so something easy to do.
- I could find no examples of treadmills being used for exercise before 1938, though there was a patent for a training machine from 1913. Of course, that doesn't mean that no one ever plonked a dog on one to keep him slim! They were previously used in prisons as punishment and in order to power machinery for grinding grain. There were even horse-powered boats in the nineteenth century, with the poor beast galloping on a treadmill to power a screw propellor, and treadwheel cranes

date back to Roman times. Perhaps even more disturbingly, in Britain from the sixteenth to nineteenth centuries, "turnspit" dogs were forced to run on giant wooden hamster wheels in order to turn spits to ensure evenly cooked meat. Poor puppies!

- The seafront village of Dawlish, which is close to Torquay, was home to Brunel's atmospheric railway. I love this concept – though don't fully understand how such systems worked – but it was not a success and, after a year of expensive and faltering operation, the machine designed for shuttling people to the seaside from the town of Exeter, thirteen miles away, was replaced by a train.

I looked up Torquay town hall because... well, that's my job, isn't it? Though not, from what I could see, greatly admired at the time, it has had an interesting history. It was opened in 1913 and soon became important to the war effort, as it was used as a hospital by the Red Cross. Can you imagine who worked as a nurse there helping soldiers from the front? Well, I'll tell you, it was Agatha Christie, and that period of her life became very important as it gave her a medical basis which would be very important in her writing career. In fact, it was at this time that she also volunteered in the hospital dispensary and learnt about poisons (and medicines, I should think). In all, she gave 3,400 hours of her time and would take the Apothecaries Hall exam before the war was done.

Arthur Conan Doyle appeared at the hall to discuss his beliefs on spiritualism in 1920, and it would go on to play host to all sorts of famous names, from The Who, The Rolling Stones, and David Bowie to The Clash and The Jam. And where do you think that Jagger and his mates stayed when they played their five-night residency? That's right, Agatha Christie's house... well, that's not actually true. They stayed at the Grand, but it's still a pretty good connection. Incidentally, Mick said of Torquay that it was "a great town. But I shouldn't think there's much to do in the winter".

The speech Lovebrook gives at the town hall really is adapted from H.H. Asquith's address to Parliament. Asquith was the last British Liberal Party Prime Minister and oversaw Britain's entry into the First World War, the issue of Irish Home Rule and the growing demands for women's suffrage. In fact, he was assaulted by a woman called Elsie Howey who was the leader of Torquay and Paignton's Suffragettes! She was evidently a committed political agitator as she was arrested six times for her various campaigns and went on hunger strikes. The force-feeding she endured by her captors was so violent that it broke most of her teeth.

Staying in Devon, all the foods that are served for the afternoon tea with Robert Milton are common there. I found two different recipes for Devonshire Cake in the twenties. One is with and the other without apples, but they both have cinnamon and dried fruit. One of the most famous things about the county, however, must be cream teas. According to Wikipedia, the term wasn't used until 1931, and the OED lists the first mention in a novel from 1964 but, breaking news! I found references to Devonshire Cream Tea in various places through the twenties, and they don't just seem to be referring to tea with cream in it. For example, the *Westminster Gazette* from Thursday, 8th April 1926 says "see that your visitors are offered, along with the bread and butter and jam, plenty of Devonshire cream". And there is specific mention of Devonshire cream teas on Friday, 14th June 1929 in the *Uxbridge & W. Drayton Gazette*.

To be on the safe side, I didn't use the term in this book, but it seems safe to assume that clotted cream was served at afternoon tea in the region in the late twenties. One thing that I accept is probably anachronistic – and which a lazy author stuck in anyway because he found it quirky – was any rivalry over the correct scone-based protocol between the neighbouring counties of Devon and Cornwall. It is funny that merely the order in which cream and jam are added should cause any discussion – I'm a Devonshire man myself, sorry – though I was recently a touch horrified on my mother's behalf when my Spanish friend made her a cuppa and poured milk into the mug before the tea. Ricardo, how could you do such a thing!?

Oddly, sticking with... ummm... dairy products, I found a puzzling advert for St Ivel's lactic cream. It claimed that there were 187 times more people who lived to a hundred in Bulgaria than Britain and it was all thanks to the sour milk they consumed, to which I thought, *Yeah, right! A likely story!* So then I had to investigate this mad fact which turned out to be... sort of true, I suppose.

It is believed that the Rhodope Mountains in southern Bulgaria have the highest per-capita occurrence of centenarians in the world. And scientists have, at times, put this down to the population's consumption of yogurt, which goes back to the Thracian tribes that ruled the region during Roman times. The natural, fermented yogurt supposedly protects people from various illnesses. Or at least that's what they said in the twentieth century. More modern scientists put the impressive longevity down to the hard physical lives the people of the region live, the age of first-time mothers being relatively young, stable family life and a genetic history of long-living. So perhaps St Ivel weren't lying altogether, though I still doubt that Bulgarians were 187 times more likely to live to a hundred than we Brits. Two other funny things about the advert are that they recommend making Devonshire splits with their product and they boast about putting best-before dates on the packaging, a major innovation which they say other companies are bound to copy!

Right, I've been putting it off for long enough, it's time to talk telephones! In 1928, manual operator systems were still widespread in Britain. However, I got in touch with a hobbyist telephone expert, in order to check for the Grand Hotel's actual telephone number, and he dropped the bombshell that Torquay was an early adopter of automatic dialling, so any calls within the town from 1925 onwards would have been handled by a machine and Irene wouldn't have been able to listen into them so easily. However, any calls outside of the town would have required a manual operator, so I didn't feel too bad about this slight anachronism. The first automatic exchange was installed in Epsom, Surrey (near where a certain author you know went to school) in 1912, but there were still manual exchanges around the country for decades after, with the last switching over in 1960.

Once again, as with the Pullman dining carriages, it was an American innovation that brought about this advancement. Strowger automatic diallers became the standard in Britain for small- and medium-sized towns, but, a little oddly, Mr Almon Brown Strowger was an undertaker from Kansas. He believed that the operator was diverting business to one of his rivals and so attempted to make a "girl-less" system. His invention required a rotary dial to step up from one line and region to another until it delivered the call to the exact right recipient. Each turn of the dial sent an electrical signal down the line, and the whole thing functioned like an immense tree diagram. Strowger received his patent in 1891 – the same year as the first named Crufts dog show – and he quickly set about automating his town's exchange, thus, somewhat sadistically, making his enemies on the exchange board unemployed. The last Strowger switch on the public phone network in Britain was turned off in 1995, but there are still rumoured to be some in use for various functions in power stations, shopping centres, on warships and the railway network. As you can see from the Grand Hotel phone number, Torquay 2234, and Marius's Mayfair 6040 – which in real life was the number of the local Rolls-Royce showroom – they were a lot shorter back then, so it's not surprising that the technology had to be updated later in the century.

Because of the Southern Rhodesia (modern Zimbabwe) plot in the book, I had to check whether you could call internationally in 1928. In short, most people couldn't, though the first official transatlantic call occurred on 7th January 1927, between New York and London. The call was a scripted conversation that you can listen to online between the heads of two major phone companies. The line was then turned over to businesses who apparently conducted six million dollars' worth of business in the very first day. In actual fact, there had been a test call the day before, in which one of the callers exclaimed, "Distance doesn't mean anything anymore. We are on the verge of a very high-speed world..." Nineteen years later, the first transatlantic wedding took place when Emma Elizabeth Weatherly married Lieutenant Dwight L. Baker. She was in Texas, he was in Germany, presumably still serving after the war, and the ceremony was conducted by his reverend father. I bet their phone bill that month was massive!

I don't have to credit any songwriters in this book because there's only one song, and I wrote it. That's right! My talents know no end! If things go to plan, my good friend Dawn O'Leary Husain will be recording Clemmie Symonds's song. Having said that, my cousin Rhodri was supposed to record the last one, but I turned up at his house too late and he was already at the pub, so my music-teacher cousin Rowland had to do it instead (with help from his students at the Aberdare Community School). Rowland is an ardent listener to the Marius audiobooks – often jumping ahead of his poor family to find out what happens – so thank you, Row!

Furthermore, it's handy having a friend with a 1920s and 30s style cabaret act, and my brother happens to have two.

Dawn was the backing singer for his band when they played at my wedding, and I also saw her singing at her own wedding with their other friend, Alison, who I've no doubt I'll be calling on before long. Yet another brilliant coincidence occurred when I visited the website of the house that featured in my novel *The Snows of Weston Moor* and saw a photograph of Alison singing there. It's a small world.

The smallness of the world is illustrated by my final topic of this chapter, as promised some thousands of words ago, white storks! Thanks to my feathered morning visitor, I had to look up these incredible creatures and they did not disappoint. When I first moved to Spain, I couldn't believe how blasé everyone was about the giant, almost mythological-seeming birds that nest all over the roofs of old buildings and tall chimneys. Now that I see about ten of them on a daily basis through the warmer months, I'm not quite so awestruck, but they are fantastic. The reason they had such a big impact on me the first time I saw them was because, though previously commonplace, they have been effectively extinct in Britain for 600 years due to habitat loss and over-hunting. In fact, 2020 saw the very first pair to reproduce in all that time at the reintroduction project at the already incredible Knepp estate in West Sussex (check out Isabella Tree's book *Wilding: The Return of Nature to a British Farm* to discover more). They hope to have thirty breeding pairs by 2030.

There are all sorts of amazing things about the birds. They are monogamous and build their nests and care for eggs and chicks together. They are also mute but can make the most wonderful clacking noise with their beaks which echoes around my village each day. White storks winter in Sub-Saharan Africa and parts of India before flying for thousands of miles to nest as far north as Estonia – with an average journey length of twenty-six days on the way and forty-nine on the way back. On the main route, the flock of over half a million birds is so big it can span for 200km. But before the nineteenth century, none of this was known, and one of the things that finally helped naturalists understand how birds migrated was what, in German, is known as a *Pfeilstorch*, or arrow stork. There have been about twenty-five of these unfortunate creatures sighted over the last two hundred years, but the presence of an African hunting arrow through their bodies – that evidently didn't kill them – helped scientists to form a theory of migration. Before this, zoologists attempted to explain the sudden disappearance of millions of birds every autumn by imagining that they turned into rodents or hibernated underwater.

All that, and they bring babies to expectant parents... How do they do it? Fine, they don't actually deliver human babies down chimneys, but that myth goes back centuries and perhaps even millennia in European folklore. Hans Christian Andersen wrote a story called *The Storks* in 1839 which not only describes the storks' migration to Africa, but "the pond in which all the little children lie, waiting till the storks come to take them to their parents". Of course, as there were no storks in Britain when I was growing up, I considered this myth an American invention, as I mainly knew it through old-fashioned cartoons like *Dumbo*. Perhaps if the conservation projects succeed, future generations of British kids will believe such pleasant nonsense.

That's all I have to tell you for today. I hope you enjoyed it. I'm off to write some more pleasant nonsense of my own.

WORDS AND PHRASES

Woodenhead – a not so clever person.

Fire-swift – a rather poetic term meaning fast, which I thought neatly matched the coal-powered trains.

Lamping – British slang meaning to punch someone!

Commissionaire – the British word, now uncommon, for the man who stands at the front of a hotel to help people with luggage, taxis, etc.

Jenny Lind – a Swedish operatic singer from the nineteenth century who was considered the finest of her day. You may have seen her depicted in the movie *The Greatest Showman* but, like many things in that film, the role she played was largely fictional – though P.T. Barnum did pay an enormous sum to have her tour the States, she certainly wasn't in love with him. Until recently there was a pub called the Jenny Lind in my town in south London. I always assumed she must have passed through there, but no. It turns out that her presence in London in 1847 was such a sensation that places renamed themselves in her honour. It must be a bit like the Eras tour today. Incidentally, that pub is now called the Nightingale, so it hasn't turned its back on her entirely.

Bissell – I often use newspapers to find inventions that were on sale at the time, and the American manufacturer Bissell patented its carpet sweeper way back in 1876.

Natational – the Spanish word for swimming is natación, so I knew there would be some kind of similar old-fashioned adjective in English. It turns out I was right!

Par excellence – the very best.

In a crack – in no time at all.

Blood and thunder – my mother often says, "Blood and sand!" as a very mild swearword, so I was happy to find a similar one to use here.

Jam-full – an earlier expression for jam packed.

Filthy look – I was very happy to use this as it turns out it has a particularly 1920s connection. The OED has this quote: "In this jargon [that flappers speak], 'brutal' means very nice... 'Filthy look' means scowl or disapproval."

Trashy – I thought this would be a much more recent word, but it actually dates back to the 1860s to mean low-class.

Flannel – a nice expression for nonsense.

Spills – a word I stole from a Gladys Mitchell novel, it meant long pieces of paper or perhaps wood that would be kept beside the chimney for lighting the fire.

High-keyed – high-pitched.

Reptile – a bit of a scumbag!

Spit and image – it's not a typo. This was the more common expression at the time for "spitting image" that we would use today.

Permanently waved – something else I found a lot of adverts for in the late twenties. It was a process a bit like perming to give women wavy hair.

Busy (noun) – an old-fashioned word for a detective.

Unmentionables – underwear.

Twitchety – nervy, jumpy.

Mauvais sujet – a disreputable person.

Souchy – a fish stew.

Suédoise – a dish I found in Mrs Beeton. I'm not sure what a Suédoise is except that it means Swedish and was presumably some sort of sweet sauce.

Vamp the current bar – with thanks to my saxophone-playing cousin Charlotte for this term. It means to repeat the current part of the music that is being played over and over until you can proceed.

Joe – a guy, fellow, chap – dates back to 1846.

Get-a-way – the old-fashioned spelling of the noun, e.g. a weekend getaway.

Coxy – arrogant. A good word!

Zut – French word meaning, bother! They do express their frustrations so well.

Glad rags – meaning your fancy clothes, it dates back to 1902.

Peu importe – more Frenchiness, it means *never mind.*

Losing his rag – British slang for getting angry from 1928, but presumably already in common usage before appearing in print.

Lunatical – a nice antiquated word for mad.

CHARACTER LIST

New Characters

Man in the red suit – who knows?

Augustus Black – the man in black. I'm not giving it away here!

Jennifer Capshaw – beautiful young woman who assists Mrs Thistlethwaite in the running of the Torquay Mystery and Detection Society.

Timothy Travers – manager of the Grand Hotel.

Mrs Angelica Thistlethwaite – intimidating head of the Mystery and Detection Society.

Sergeant Dennis Stainsbury – Torquay police officer with a chip on his shoulder.

Robert Milton – Mrs Thistlethwaite's rival in the society.

Sylvester – taxi driver.

Alexander Fraiser – playboy socialite tipped for politics, engaged to rich heiress.

Clemmie Symonds – beloved singer.

Irene Adams – the local telephone exchange operator.

Jules Laverne – charming New York band leader.

Returning Characters

Marius Quin – his face is on the cover... what a handsome chap!

Lady Isabella Montague – his lovely assistant/the love of his life who got away/the daughter of the Duke of Hurtwood/a capable detective in her own right.

Gilbert Baines – Bella's beloved.

Uncle Stan/Auntie Elle/Mary – Marius's uncle, aunt and mother (who finally has a name!)

Inspector Valentine Lovebrook – Marius and Bella's police officer friend (who also finally has a Christian name!)

Bertrand Price-Lewis – Marius's jolly publisher.

Lucien Pike – a shadowy figure who may be involved in the disappearance of Marius's father ten years earlier.

ACKNOWLEDGEMENTS

I must always start this section by thanking my brilliant editor, Emily. Working with her feels like I'm part of a special club in a book about child detectives. The series wouldn't exist without her, and I always have so much fun when we're working together. So thank you, Emily. You're the best.

Most of the rest of you who deserve thanks know who you are. All my ARC readers who chip away at each book to make it ten times better (especially Joe and Kathleen Martin). My daughter Amelie for asking the most astute and challenging questions that any six-year-old has ever formed. My son Osian for tottering into my office so often and bringing sunshine in with him, and my selfless, kind and inspirational wife Marion who makes me catch my breath ten times a day whenever I realise that she's made my every dream come true. None of this would be possible without you, my angel, so thank you.

And, of course, thank you also to every person who has read this book. I couldn't do it without you.

Printed in Great Britain
by Amazon